THE ANGLE OF FALLING LIGHT

THE ANGLE OF FALLING LIGHT

a novel

BEVERLY GOLOGORSKY

SEVEN STORIES PRESS
New York • London • Oakland

Copyright © 2025 by Beverly Gologorsky

All rights reserved. No part of this book may be reproduced, stored in a retrieval system, or transmitted in any form, by any means, including mechanical, electronic, photocopying, recording, or otherwise, without the prior written permission of the publisher.

Seven Stories Press
140 Watts Street
New York, NY 10013
www.sevenstories.com

Library of Congress Cataloging-in-Publication Data

Names: Gologorsky, Beverly, author.
Title: The angle of falling light : a novel / Beverly Gologorsky.
Description: New York : Seven Stories Press, 2025.
Identifiers: LCCN 2024058725 (print) | LCCN 2024058726 (ebook) | ISBN 9781644214633 (trade paperback) | ISBN 9781644214640 (ebook)
Subjects: LCGFT: Novels.
Classification: LCC PS3557.O447 A85 2025 (print) | LCC PS3557.O447 (ebook) | DDC 813/.54--dc23/eng/20241209
LC record available at https://lccn.loc.gov/2024058725
LC ebook record available at https://lccn.loc.gov/2024058726

College professors and high school and middle school teachers may order free examination copies of Seven Stories Press titles. Visit https://www.sevenstories.com/pg/resources-academics or email academic@sevenstories.com.

Printed in the United States of America

9 8 7 6 5 4 3 2 1

for Georgina

And with deep appreciation

for Dònal de Burca
and
Liz Geweritzman

It was a cold dark November
morning
breaking slowly into light.

—JANE LAZARRE, "Chiaroscuro"
from *Breaking Light*

I.

1

The hearse is parked in the driveway, back doors wide open. A few of us wait around for the body to be brought out. A crisp black mourning ribbon hangs on the front door of the house with Kevin's army medal pinned to it.

He and I sometimes walked into town together but didn't spend gobs of time with each other . . . still . . . his suicide was sudden. Aren't all suicides? Rumor has it he shot himself; others say he OD'd. Does it really matter how he did it?

The last time Kevin and I talked he was thinking of enlisting for a third tour. I should've just listened. Instead, I unwound a long string about how the war was a waste, a travesty, a killing machine. I wish now I hadn't sounded so dismissive.

It's ghoulish, waiting here to see the body. I head to the beach. Someone calls, "Tessa, where you going?" But I don't respond.

The beach is cold and wintery. Occasionally someone walks a dog or a jet plane flies over, otherwise there's only the faint shushing of a lazy ocean. Actually, it's the Long Island Sound, the real ocean with its noisier, cresting waves is around the bend, though exactly where the water bends, I can't say.

As the sky darkens, the wind picks up, and the cries of the seagulls lessen. I phone my sister. Again, it goes to voicemail. Again, I text her: "Marla, where are you? Mom isn't home yet. I'm starving, going to the diner, meet me there."

Beams of light from the old-fashioned lampposts hopscotch along the streets that make up the small forgettable town. The diner is squished between a bank and post office. Our mother worked there when we were little. If Louise is serving, she'll feed us for free. Let's hope.

The little bell tingles when I push the door open. A few people sit in the wooden booths. I take a counter stool next to an older man.

"You alone tonight?" Louise asks, one hand gripping an empty glass, the other pouring water from a pitcher. She and my mother are close.

"Marla's supposed to meet me."

"You want to wait or . . . why don't you order . . . how about the special, meat loaf and sweet potato?"

"Thanks, sounds great." In the adjacent blue-tinted mirror I notice the man glance at me and smile, which I ignore.

Each time the front door opens I turn with renewed hope.

"Waiting for someone important?" the man asks. Not wanting to be rude, I nod at him in the mirror, then turn away, but not before noting his determined chin and white shirt open at the throat.

"How's your mom?" Louise places the food before me.

"She's good."

"The woman never takes time for a deep breath. Let me know if there's anything more . . ." But already she's moving down the counter to clear plates.

"Enjoy the meal, you're a beautiful woman," his tone serious but not flirtatious, then he's out the door.

People have remarked on my being pretty. Beautiful, though, that's a bit stronger.

Louise, her tired dark hair pulled into a ponytail, refills the water glass.

"Who was the man on the stool who left," I ask, because Louise doesn't miss much.

"He's house sitting somewhere up on the beach. How's the food?

Nina hauls the sack of wet dishtowels to the hospital autoclave. The towels reek like the stray dogs her husband brings home. When she complains, Scotty says no one's asking her to take care of the mutts. True. Except the dogs' nasty odors drive her mad. She can't help but plop the animal in a bathtub. How could she let her girls near such a dirty mongrel? The reluctant dog is never pleased and soon runs into the wettest dirt it can find, and there's plenty around the house. Come to think of it, it's been a while since he's brought home a dog.

She drops the sack in the autoclave, last chore of the day, and heads toward the path out that avoids the wards, which are filled with wounded soldiers who leave holes in her heart. The sweet, young blasted-to-pieces kids are hooked up to contraptions or lie there too depressed to even blink. They aren't much older than her girls. If someone calls out to her, she always stops to say a few words, which can end up being a bad night, their helplessness a reminder of her own.

On the lawn beyond the sun porch where patients convalesce or meet visitors, she pauses for a breath of air.

"Hey, no one's come to see me. Say hello."

"Such a young, handsome man without visitors, how's that possible?" He has all four limbs, thank God.

"If you sit I can tell you about it."

"It's a bit cold to sit outside." But she takes the chair next to his. A wintery breeze scatters the dry leaves on the grass.

"Why are you here?" He doesn't look sick; maybe it's stuff in his head. She's seen a lot of that in the waiting rooms. "A bit of something, all fixed now. I leave in a few days. I have a question? Who are you?"

She laughs. "Big question."

"How about a name?"

"Nina. And you?"

"Peter."

"Where were you stationed?"

"Finished one tour in the I and two in the A, those exotic places being destroyed in the name of goodness called Bush. After 9/11, thought it was my duty to join the Marines. One has only to walk through the vet hospital to see the results of such foolishness."

"Sadly, they keep the place busy."

"I bet you could use a drink?" His smile is pretty, strangely gentle.

"Why do you say that?"

"Anyone who works here would. You do work here?"

"In the cafeteria kitchen. Awful job. Pay's okay, sort of."

He produces a small silver flask. Offers it to her.

"What's in it?"

"It won't kill you. Scotch."

"It might. I'm just that tired." But she takes the flask and after a small sip, takes another longer one.

He watches her closely. "Someone like you should be able to get an easier job, no?"

"I'm a mother of two with a war-wounded husband and I'm grateful for the salary." Why would she say all that? Jesus!

"A mother of two. How's that possible?"

"Very."

"But you're so young."

"Yes, that's still true, I suppose."

"Do you live nearby?" he asks, as if it matters.

"Grew up in Long Island, not far from the hospital and now home is in the next town, a few miles east," she says, not sure why.

"I'm here for awhile now. But I have a cabin in California that I built myself. Imagine if you will a secluded wooded area, a bottle of whatever, two hammocks swinging gently as the night sky fills with enormous diamonds, where the mornings arrive offering promise without consequence. I wish you could see it." He holds out the flask.

Ashy darkness begins to blur the sharp edges of nearby houses. She should get going, and she will, soon.

Driving the empty stretch of road home, Nina rolls down her window, the night air cold. Gnarled trees and scruffy brush fill one side of the road, on the other the sandy embankment of the beach. The ease between a man and woman, she forgot it was possible. He asked a lot of questions yet wasn't intrusive. How did he manage that? His rather poetic description of his California cabin surprised her. She isn't used to a man sharing feelings so freely.

She drives slowly, lingering in the unexpected haze of the past hour or so, which will dissipate soon enough with the push and pull of the needs at home. Hopefully Scotty won't provoke Marla who feels duty-bound to let nothing pass unchallenged. Tessa, a year younger, is more circumspect.

Turning onto the dead-end road, the car coasts down the rutted driveway to the house at the bottom. The buzz of Scotty's chain saw greets her from out back. He likes fixing stuff, and there's plenty to keep him busy. Their furniture is old and breakage is constant; he won't toss anything out. Except for now and then tending bar for Rico, his shattered coccyx keeps him at home. He doesn't complain. In his own rough mind, he believes most things in life are supposed to be difficult.

"Where've you been?" Tessa calls out as she enters.

"What?"

"Kevin died and Marla didn't meet me at the diner and why are you late?" Green eyes steady on her.

Crime and punishment, it never fails. "I worked overtime, extra money. Awful about Kevin, terrible. I'm sure Marla will be home soon."

Tessa stares at her, mute.

"Maybe Marla mentioned something to Scotty," she mumbles.

With Tessa shadowing her, she strides through the railroad of rooms and opens the back door to a small plot of woodsy land that Scotty owns with his kid brother, Hack. Scotty wants them to clear-cut some of it to make space for a storage shed. Yellowed leaves are raked into neat piles. The thick roots beneath two old trees are coated with the sand that's been trekked through the house.

Under the dim backdoor light, Scotty works on a broken wicker chair, and gives her a don't disturb-me-look.

"Did Marla say anything about where she was going today, any appointments or stuff?"

"Nope, probably cavorting with some sex-starved boy. No point treating her like a baby." He glances at the screwdriver he's holding, then down at the upturned chair. Dismissed. She goes back inside. He doesn't give a shit about Marla. Not his daughter. The human condition: what's not yours reaches in, but not that deep. Oh, God, she hates these kinds of thoughts, and shakes her head, catches Tessa—also not his daughter—watching her the way she always does, skeptically, as if Nina knows more than she's telling. "It's okay, lovey, if Scotty knew anything, he'd say."

"Why are you so worried?" Nina asks.

"I'm going to the beach. Maybe Marla's there with friends."

"It's dark out, and . . ."

"I won't be long."

"I'll go with you."

"You don't have to."

"But I do." She grabs a flashlight from the kitchen drawer.

They follow the thin yellow stream of light along a footpath down toward the water. It's cold, cloudy and moonless, quiet, too. Clearly, no one's frolicking on the beach.

Halfway down, the flashlight picks up a faint outline of something lying in the sand. They head toward it. Getting closer, they begin to run. Nina's shoes fill with sand, as if trying to hold her back from the unbearable. "It's Marla," Nina screams and drops to her knees. She shakes her daughter's slim shoulder. Has to be alive, must be, she prays, refuses anything else, and continues to shout "Marla, Marla," again and again because this isn't happening. Tessa tries to get past her, get closer, but Nina can't move.

Marla's eyes open, not dead, oh God, not dead, but unseeing. She's sleeping off something. Nina's heart continues its triple beat, but the initial fright now fury.

They get Marla upright, walk her back to the house. Once inside, Nina lights into her daughter, what is she on, who gave her stuff, her voice loud in her ears, but she can't help it. Threatening, scolding, she orders Marla to remain at home after class or Nina will find her, wherever she is, and drag her back. Marla wears a stony expression, clearly too zonked to take in any of it.

2

From bed I hear the front door bang shut, my mother gone to work. The image of my sister lying there on the dark, empty beach, like something the ocean had no more use for, filled me with cold numbness. During the night I grabbed her hand and held it for a long time. Awake or asleep, she didn't pull away. We've shared a bed since forever. Our stuff crowded into knob-less drawers in the knob-less dresser, our clothing hung together in the closet. I lean over, "I'm cutting class today." Marla stirs but says nothing.

Slipping into jeans and a sweatshirt, I grab my jacket off the chair, and tiptoe toward the front door, hoping Scotty doesn't ask where I'm going. On the spot lies are easy enough, but who wants the bother? He couldn't care less.

Pulling the worn jacket tightly around me, I head up the cul-de-sac road to the bomb-size but not-too-steep sinkhole, and slide down, landing on the makeshift nest of branches. A muffled silence, yet it's the noise of possibilities I crave. Whenever Marla scraped up enough money, the two of us took a train into Manhattan and wandered around. People there walk with purpose, destination written on their faces, different from the purposelessness here.

When I try to explain this to my friend Raff, he shrugs, says people are the same wherever. Not true, but why argue? If he's content with his present and future lot, so be it.

"Tessa? Come up. Take a run on the beach."

"In a while. Come down."

Marla's long legs reach the scruffy bottom before the rest of her shapely self. "It smells awful down here. Did something die?"

"What a pleasant thought. What was last night about?"

"Nothing." Marla says.

"You were stoned flat out on the beach."

"So?" Her arm slides around my waist in a quick squeeze.

"So you're not going to share?"

"Run on the beach with me. Why did you cut class?"

"I figured you'd stay home today."

Marla takes a half-smoked joint from her pocket, lights it. "Want?"

"No."

She plops down beside me, inhales deeply, and looks around at the absurd décor of dirt, leaves and twigs. "No kind of life," she shakes her head. "People here expect so little, Mom, too. Maybe they believe it's all they deserve, or all they can get, not me. Not you either. We'll find a way out. Sheer will if nothing else."

"Amen," I say.

"Did mom ask about me before she left?"

"No, but I'm sure she's pissed at you."

"Won't last."

"She came home late yesterday, never had to do overtime before."

"Shitty she has to work so hard," again inhales deeply. "Glad for us she can do what she does."

"That's mean."

"No one asked her to marry a stay-at-home lump."

"They must've been in love, right?"

"Ugh. I'm meeting a man later with long braided hair . . . and connections . . ."

"Is that who gives you . . . What's so great about getting stoned?" I ask, disappointed not to hang out together.

"Don't put down what you haven't tried."

"I've smoked weed."

"Not the be-all of drugs. What's your day plan?"

"I have stuff to do," I lie.

"Run with me. I need to get my blood going. You know I always like you close. We'll figure out something un-boring to do together later. I'll be back before Mom gets home."

"You sound very determined."

"My middle name."

Nina leaves the car window open; the cold air keeps her awake. She couldn't sleep last night. Marla worries her. What did she take? Who gave it to her? Hack? Doubtful. Who, then? A friend? A stranger? Was it someone outside the school, on the beach? Drugs are passed among friends like pennies. She needs answers and won't stop asking till she gets them. And then what . . . that worries her too.

In bed Scotty wanted to know what all the yelling was about. She told him. He chuckled, which infuriated her. "What's so funny," she asked not wanting to hear. "Being stupid is part of growing up," he'd said.

It's true, she thinks now. Pregnant and married at seventeen was stupid. Her girls are too smart for that. She remembers once asking her father what he did for fun as a teen. Fun? He looked at her as if she'd lost her mind. Said he didn't think that way and she shouldn't either. Life wasn't supposed to be about fun. It was about getting through, and doing so without help from anyone, because to expect that would only disappoint. Even then she didn't want to believe him, but his words never left her.

The hospital parking lot is crowded. Driving in circles till she finds a spot, the pleasant memory of yesterday's late afternoon scotch comes to mind. Well . . . today is today, and she feels a shadowy disappointment. Is her life that desolate? Don't answer that.

Peter snags the same two lawn chairs as the day before in the hope that Nina will pass by. An undefined sadness dogs him, as if he'd glimpsed someone who could matter but let her vanish. He rarely talks about his California cabin because, mostly, who cares. But her green eyes fastened on his words as if they were state secrets. It made him want to share more stories with her.

Crazy they even met, though crazy defines the last two weeks. He came east to visit his best buddy in the hospital then his appendix burst. He blamed the previous days of stomach pains on whiskey waking his ulcer, souvenir of the last tour. Then walks into a hospital lobby and collapses. After surgery he did get to spend quality time with Richie, who refused to discuss his own pain and suffering. "Marines don't cry."

Marines also take action, he thinks. If Nina doesn't appear today, he'll go to the cafeteria kitchen tomorrow and find her. Patience was never his thing.

3

Hack pulls a beer from the cooler, eyes Tessa's scarf splayed on the couch where it's been since she shrugged it off. No doubt the girl will visit again to claim it. Does that make him happy? It makes him nervous.

When she knocked at his door. He thought to ignore it, then reconsidered. Anyone but Scotty at his door is a rare occurrence, so he hoisted himself out of the chair and to the front door, which he opened to reveal Tessa, who stated she came to hang out for a while. He thought to gently push her back out the door, except she ran a stream of words at him with the kind of enthusiasm he couldn't summon out of himself not for a million dollars. Not that he cares about money. He doesn't. Then she set her pretty bottom on his couch-bed like the place was hers. It did give him a kick, seeing that kind of spunk. He gave her a beer, how could he not when he was drinking one himself? One or two beers don't make a drunk. What does? That's a different question.

Thing is, why come here? Why spend time with stoned Uncle Hack, twice her age? Uncle? She exclaimed in her breathy rush of words, no, he's not blood. She's Scotty's stepdaughter, he's Scotty's brother. So . . . and went on in her crisp, quick way, one word blowing out the next with barely an intake of breath. He caught one remark about being bored. It seems the girl doesn't have too many other places to be.

Is she seventeen, eighteen or fifty? Either way, she looks mature. It's the curvy body. Carries herself like queen of the night, except she's not, and knows that, too. Nina would have a fit if she knew Tessa was hanging out here. Why tell her? The woman works hard. He doesn't add burdens, doesn't remove them either.

The girl had no good word to say about Scotty, instead talked about a missing father like he was important. She can't possibly remember the man from way back then. Said she sometimes looks through obit sections of newspapers for his name. Doesn't sound like the kind of dude who'd be important enough to get his name in an obit. The man's a bastard who never tried to find his little girls. Even he'd be a better father than that. Maybe.

Unlike the missing father, his rented bungalow is easy to find. He rarely goes out. Whatever's out there, he's not interested. Scotty's been after him to do some work on the back property. It's Scotty being the concerned big brother. But he doesn't want to exert a thimbleful of energy in this insanity called America, except maybe to pick up his drugs. He may be a bucketful of negatives, but doesn't lie to himself, not anymore, and knows that out there nothing can push past the shit inside him.

Too bad he goes through his stash like it was candy. And does that matter to him? Not especially, not like it might've before the desert, but after, after, after. What was before after? Kill the Haji, save the land, protect the people, love your brothers, save the oil, keep distance from that car, cover your face man, get off that road and that road and focus your eyes on the road for mines, watch out, it's a . . . no, it's a woman, no . . . it's . . . shoot . . . don't shoot . . . The list his brain still sings, especially when his head hits the pillow. Actually, hopefully, he'll pass out before that happens, but even then, the images swirl.

Outside the small, fractured window, darkness, sweet darkness, inside, the scarf still on the couch. On screen, TV images blink at him. Doesn't matter, the messages suck.

4

Nina hurries to the parking lot. Hurrying isn't new but rushing toward pleasure is. The weather is colder now, her old coat worn thin, but there's a heat inside her.

Since the day, three weeks ago when Peter walked into the hospital cafeteria, the usual has become unusual. They see each other weekdays from three, when her work ends, until late afternoons edge toward darkness. At first it was on the hospital lawn. Discharged, Peter booked a motel where three days ago they made love for the first time. Tender, but strange, too. Sex was not part of her life with Scotty.

Now, each evening, on the way home she replays their moments together like a favorite piece of music. He makes her feel it's still open, her life, except it isn't, not really, not when, amidst any moment, truth grips her: It can't last. It will have to end, this double life. Lying isn't her thing: one lie begets another and soon the truth is too far out to reach. It all makes her anxious. How could something that began so innocently escalate so quickly? She's too old—even if she is young—to be taken in by another man. So why doesn't she stop seeing him?

He's waiting near her car, a duffel bag at his side, which he tosses in the trunk. They head to his buddy Richie's house, which he offered them the use of until he gets out of the hospital. They stop at a supermarket, walk the aisles together. Whatever appeals gets into Peter's cart; money doesn't seem to be an issue. She, however, shops like a crow, hunts and pecks, one tomato, two potatoes, never a pound, yesterday's bread on sale, only enough to get through the day. Scotty buys the beer he drinks. At least that.

Richie's house is a tan bungalow with no porch. Inside, she opens windows to dispel the musty smell. The furniture weeps with neglect. Out back is a patch of yard with a barbecue on a table. A few tufts of grass sprout hopefully between the bricks beneath. Two deck chairs and a card table lay folded on the ground.

"Richie said it was fine to grill out here. I'm dying to cook outdoors. I'll wrap you in a blanket if you get too cold," All the while setting up the chairs and table, wiping off the grime and dust with a towel from his duffel.

"I can't stay any longer than usual . . . my girls . . . "

"I know, though I'd rather keep you here. Be right back."

Scotty and the girls believe she's working overtime; that is what she told them. Though no one is about to check her unchanged pay stub, Tessa wants to know why she has to work so late. She's glad the girls have each other. She was lonely as an only child.

A streak of yellow sky promises November's early darkness. Lights go on in nearby houses; indistinct voices reach across the space. Some are high-pitched like children playing. Peter carries out a tray with plastic cups, a chunk of cheese, and a bottle of scotch. He sets the tray on the card table, then leans over to place his lips on hers and their eyes open, as if musing on their luck.

He starts up the grill. It's not long before the coals begin to glow. He cuts up some cheese, pours them each a drink, and they click glasses.

Her cellphone rings. She doesn't want to answer but does. Tessa: "Hi honey."

"Marla's not home yet."

"She's with friends. You know your sister, she . . . "

"Can you get out of work now?"

"Why?"

"I have a bad feeling. Can you leave?"

"Yes."

"When will you get here?" Insistent voice.

"On the way."

"Nina, it's okay," Peter slips an arm around her shoulder. "I understand."

And if he didn't, she thinks, gathering her stuff, she'd have to leave anyway. Anger flares at Scotty, then subsides—not his fault—and once more guilt tightens her throat. Lord, how did her plodding, uneventful life become so complicated?

The house is brightly lit which means Scotty must be out working at the bar. He watches heat and electricity like it's being rationed. Tessa is wearing her jacket and is curled into a corner of the couch, signaling disapproval, or is it distress?

"Hi sweet pea, any word from your sister?"

"Can they keep the cafeteria open so late?" Tessa's eyes search her face.

"I guess so. Did you call any of her friends?"

"That's your job."

"I get that you're pissed at me, but Marla going off to do her thing isn't my fault."

"Maybe it is . . . Anyway, if you'd been here, we could've eaten at the diner. Nothing in the fridge."

"I'm here now."

"Mom, you should be worried about my sister."

"Why are you so upset? Marla rarely gets home before eight. It's just after seven now."

"She wasn't around all day."

"What?"

Tessa stares at her.

"Do you know why?"

"She usually tells me if she's going to take off somewhere."

"Take off! Since when?"

"Mom, I don't know. Something's wrong. Stop with the third degree."

"Any idea where to look?"

"Too cold for the beach . . . let's drive around the school yard."

"Unlikely," she says.

"Mom, just drive into town."

Tessa's anxiety settles inside her as they head to the car. Scotty's going to have a fit with all the lights on. Can't worry about him now.

Neither of them speaks as the dark road speeds by. In town, most shops are shuttered, the streets empty. So, too, the school yard.

"Now where?" she asks.

"The bar?" Tessa mumbles to herself.

"What bar?"

"Can't remember."

"You went with her to a bar?"

"Mom, please let's not."

"Tessa, I need to know. Where's the bar?"

"No, Mom, that's not a good idea."

"Why?"

"She'll never forgive you for embarrassing her."

"Why would I embarrass her?"

"Jesus, Mom. Her friends see you come in to take her home? Really? Weren't you young once?"

And still are, Peter says.

"We'll go in as customers. I'll buy a beer, you a coke. If Marla's there, she'll come to us. How's that sound?"

"I don't know . . . "

"Where's the bar?" No nonsense voice.

They pull into a small lot, park between a pickup truck and a motorbike, enter a back door, and follow a long, musty-smelling hallway to a dark room of crashing loud music, teeming with people. A neon-lit sign in the window flashes on and off. Deranging.

She spots Marla on a corner stool, semi-slumped, head down, ready to keel over it seems. A cold calm sends her elbowing through the crowd till she reaches her daughter.

"Marla we're going home," she says and slips an arm around her tiny waist.

Tessa accidently-on-purpose knocks two empty glasses off the counter, which shatter. "Tessa," Nina warns.

"Need assistance?" The bartender asks nonchalantly.

"Asshole," Tessa snarls. Marla giggles.

"Let's go," she says.

Marla looks at her with only faint recognition.

"Try and stand up. I can't carry you, for God's sake."

Marla gives her a scary grin but doesn't resist.

In bed, unable to sleep, the image of Marla's slumped body awakens a memory of stopping her stoned first husband from kissing the new baby on the mouth, lest he transmit his addiction. Oh Lord. Marla will not follow in his footsteps; it's not ordained. She won't allow it. In truth, though, Marla's curious mind is driven by needs without parameters, needs that can't be met in this small town. So, what then?

She hears Rico's pickup truck dropping off Scotty and thinks to pretend that she's asleep but doesn't.

"Hi," she says. "Was the place busy?" He looks exhausted.

"Yeah. Made good tips."

"I was at a bar, too."

"Yeah."

"Looking for Marla. Found her in a place called the Zanzi-bar. She was stoned and drunk."

"Is she all right?"

"Asleep."

"Well, there you go, nothing to worry about."

"Nothing to worry about? She's taking all kinds of stuff."

"It's a phase."

"It's not a phase."

"Have it your way."

What's the use? Scotty's not going to get worked up. He believes the life a person's born into is the one he'll die in, so why bother. She shared this with Peter who said it's a philosophy of death at an early age. Lately, Peter comes to mind no matter what else is happening. She can't have him there now, and turns to gaze at the photos on the wall: her girls at different ages, her dead parents, a few friends she no longer sees. , And why's that?

There's one of her that Scotty took at a fair, holding aloft a large frankfurter. That was soon after she met him, almost fourteen years ago. She thought him attractive with his bushy, gray, shoulder-length hair; deep-set, deer-black eyes; and most of all the I've-been there-done that attitude he emitted like perfume. She was twenty-one and he nearly fifty, a veteran of the first Iraq war. He courted her closely, escorted her home after her shifts at the diner. Not a talker, but reliable, honest, and not a man who would think to bring her flowers or comment on the way the stars laid out a path toward heaven. That was her domain and he let her have it.

Her parents were delighted with Scotty, a man who didn't care that she had two little girls, who owned a house, who wasn't an alcoholic, and—as her mother put it—who wouldn't raise a hand to her. What could be better? Her parents were eager to get her under someone else's roof. Their own barely met their needs.

Scotty already asleep, she gets out of bed, slips into her old chenille robe and traipses across the cold floors to stretch out on the living room couch. Only the faint rustle of the house settling disturbs the silence.

How much would a good drug rehab program cost? Scotty would be against it. Too many of his buddies went through one program after another only to return to the same behaviors. Probably, Marla wouldn't go, but any move out of here, away from whoever she's getting stuff from, would help. Change takes money, of which there's none, so dream on.

From the couch, she can see the shifting light outside the window that which promises another day. And yes, she'll see Peter. He knows little about her family problems. Their time together is protected, fleeting, and filled with joy and comfort, a fairy tale. But fairy tales are short stories that end.

5

A cold wind comes in with the tide. I pull Marla back from the spray. Her thick, dark hair whips wildly about her face, under her eyes, kohl-like dark smudges. Hangover? Tiredness? I refuse to think deeper.

"Gave you a bit of a tour last night," Marla's voice low, hoarse, downcast.

"We couldn't find you," an accusation."

She remains quiet.

"You should've at least called me. I worried. I didn't know where you were." I mean to sound irate, but it's hard for me to be angry with her. "What happened last night?"

Marla laughs without joy. "I happened. I happened to myself and fucked up with some guy who isn't worth discussing."

"But you were stoned . . . "

"I needed to feel good and getting high feels good, not just good-good, like a passing pleasure, but substantial, as if I have weight—not pounds—power. Everything around here is light-weight. Can you understand?"

"Of course I do." No lie. But what I really want to say is that I fear for her.

"Come on, let's jog."

We run a zigzag path to keep our sneakers dry. The sky, white as a sheet, offers nothing. The seagulls wheel lower and lower, their cries a constant protest.

A dog comes bounding toward us, and stops, black-and-white, silky-haired with large sympathetic eyes. A man calls out, "He's friendly."

It's him, the man at the diner.

"Marcus, Marcus Roland." He extends his hand, which we ignore. He seems taken aback as if we're supposed to recognize the name.

"What kind of dog," Marla strokes its head.

"Border Collie."

"Is he yours?" Marla asks. Marcus nods and stares at her face. If he says she's a beautiful woman . . . "

"Marla, let's finish our run," I urge.

"Yeah, in a minute."

"Would you be interested in posing for headshots, seventy-five an hour? It's all on the up-and-up. I'm a photographer, a bit famous, I don't mind admitting. Look me up on Google. Your pale face with its dark shadows interest me. You can bring your friend with you."

"I'm her sister," I assert.

"Yeah, okay, bring your sister. Whoever you want. It's safe. I'm safe. I'll be in the studio below the house till noon. I'm house sitting for a friend. The place has a glassed-in front and is perched above a dune. It's about half a mile up on the beach. Enjoy the run. Come, Argo."

The dog follows him, leaping in and out of the water.

"I'm going," Marla says.

"Where?"

"To his studio. Why not? Seventy-five dollars, what's wrong with that?"

"A maniac, a . . . "

"Oh come on, you'll be with me. I need something to perk me up."

And already she sounds more cheery.

Marla begins to walk up the beach, calling over her shoulder. "Are you coming?"

We catch up with Marcus as he's unlocking the studio door. "Wonderful, come in," he says, and holds it open. "Not you, Argo,"

30

then shuts the door. It's a small, square, dimly lit room with a few chairs, a table, and a three-sided window with drawn shades. Eerie, I don't say.

"Have a seat, get comfortable," and touches something on the wall. The shades slowly rise, flooding the room with white beach light.

"Cool," Marla says.

"Where's your camera," I ask.

"Tess, give him a moment."

"Your name, Marla, is it?"

"All the time," she says.

From the taxi window, the town passes in a darkening blur. "Are we going to that same place?"

"Look at it this way," Marla says, "A few hours ago I lent out my beauty, earned money, nothing evil occurred, and, Tess, it's going to buy us a few drinks, music, talk. It's healthy. Smile, it's all good."

"How will we get back?"

"Someone with a car will drop us or we'll call a taxi."

"Mom will . . . "

"Stop worrying about her worrying. We have some life to live."

It's as crowded and noisy as it was that awful night. I wait at one of the small tables for Marla to return with our drinks. She doesn't. I scan the room; can't find her, the crowd tightly packed. Shit! I call her phone, it goes to voicemail. I text: Where are you? Nothing back. I get up to go look for her. The noise is loud, high-pitched, almost frenzied. Who can hear a phone ringing? I find the restroom. The door's locked. "Marla, are you in there?"

"Not Marla."

Once more, I scout the room and catch sight of her coming in from outside. She's heading toward the bar. "Marla," I shout. She stops.

"Tess, my best sister, hey."

Already she sounds buzzed. How is that possible? "Where've you been, I was looking for you."

"Yeah, met someone in the ladies, had a few tokes, a snort, you know? And heard that someone outside was selling a bit of something, which I thought to check out. Don't look so concerned, Tess, it won't last."

"What?"

"The high. It never does, alas. It's only temporary. Then the colors dull again, voices sound annoying, words have no matter, days feel endless, and too soon I'm back down with everyone else who never leaves this town."

"We should go home."

"Nothing happening there."

"Okay, maybe have a drink and then go?" I say.

"Yeah, maybe."

"But text me the number of the taxi place."

"Are you leaving me?"

"No. It's for later," I say.

6

At first Nina said no, still too upset by Marla's behavior to imagine enjoying herself. But Peter continued his gentle urging. Finally, she did call into work sick and took the day. In bed together now, his shoulder warming hers, she's not sorry, not at all. The TV news drones on its daily disasters, Dow down 700 points . . . housing crisis worse . . . more troops being sent. Peter seems engrossed, but she allows her mind to replay the last splendid hours. Kicking through a mat of leaves in a woodsy area, Peter calling out names of trees, of tiny winter wildflowers, sharing his love of nature. The sun was white, the cold undeniable.

He took her to an old bar to warm up with Irish coffee, the tables as rickety as the bartender. They shared stories and anecdotes about their lives. Beginnings are like that, filled with mystery, curiosity, and excitement, plush as sable coats, though how would she know?

Peter said he grew up near Portland, Oregon, that his father was killed in a motorcycle accident when he was ten. His mother whom he loves still lives there. But she is and was an alcoholic as far back as he can remember. He sends her money to keep the booze at home and her out of the bars. He said he was a lonely kid who wandered among the big trees after school till hunger sent him home.

She told him about her dad who'd been out of work a lot, at home more than her mother, who worked as many jobs as she could. How glad they were to have Nina squared away in marriage even at seventeen, that they'd died relatively young. She talked some about her brief first marriage, that her husband had been handsome, attentive, and talented. That his drug habit didn't alarm her smitten heart, though soon enough the haze lifted.

She didn't say so, but remembers those days and nights as chaotic, finding herself in one sleazy club after another, listening to his band play. Sex was the culmination not of love, but of titillation. Yet she wouldn't have known to say so then. How could she? Who would have schooled her? No wonder Peter's uncomplicated affection is so satisfying, healing. Actually, everything about him pleases her. Such perfection scares her.

Sunlight deserts the small bedroom. She considers switching on a lamp, but the warmth of his closeness keeps her still.

"I've never felt this way about a woman. It's scary," Peter suddenly whispers, and it feels as if he's crept inside her head.

"It is."

"But we mustn't be afraid," he adds.

"Why not?" she wonders out loud.

"We've lived through much. We're better prepared. Drinks." he declares, interrupting the solemnity to slip out of bed and head to the kitchen.

Outside the window the sky will soon alert her to evening and send her home. She finds the remote, powers off the TV.

He hands her the tray of drinks and slides in beside her.

"I bought you a present," a boyish grin. He takes a tiny package out of the drawer.

"Peter, I can't . . . I . . . "

"Hush. Open it."

On a bed of satin is a delicate bracelet of tiny blue iridescent beads, which she slips on her wrist, the clasp easy.

"From India," he tells her. The beads, that is.

"It's beautiful. Thank you." Ridiculously, the gift saddens her. What is she doing?

Peter stands in the doorway, waving till her car vanishes from sight, then returns inside: a magnificent day followed by a desolate evening. Though they spent more time together than usual, the moment she leaves, he's lonely for her. He wants more of her time but is afraid to say so. Also, it scares him that she disappears into a whole other life, one so separate from him. She once said her girls wouldn't understand their relationship, that mothers must remain in their role as mothers, not lovers.

As a kid, his own flawed mother's power over him sent him out each night to wish on a star to stop her drinking. When he shared this with Nina, she hugged him. What he didn't say is that being in combat taught him that wishing has no power, none at all. In Afghanistan, death at his elbow, he buried all thoughts of a future. It was the wise path to take, but the burial lasted past his return stateside. Until Nina, that is. Now, his emotions seem to overflow like a shaken soda bottle.

I'm flipping pages in the free town paper that mostly offers ads for elsewhere. Marla's curled into the far corner of the couch speaking low on the phone. I have no idea who she's talking with.

"Tess, what time will mom get home?" she asks, grabbing her jacket off the chair.

"Soon. Why?"

"That was Marcus. He's developed my headshots, wants me to see them, said some people are beautiful but not photogenic. I'm both. Going to jog over, take a look, and then I'll return. Tell mom I'm out with a friend."

"I'm going with you."

"Tess, silly, you met him, you saw nothing bad happened. I won't stay long," she says.

"I don't want you there alone."

"Are you strong enough to strangle him if he tries to rape me?"

"Marla, not fair."

"Listen. A stranger walks into our life, my life. That's an unusual occurrence. An omen."

"Of what?"

"I don't know yet, but I'm going to find out."

I slip into my jacket and follow her out the door, then jog alongside her. She laughs. "You are one ridiculous girl, but I'll be completely safe. Go back, please. It's embarrassing to have you tag along. I'll be home before you know I'm gone. Okay," and jogs ahead.

I stand there. No way she'll be home soon. It's true; the man was perfectly polite. Still . . . I head back. The beach is dark, the moon is out, and I use the light from my phone to avoid the incoming tide.

I'm in the bedroom when my mother returns from work, late as usual. Too edgy to chat, I call through the door that Marla's out with a friend, will be home later. I try to read. The words won't sink, and close my eyes, hoping sleep will erase worry.

Useless, and I continue to check the time. It's been almost three hours. I lie there imagining the worst, but resist phoning her. She doesn't want a caretaker; I get it. But what is the worst? That he'll hurt her, assault her, imprison her; she'll never be . . . stop, Tessa. That's my nightmare, not hers. I will phone her; I have to; ten more minutes and . . . I hear the front door; close my eyes again.

"Hey, Tess. Wake up."

"Why?" I say in a pretend sleepy tone but open my eyes. She's perched on my side of the bed.

"I've things to tell you, all great, great, fabulous, listen. Head-shots were gorgeous, is that not wonderful?" the words quick, loud, excited. The smell of whisky comes off her breath. I'm used to the scent of weed on her jacket, which she's still wearing.

I sit up. "Did you have some drinks?"

"We socialized a bit, divine. And tomorrow, Tess tomorrow we're going out to celebrate. You and me out to dinner, not the diner, no, no, someplace fancier. Okay? You'll order the most expensive dish, me too."

Her high can be infectious and she is high.

"He gave you money?"

"I posed for a few more headshots, got paid. Is that not glorious?"

"Can I see some of the headshots?"

"He won't part with them, not yet, says he looks at them even when I'm not there. Is that not a compliment or what?"

"Don't know, but you're flying."

"Correct, Tess, damn correct. And it feels good to fly above the crap. Because I have a new friend, a smart, talented man interested not only in my present but . . . hear this . . . my future!" her eyes wide, bright, glassy.

"You're going to see him again."

"Why wouldn't I, something good finds you, hold onto it, tight. My new motto: Be bold. It pays Tessa, it does. So, I'm giving it to you, a gift, because you're my great sister. I'm starving, come to the kitchen."

Food, coffee might help, wishful thinking. I slip out of bed.

7

Heading home from Raff's I'm as restless as I was going there. No one is around. Marla left home early, which she's done now for weeks, won't say why, just says be patient, wait, I'll tell you all, but wait. She texted me only once today: sheer joy, she wrote. What does that even mean? At least Raff was available. I hoped he'd come up with something exciting for us to do. He didn't. Smoke weed and smooch. He had the privilege of my deflowering a while ago, something I pursued, needing to get it over with. But smooching with him, which he calls having sex is entirely lackluster. Today, he came in two seconds, and then lay there with a stupid grin, half asleep. That's it for me with him.

Passing Kevin's house, I notice Kevin's army medal is no longer pinned to the mourning ribbon on the front door. Did some horrible person pocket it for God knows why? For Kevin's sake, I choose to believe one of his sisters took it as a memento. Raff said none of Kevin's sisters has been seen in the usual places. He said they're ashamed. On seeing my face, he added it's what people are saying. Jesus, I hate this town of small minds.

How desperate Kevin must've felt, I think. Scotty said suicide is cowardly; I don't agree. It's brave to make a decision to leave the future before it happens. I don't know if I could be that brave. But what if everyday felt as hopeless as today?

I cut down the path that leads to the beach. It's cold and damp and I'm hungry and tired, but the gulls and lapping water speak to me, and I need to hear something beside my thoughts.

The car coasts slowly down the rutted driveway. Peter asked her to make tonight an exception and stay to have dinner; it upset her to say no. Since the day weeks ago that she took off from work their usual hours together no longer feel enough. Oh Lord.

Pulling up in front of the house, she sees no lights, no girls, no Scotty. Is she being a fool? Thinking her family need her every minute? Marla texted she'd be sleeping at a friend's place, they're going to a late movie in another town. For weeks, Marla's been out and about with no repeat episodes thank goodness. Though in and out of the house, she's been in an up mood. One recent morning, she asked her daughter if she'd found herself a boyfriend. Marla's sheepish grin said it all. When Nina mentioned it to Tessa, no response. They keep each other's secrets, which doesn't upset her; their closeness pleases her. What does upset her, though, is how quiet Tessa's been lately. Does she feel left out? Not sure it's the right thing to ask. Anyway, Tessa will be home soon, no night owl she.

Wispy clouds sweep a darkening sky as she unlocks the front door, then flicks on lights. A note is taped to the fridge: *"I'm at Rico's. Drive up, have a drink. I don't see you much."*

A stab of conscience stills her. Scotty requesting her presence, that's rare. Is he feeling neglected? She continues to do everything at home that she's always done. Does he feel guilty about all the overtime hours she's allegedly working? That would be awful. Maybe he's become suspicious? Does she want to know? Does she have a choice? She leaves the note for Tess to see and walks back out.

In the car, the radio on, she tries to hear the music and ignore her anxiety, but if Scotty knows . . . she's not ready to uproot her girls or to commit to Peter. It hasn't been long enough. She can't make another mistake.

On the beach road as she nears Hampton Bays the houses owned by the summer people grow larger. The locals are kept busy serving them and make a decent dollar for the eight weeks or so. But in winter it's the locals who frequent the few bars that remain open, like Rico's.

She parks in the small lot and sits for a moment wondering if coming here is a mistake. Too late, she decides, and leaves the car to head toward the square building with its wooden façade and two bay windows. Inside, the dimly lit room alive with voices, every stool taken. She watches Scotty work the bar. He moves quickly, two beers in one hand, two in another, serves them, takes the money, nods thanks for tips, doesn't chat, no surprise, a man of few words.

"Nina, gorgeous," an arm around her shoulder.

"Hi, Rico."

"Your man is a hard worker. What can I get you?"

"Scotch, neat."

He tugs her through to the lip of the bar. "Scotty, a very special scotch, neat." Scotty looks up. "Hi Nina."

Rico pats a young guy on the back. "Give the lady your seat."

It's best to comply, because it's Rico. She nods her thanks and slides onto the leather-padded stool. Scotty places a scotch in front of her. "Glad you came."

Instead of being calming, his welcoming words raise her anxiety: too many lies can do that.

"Are your girls as beautiful as you?" Rico stares at her face in the adjacent mirror.

"More so."

"Hey, name a song . . . we have the oldies . . . and it's yours," Rico says.

"I don't know, I . . . "

"Hey, Scotty, what's a good song for Nina?"

"Let the man work," someone shouts.

"Shut the fuck up, this is my bar."

Scotty pauses, "If I Should Lose You."

Her insides tighten.

"Grab a break, man," Rico orders. "Have a drink with this gorgeous lady. I'll take over for ten or fifteen and not a second more."

They sit at Rico's table against the back wall.

"Are you surprised I came?" she asks, her head starting to ache.

"Should I be?"

"Actually, yes. I was tired. But the girls weren't at home, so I came."

He nods.

She searches his expression, which tells her zero, but there's definitely something on his mind. She knows him long enough to know the invite is proof of that. If only she could close her eyes and vanish like the bad witch in Oz. If somehow he's found out . . .

"Where've you gone?"

"Oh, did you say some ..."

"Not yet, but I will."

Her tension mounting, she takes down the rest of the scotch. "Where's your drink?" is not what she wants to know.

"I don't drink much while working. When the place shuts, I have a few with Rico."

"What's on your mind?" she needs to know.

He looks at her. "I saw Hack. He's thinner than a line, doesn't eat. What if he moved in with us for a while?" His words roll out slowly and only then does she take a breath.

"Of course. No problem," relief flooding her. "Tessa likes him. Marla won't care."

"He gets disability and will chip in, and the couch can . . . "

"Sure, invite him." Her tone more measured; she'd normally resist another mouth to feed.

"I already asked. He refused. If you ask, he'll come."

"You don't know that."

He shrugs. "Thinks you work too hard, wouldn't want to bring more pressure."

"Okay, I'll talk to him." Hack won't be a bother; he'll watch TV stoned. And with Marla out so much, it'll be good for Tessa to have another person in the house. "Is that why I'm here, about Hack?" Braver now.

"I get home half asleep and you're already asleep."

"True."

"Want to stay till closing?"

"I'm tired, should get back. Why'd you pick that song?"

"It was the one at our wedding party."

"Yes," she murmurs. "I remember now." She does. Scotty chose it, a song she didn't know, one from his generation. It was slow and long and they danced to the very end of it, Scotty holding her securely, she, wondering what would come next.

8

Dropping my book bag, leaving my sandy sneakers in the vestibule I head toward the voices in the kitchen. He's here, that man. Marcus. He stands with his hands clasped behind his back like some fucking diplomat. Still in her outdoor jacket, Marla sits close to my mother at the kitchen table. She speaks quickly, one word abetting the next, her eyes wide, aglow, her excitement obvious. How long have they been here? What have I missed?

"Mom, he's doing a portfolio of me, which many modeling agencies will see. That's a fact. He's going to mount a show in which photos of me will be the main attraction. That's a fact. Marcus is famous. He's done many shows. That too is a fact. Mom, it's an opportunity that will never happen again."

He remains wordless, a statue. I don't trust him, I don't. The kitchen with its tightly closed windows is darkening, but no one thinks to switch on a light.

"Is it Marcus who you've been seeing these past weeks?" My mother's voice all wrong, too soft, too iffy. Unassertive.

"Of course. He's already taught me how to sit, pose, use my profile, and a thousand other things. He's so talented."

My mother glances at Marcus, who offers a brief smile.

"Mom, I have to live there, 24/7 in order for this to work. Photos at dawn, at night, please, Mom, wish me luck and don't stand in my way. I'll be less than a mile away."

Objections scream in my head, but would anyone listen? It'll sound self-serving and God, maybe it is. Do they even know I'm standing here?

"What about school? You have only a few months left."

"All taken care of, not to worry." Marla's quick to say.

"Marcus, why are you doing this for my daughter?"

"Mrs. Boyce, she is a photographer's dream, her bone structure, her moody lovely face with its colors and shadows. Others will see that and more, but not if she stays hidden here."

Don't listen to him, I plead silently, though I can't disagree with his description of my sister's photogenic potential. She is, as he says, extremely interesting to look at and I'm not alone in thinking so. Wherever we go, people are drawn to her. Even when she isn't stoned, there's nothing quiet about her.

"Remember,"" Marla takes hold of my mother's hand. "I'll only be a short distance away. What can be wrong with that?"

"True," my mother murmurs, then turns to Marcus. "Promise you'll take good care of my daughter."

"Of course," he intones, then pats my sister's shoulder. "See you in a bit at the house."

As soon as he's gone from sight, and before I can even think to say a word, Marla gets up, grabs my arm, tugs me after her. "Come, help me pack a few things."

I sit on the bed as she flits like a caught bird from drawer to closet to dresser top.

"When I'm successful, you will benefit too. I'm not going to leave you here alone, no way," a quick glance at me. "Once I make enough money, I'll get an apartment in Manhattan. You'll come live with me. Won't you," she suddenly asks as if I'd possibly say no.

"Of course." I nod madly, close to tears, which she doesn't notice.

"Then you'll decide, college, job, or whatever? Money can do that, Tess. Don't you agree?" again she glances at me, as if to make sure I'm there.

"Yes." I want Marcus to disappear.

"This is my opportunity to make it all happen for both of us.

Never for a second think I'd forget you." She's speeding; she's on something. Talking fast, moving fast, she stuffs clothes in a bag that I've never seen before. "Tessa, tell me you get that."

"I do," my voice barely above a whisper. I want to stop her but remain on the edge of the bed, helpless in the face of her happiness.

Then a quick hug and my sister's gone from here, from me.

Left to stare at the mess of half-open drawers, stray shoes, underwear left wherever, and the dark spaces of empty closet hangers. Even if I managed to speak up it wouldn't have mattered. Marla didn't want my opinion. Maybe she already knew what it would be. But do I really know what's best for my sister?

Shouldn't I be grateful that Marla's able to pursue the career she wants? I love her. Why, then, am I so miserable? Perhaps it's envy: Marla's getting out of here. And I'm being left alone to bear the brunt of each day without her.

❋

In her robe at the kitchen table, an old cardigan wrapping her shoulders, Nina can't help but wonder if she made the right decision. The house is cold as usual. Tessa, sequestered in her room, wouldn't talk to her, a statement of her disapproval. But could she object to Marla going just to satisfy Tessa? Asleep now, Scotty too, wouldn't talk to her. She tried to discuss Marla's decision, shared her conflicted emotions. He wouldn't engage, said as he too often does Nina knows her daughters best, his proverbial shrug.

Who can reassure her? Even if she forbade Marla from leaving, her daughter wouldn't listen. Marla's a most determined girl. What good would that be: A run-away daughter?

Marcus is a known photographer not a fly-by-night predator. He's offering to open doors for her daughter. His appearance in Marla's life could be a gift. If his word is as good as Marla believes it is, she will have an opportunity, a career, and a better life. It would be sinful to keep her at home just to keep her here where there's little to gain. Still, it saddens her; Marla now lives elsewhere. How strange.

Opportunity may have once been hers, too, she remembers. She was a few years younger than Marla, about to enter high school. Her English teacher visited her parents to urge them to allow Nina to attend a special high school in Manhattan for gifted students. He told them it would help Nina's future. Her parents couldn't have been more polite, a teacher was to be respected. As soon as he left, however, they put an end to the idea, citing cost of travel, plus a list of whatever. Point is, she didn't attend and can't know if going would've changed all that came after. She couldn't do that to Marla; stop her ahead of a chance.

Outside the closed windows, the beach, which flickers lights in spring is shrouded now in dense, foggy darkness.

9

Snowflakes float in the wind as I traipse across the damp sand hunched into my jacket, which does little to keep me warm. Home without Marla feels more desolate than ever. She's only gone a week, but who's counting? Me, hoping she'll change her mind. I know my sister. If she disapproves of anything there, she won't stay. Though on the phone yesterday her speedy voice did sound happy.

The distance between his place and ours is less than a mile and soon enough I can see the beach house. It must be new; it's not weather beaten like many other beach houses. It's long and low and the shiny wooden front door is ajar. I stick my head in. "Marla?" I call, praying Marcus isn't there. No response. I step into a large room with one windowed wall, tiled floor, long cream-colored couch, driftwood beams cross the ceiling, fireplace and kitchen at the far end.

"Marla?" Louder.

"A door in the paneled wall, touch the knob."

I do. It opens onto another huge room with another windowed wall, now shuttered.

"Wow!"

"Nothing like back home, is it?" In bed in a short black nightie, hair mussed from sleep, Marla slides a hand across the sheets, "Come in and luxuriate."

I kick off my sneakers, climb into the huge bed.

"Marla presses a nearby button and the window blinds rise, revealing beach and water close enough to touch.

"Where's Marcus?"

"Out doing research for a Manhattan and then Florida show. He's fretting that he hasn't nailed down a theme yet." Marla extracts pills from one of two bottles on the bedside table.

"What are those?"

"Marcus is generous with his supply. He allows me two pills in the a.m. and two others in the p.m. And, Tessa, these little babies make the present feel fine. So why suffer it?"

"You sound like Hack."

"You worry for naught, sweet sister, only the undisciplined become addicts. I'm in the driver's seat. Anyway, if I take more than what's allotted, Marcus will remove them all. He explained it clearly."

"Are you nuts! He's feeding you drugs daily! You took stuff before but not every morning and night, it was . . ."

"Tessa, I'm not stupid. I understand his need to control. It doesn't bother me, doesn't hurt me. I'm not controllable. We have good times. He takes me places I could never go otherwise: fancy restaurants, art galleries, museums, and shopping for expensive clothes. Who cares if he enjoys choosing what he says will enhance my beauty. He's an artist. How does any of his generosity hurt me? It doesn't. I'm his pretty little model, and one day after I've had enough, I'll leave with more culture, clothes, and probably money. What's the fucking downside?"

"I don't know," I say miserably.

"I'm not going to end up like mom, having to work overtime for an extra few dollars."

"We don't have to repeat her life."

"Of course we do, maybe not in a cafeteria kitchen, but in some other dead-end job. There's no stairway to heaven from poverty town. No one opens doors for people like us unless we do something outrageously special. Marcus is going to do for me what I could never do without him: help make me a known model. Hey, smile. I'm happy."

"So, everything is just perfect?"

"Perfect? Who expects perfect? I don't always understand what he wants from me. He's moody, but still, I'm grateful. He's famous, cultured, handsome, experienced, and he chose me."

"He gives you cash?"

"He takes care of anything I need."

"Isn't he going to pay you for modeling?"

"He will. As soon as he settles on a theme for the show my work begins." Marla's tone dips as if threatened by a thought. She slips out of bed to stand at the window.

"I miss you at home," and slide off the bed to join her.

Seagulls wheel past, their cries inaudible through the glass.

"I miss you, too. Visit as often as you want. Marcus won't mind."

"He makes me uncomfortable." I say truthfully.

"Suit yourself."

"Why was the door ajar?"

"For Argo, sweet dog gets tired of being outdoors and comes home."

"Remember how badly we wanted a dog?"

"I do. But there was never enough money, though mom works her ass off. With Marcus, that's not a problem," her voice speeding up. "Hey, I'm going to serve us a majestic breakfast: eggs a la something, or would you prefer French toast, my dear? Espresso is on the house."

Her perky tone saddens me. It's as if she's leaving me again.

Trudging home on the darkening beach, it's colder, the wind angry. Marla's gleeful voice extolling her great adventure echoes in my head. She talked nonstop. Do the pills make her think only happy thoughts? At some point she's bound to crash, and than what? She's wrong about Marcus, wrong about all of it. A man twice her age, pills to adjust her moods, it can't be good. It isn't good, no matter what she says. My sister, a princess locked in a palace, but instead of feeling imprisoned believes she's privileged. It's scary as hell. I tried, I did, to say some of this, but she shrugged me off.

Small, anchored boats bob precariously in the current, the tide coming in. Low tide, high tide, it never stops, endless and without meaning. A distant slice of moon peeks through fast moving clouds. I don't want to go home. My mother still at work and dinner alone with Scotty is torture; he can sit there without saying a word. Yesterday after some lame excuse, I ate in my room. He didn't object. He's only interested in me to appease my mother.

I head to Hack's bungalow. Stoned, yes, but he's communicative, sort of. Truth is, he doesn't care enough about much to pretend, impress, or lie. Tall, wiry, he's built nothing like Scotty. Marla and I don't look alike either. While I favor my mother, rumor has it that Marla resembles our father, that shadowy figure I can't bring to life. When I told Hack that my father had been a Grateful Dead follower, he wasn't impressed.

I knock. No response, and push, the door opens. "Hack, it's Tessa, I'm walking in."

Under a dim lamp and the flickering light of a muted TV, he's a blurry figure on the couch.

"What brings me the gift of you?"

"How stoned are you?"

"Deep."

Marla on drugs, Hack on drugs, who knows who else? What am I missing? I need Hack available now to hear about Marla. I need to tell someone. If I tell my mother, it won't end well, and Marla will never forgive me.

"Are you about to pass out?" my voice loud.

"Whoa, girl, I can still hear, a soldier pays attention. The captain said so. Sent me out to check the bodies. Were they breathing? Would not trust fingers on a pulse for such a serious decision, I bent my ear close to the bloody mouth to wait for a breath. Is that determination?"

"Oh crap, you are wasted."

"Alive and wasted. What does that mean on a daily basis. You tell me?"

"Hack, I haven't come here to talk about you."

"Words mean shit."

"I'll visit another time."

"Sorry to see you go."

As I reach the house, my mother's getting out of the car.

"Is the cafeteria open all night?"

"It's cold, Tessa. I'm going in, are you coming?"

"I hope there's food in the house. I haven't eaten forever."

Scotty's in the living room, I hear the TV voices.

As my mother flicks on the kitchen lights and takes out some dishes, I follow her like a hungry cat. It's more than food I crave.

"Tessa, what's with you? Bad day?"

"Do you care?"

"Yes. I do."

"Then why aren't you home more?"

"I'm trying to make extra money. So, tell me . . . "

"What exactly," I snap, my tone upsetting her, but it's that or loud, gawping sobs.

"I'm too tired for your mood. Do you want an omelet? If not, I'm going to watch TV."

"Yes, I want an omelet."

In no time my mother puts the food on the table and sits next to me. "Have a few bites, then, please . . . tell me what's troubling you."

"I stopped in at Hack's. He was wasted. It's depressing."

"Scotty says his brother's not eating. Would you mind if he stayed with us for a while?"

"Fine by me. But why would he want to?"

"Don't know. I'll ask him, see what he says. Tell me why you're upset? Was it Hack? Was it hunger?"

I'm shoveling food in my mouth.

"You miss Marla?"

"What do you think?"

"Me, too. But when I was in Junior High . . . "

"Mom, you told me that story."

"You haven't brought friends home in a while."

"This isn't a hospitable house. And my friends bore me during the day. Why would I want to spend more time with them? The girls can't wait to marry and get pregnant. Then their whole future will be taken care of. No more big decisions, just daily ones. I'm going to bed."

In my room, I open the laptop and write, "What kind of drug makes you feel everything's fine," and wait for Google to reply.

10

It's always fucking freezing here; I pull the old quilt tighter around me. No use complaining out loud. Scotty will say to sleep in a heavy sweater. Electricity and heat are the means by which Scotty exhibits his unspoken hostility. I said as much to my mother, who didn't reply. Good, because I didn't want to hear that he's keeping expenses down, especially not after Marcus's generosity was laid out so clearly a few days ago. He's taken my sister on a jaunt somewhere. She didn't say where or when she'd return. I had a feeling she didn't know.

Wherever she is, she can answer the phone, can't she? I call her.

"Hey Tessa."

"Where are you?"

"A few dunes away," she sounds too cheery for my mood.

"When did you get back?"

"Does it matter, lovely sister?"

"I'm not going to class. I'm available."

"Excellent timing. Marcus is out working. Meet you on the beach in ten minutes."

Suddenly, seeing her makes me anxious. What's that about? Must be my night of anxious dreams dogging me. Dressing quickly, warmly, heavy socks, I can't seem to put on enough clothing.

Marla's there at the water's edge, her jacket unzipped over a low cut, silky blouse I've never seen. The wind whips her thick hair every which way. She looks wild and strangely otherworldly, a spirit source arisen from the sea, delicate, untouchable, a picture without a frame. "You'll freeze," I say, embarrassed by my thoughts.

"We're going to Central Park. I have money. We'll be like little kids on an outing alone for the first time," her words quick.

"Are you okay?"

"Why not? We'll walk to the train station. Not that far, no I remember not. Hurry, the next train could be pulling into the station any minute."

I hold back the questions gathering like a knot in my stomach. Did she fight with Marcus? Did something happen on their trip, but what, because though present, she's elsewhere.

On a fairly crowded train we find two seats near a man who gazes out the window. Marla talks to him about scenic views and other nonsense. The man says not one word. I poke her to stop bothering him, but she ignores me.

We exit Penn Station and head up Sixth Avenue to the park. She's walking so fast I can barely keep up. She can't stop talking, commenting on everything in sight: women's attire, building height, street smells, even the traffic light she swears favors red over green.

"Marla, stop. Just stop. You're too jumpy."

"I have to keep up the energy."

"Or what?"

"Not to suddenly crash while we're at the park. Marcus took away my coming down pills because I snagged an extra one last night. Don't look so shocked. It's my fault. Let's just go and do and be and enjoy whatever. Tessa?"

She wants me to say okay, but I can't, and I'm having second thoughts about going to a park. If she crashes, what do I do?

As if reading my thoughts she slings an arm around my neck, whispers, "It's going to be fine. It always is fine."

The carousel, open for one more week, will close until April, the sign reads. Though the music plays, no one is on it. Marla buys us five rides apiece. We mount two adjacent ponies. The music, the up and down motion, being the only two riding, I find myself laughing along with Marla despite the absurdity of the moment. The ticket man comes out of the booth to watch us. We are on stage, two stars, the place is ours and it's both ridiculous and wonderful.

Marla's excitement infectious we hold hands, run up and down hills, and then across the grass in search of food. The venders parked in a clutch are happy to see us. We buy something from each one: cookies, peanuts, ice cream, lemonade, popcorn, and with arms filled find a flat rock to sit on.

"Is everything okay with you and Marcus?" I finally ask.

"Of course."

"Mom wants to visit you."

"Not going to happen."

"Why not?"

"I need to protect my environment from judgment."

"She wants to see you," I persist, needing my mother to go there.

"I'll come see her. In a while."

Before finishing even a few of the goodies, she grabs my arm. "Up. Up. Let's go," the uneaten food dumped in a trash bin. I won't try to slow her down; I've been warned. She has the lead: I follow to the children's playground, which is without children. Of course, too cold for little kids to play here, but Marla's already climbing jungle gym, and as lithe as a monkey gets to the top in no time, calls down, "Lovely view. Come on up, chicken."

I gaze up at her with a dumb smile until she descends, and again follow her to the swings. Side by side and pumping high, I'm waiting for the crash, it has to happen. She doesn't stop talking though I'm no longer listening, feeling helpless.

Jumping off the swing, she shouts, "Let's go," and heads toward the nearby zoo. I'm not a fan of watching caged animals prowl around in small spaces, especially ones from hot climates exposed to winter weather. But I know now we'll only be there a minute or two. Most of the animals are not outdoors, only the seals and penguins oblige us with their presence. "Funny little men in tuxedos," Marla says, her voice slowed, slurry, and lower.

"I'm cold, let's get some coffee," I say.

She shakes her head once quickly, begins to walk. "I must get back to Marcus."

"Come home with me, I plead. "You can sleep off the crash. I won't leave you alone."

"I can't. I won't be able to sleep, not at all, not without the pills. Marcus will understand. I'll promise. I'll swear never to disobey again. I'll tell him he's made his point. Need to go back now, Tessa."

On Fifth Avenue, Marla hails a taxi to Penn Station. She's no longer talking. Now it's her silence that freaks me.

It's rush hour. Everyone pushes into the train to secure a seat. Marla stands inside the open door, letting people move past her. When the door closes, she slumps against it.

I want to shout seeing what these fucking drugs do to her. But her trembling hands, pale face, and anxious eyes silence me. "Is there anything I can do?"

She shrugs and says nothing.

On the beach, walking quickly and silently toward the house, Marla tugs me to a stop. "There is something you can do," her voice desperate, still slurry. "A favor. Come back with me. I'll tell Marcus you haven't slept for a few nights, that I promised he'd give you something to help, do that for me, Tessa, please. Tomorrow, things will go back to usual, but tonight I can't bear the sleepless hours of scary images, sweats and horrid stomach pains. Please. I won't ask you to do this again. I swear!"

"He'll want me to swallow the pill there. He's not stupid."

"Pretend to put it in your mouth, slip it between your fingers. It's tiny. He'll give you water. Swallow. Close your hand in a quick tight fist to press the pill into your palm. We hold hands as I walk you to the door and you slide me the pill. It'll work. I know it will."

Desperation as invention, I think miserably. "He'll see it," I plead, as if being caught would be the worst thing. "Take one from his stash."

"Can't. He counts them."

"But I don't want to be near him." He's crazy, I don't say.

"I'd do it for you, though, right?"

She would.

Slipping her arm through mine, my reluctant body continues to follow her lead. At the house, she knocks hard at the locked door. Marcus opens it, in khakis and a polo shirt.

"Hi ladies! Have a good day?"

I nod, afraid my voice will fail me.

"Wonderful day," Marla's tone phony-breathy as if coming off hours of exhaustive fun. "We did so much, I'm beat. Listen, Tessa came for a favor. Midterms are here and she hasn't slept well in the last three nights. I kind of promised you'd give her a night pill, just this once. She'll take it here and by dark, it'll tire her. I've talked her into it. She hates any kind of pill. But she needs to ace those tests."

"I do," which sounds lame to my ears.

"No bother," Marcus says. He disappears, returns with a glass of water and hands me a tiny white pill.

I pretend to put it in my mouth, close my hand over it, take two sips of water, and swallow. "Thanks, Marcus. Marla, I have to go."

"Okay, sweetie, call me after the test tomorrow." Taking my hand, the pill successfully transferred, my sister gives me a meaningful hug.

Walking home, I'm afraid for my sister. The suddenness of her reversal from cheery to desolate was scary. What's happening to the wiring in her brain? My stomach churns with hatred for that man. I allow myself a quick fantasy of calling the police of saying Marcus's place is a drug den, that he's feeding pills to young women. If I were to really do that, Marla would never speak to me again, a difficult price to pay. She's right. I am chicken or I would do something, anything to call attention to Marcus's behavior. Thing is, she won't leave no matter what I do.

But someone needs to intervene, do something to get her out of there: Maybe a social worker? They're trained to handle addiction and other family problems. Lots of families around here get visited, though nothing changes, or nothing I can see.

Looking past the water into a dark sky, hearing the soft slap of wavelets against the moored boats, I feel even more alone.

I switch on the only lamp that still has a working bulb.

"Did you just make the sun shine?" Hack stretched out on our old couch. The TV is on, the volume muted.

"When did you get here?" I say, taken aback.

"Story too long."

"I didn't hear you come in this morning."

"Stealth, my LT's favorite word. He gave the word to me. I use it, but he'll never know. Gone. LT O'Connell, our stealth man."

"You're stoned already."

"I'm dedicated to routine."

"What are you watching?"

"Yesterday's football game."

"You already know who won." Do I care?

"Winning, losing . . . what war's about."

"I'm starving. Did you check the fridge?"

"Didn't check and don't care, either."

"Would you try the diner with me?"

"I would not."

"You never go anywhere," I complain as if that's the source of my misery.

"Girl. I'm somewhere now."

"Did my mother talk you into moving in?"

"Must have."

"Any specifics to share?"

"That you needed my company."

"Really?" I consider this. "That was smart. Lately, she's hardly at home and I don't all that much relish your brother's company."

"I wouldn't mind another beer but getting up . . . "

"I'll bring you two," suddenly glad he's here.

In the kitchen I take three bottles from Scotty's stash in the fridge. I hand two to him.

"I skipped classes."

"Yeah . . . "

"I was with Marla."

He twists off the cap, takes a swig.

"We went to Central Park."

He nods.

"My sister's a drug addict and no one cares," I say.

He nods.

"You can't be company if you don't talk to me."

"I'm retired from loud noise."

"I'm not shouting." Though I'm not talking softly.

"Also, battles," his eyes on the TV screen.

"I'm supposed to meet Raff tonight, but I'm cancelling."

"Why?"

"Don't want to leave you alone."

"Girl, I'm alone with everyone."

11

"Would you like to stop in at that old bar for some Irish coffee before . . . "

"Peter, I mentioned I have to be home earlier today. Tessa's been . . . I don't know, something, probably missing her sister. And Scotty's brother . . ."

"Yes, you did say." They're at the kitchen table, a half-bottle of scotch stands sentry.

"What's wrong? Something is. I can feel it."

He takes her hand. "Richie is getting out of the hospital. He needs his house this house back."

"Oh." Somewhere an owl screeches.

Peter pours an inch of Scotch in each of their glasses. "I offered to rent this shitty house so we could stay here. But Riche needs it in order to remain near the hospital for his continuing treatments. I've been looking for places since I heard. Whatever's available is too far from your job, traveling would cut short our time together. I don't want that. I'll keep looking, but until something better turns up, I reserved our old motel room. Not much of a place, I know, but where else can we go?" He sounds wretched.

"When do we have to leave here?"

"Three days."

"I see."

"Nina, honey."

"I don't have time to discuss this now."

"I know, didn't want to ruin our hours together. Also, I worried your response wouldn't be what I wanted to hear."

"What do you want to hear?"

"That we'll manage, that nothing as trivial as a place to live would keep us apart."

"Peter. It's not trivial, but we will manage, we have to. Okay, sweet man?"

***

As usual, he stands outside the house, waving until her car is out of sight. The darkening winter sky returns him to the kitchen, the whiskey, and the emptiness, which tonight feels worse. He pours more scotch in the glass. How long can they live happily at a motel, a room with a bed and a window? It was fine for the first weeks of getting to know each other, but their relationship has progressed, deepened. Besides revisiting a past scene can be a bummer; he learned that in each successive tour.

He wants Nina to move in with him forever. That's what he wants and he'll never stop wanting that however long it might take. But man, life is truly precarious, another take-home lesson of war. The glass drained, he pours in more.

Damn, he could offer her a paradise in California, a life of ease and comfort, togetherness. He'd get back into carpentry. People always needing this or that built or fixed or changed. It's what he did before. Between what he saved during his tours and what he'd earn, Nina wouldn't have to work. If she wants a job, it wouldn't be a problem: hospitals, diners, shops, part-time, full-time, whatever made the woman smile would be fine with him.

Someday . . . but the moment has to feel right, he'll bring up California, and not as an ultimatum. If she says, not yet, he'll remain here until she's ready. God, if someone could tell him when that might be . . . He pours more scotch, emptying the bottle. Who cares? He's only going to bed alone, except he's not ready for sleep.

If they could chat in the evenings, it would help. What if he calls her at home? Who would he hurt? She has her own phone. But what if her husband picks up? So, his wife has a friend, big deal. Or the daughter answers, he could say, "Hello, I'm a friend of your mom's. Is she there?" Mom gets on the phone; he says, "Baby, I can't bear being without you." And ... she hangs up, rightfully so. Wrong number she tells them sitting at their cozy family dinner.

He has a car now. He knows where she lives. Drive over? Nothing criminal about visiting the house where the woman he loves resides. Criminal is killing civilians for no good reason. Criminal is manufacturing enemies that don't exist. Hear that, Bush? But visiting a house is not criminal. Maybe knock at the door, ask for directions to somewhere, take a peek inside, or he could ask to . . . Millions of ruses to use for an imaginative guy like him.

Remembers how once in a while at school he'd suddenly have a premonition of disaster and walk out, go home, check to see if his mother was on the couch or the floor. Cited for cutting, threatened with suspension, expulsion, he'd make up outrageous stories that got him off the hook. He can't remember one now.

Sitting here bathing in self-pity isn't helping. He tosses the empty bottle in the trash bin, grabs his jacket and palms the keys. He walks into the impenetrable darkness, gets in the car, and chucks the jacket in the rear seat. Is misery the price of love? It sure leads to long, lonely nights, and memories he'd thought he'd buried deeply.

Check: license in his wallet, wallet in side pocket, registration in glove compartment. Okay, he's been drinking, is drunk, and must not speed. Reminds himself again . . . do not speed. How many cars can there be on a country road at this time of night? Not many. He'll be easy prey for any uniform.

The car still idling, his thoughts tangle, out the window shadows and shapes. His mood dark, the whiskey doesn't help. Drunk like his mom, isn't he? Jesus! The night's too powerful, put an end to it, and drags his ass to bed to save whatever dignity he still has.

Driving the empty road home, the move out of Richie's place worries her. In her life, change didn't end well. This is different; the motel is a temporary stop on the way to something better. She knows Peter will keep searching. He was willing to rent Richie's house just so they could stay there together. She's touched, more than that, amazed. Who in her life would've ever done something rash for her?

It galls her, it does. The beach houses left empty all winter yet not possible to rent because some owner may decide to use it on some weekend. And how often does that happen? The waste of it!

Angry sea wind shakes the tree limbs as the car coasts down the rutted driveway. She's a few minutes later than promised. The first night and poor Hack will have to wait for his dinner. He didn't want to come stay with them. Early in the a.m. she laid a Tessa trip on him, and Scotty rang later to say he showed up.

"Hi," she calls.

"Mom, I'm famished." Tessa appears, a blizzard of auburn hair framing her delicate face.

"It'll be a bit though before the food . . . "

"Hack and I had some beers. We're starving."

The back door slams. Scotty. For a moment, she and Tessa listen to the low murmur of the brothers in the living room.

"Tessa, help me scrape the carrots and tell me about your day."

"You want me to leave the men alone?"

"What does that mean?"

"With his brother here, Scotty's more wakeful."

"That's a good thing."

"Except Hack is here to keep me company."

"Join in, then."

"War talk. Mom you shouldn't work this late, it's not worth it. All that extra money hasn't changed a thing, at least nothing I notice." Tessa's glance takes her in with something more than sympathy.

"Are you going to help or not?" She places a bowl on the table.

"Their talk could be interesting. Maybe I'll learn if there are different wars or just different places to fight them?"

Dumping uncut carrots in the boiling water, she stands near the stove. If it weren't for Tessa, she wouldn't mind getting wasted tonight.

12

About to take a quick run on the beach before class, I notice a van parked further up the road. Unusual. Maybe it's abandoned. Near the choppy water, the packed sand is damp. Timid wavelets swirl up around my sneakers. In the near distance a group is playing Frisbee. So early! Who are they? I jog toward them.

"Hey." A tall, thin woman with long dirty blonde hair and dangly earrings that spark like bits of lightening greets me, a wide smile on her face, her open jacket reveals bouncy bra-less breasts. She isn't alone.

"Hey," I say.

"I'm Jeri, this is JJ, Manny, and Suzanne." The group folds themselves around me with sweet energy. "Come hang out with us."

"I'm Tessa. I'm on my way to class. Maybe later?"

"Absolutely and exceptionally cool, Tessa. We're here for a few days. Find us when you can. We love meeting different people wherever we land."

"Okay," I say, kind of excited by their presence.

"Later," Jeri calls as the group walks down along the shoreline and wave back at me. They're all wearing earrings, the men, too. They're not much older than me and clearly not from around here. I'm tempted to cut classes again, but I'll find them on the way home, something to look forward to.

I dress with an energy I haven't had since Marla left me, which is how it feels, and maybe it always will. After spending several glorious days with my new friends they invited me to join the gang, which is what they call themselves, and travel with them. It warms me to think how quickly they accepted me as one of their own. Pure Karma.

I said I would think about it. And I have, a lot, day and night. Marla's gone. My mother isn't home till dark. What is there here for me, more loneliness despite Hack? Leaving will upset my mother, of course it will, but she'll get over it. I'm not running away, I'll be in touch. We have phones; we'll talk, probably more often than we do now. This is what kids my age do, have done for eons. I'll tell her about my new friends once I'm on the road to adventures that'll teach me more than school ever could. Besides how many weeks are left before I graduate, not many? And then what, which I no longer have to worry about.

Marla will be excited for me. She'll get it. She made her choice. Now I'll make mine. There's hope in this world after all, and a strange mellow joy enters my soul. I have new, interesting friends who roam the wilds, do odd jobs and keep the journey going. What matters most to them are imagination, contribution, and creation. They aim to add not subtract from wherever they land; they've already been many places. Their jubilant vibe is infectious.

Jeri, gleeful, vivacious and affectionate, often grabs my hand like a long-lost sister. JJ, such a serious little face, but not at all serious. He's the straight man to Manny's jokes that had us all laughing till our sides hurt. Suzanne, who trails Manny wherever he goes, is the quietest, and the least curious about me. The others want to know everything. When I told them my father had been a Grateful Dead follower, they anointed him one righteous man.

Scotty is brewing coffee in his old pot with a lid and a spout, the kind that no one uses anymore.

"You're up early."

I shrug. He doesn't pursue it. Lack of genuine interest is my theory. It doesn't matter. He doesn't matter. I'm psyched to exit a future where everyone accepts things as they are. Meeting the gang is destiny.

My bag of clothing is already in the van. I gave JJ the one-time fee for food and general maintenance. Hack loaned me the money and, as expected, asked no questions. It didn't feel great taking money from him but other than booze and pills—which Hack's disability checks cover—what does he need money for? The man doesn't go anywhere. So, I'm not depriving him of anything vital, God forbid. I intend to repay. I do. I'll keep in touch with him.

Jogging down the ramp to the beach, a surge of anticipation wells up in me. Before my little girl birthdays, my mother would talk about the fun and candy and ice cream; staying up late the night before was a sense of grown-up freedom. Now more than a sense, I'm about to own it. Traveling will turn the ordinary into the extraordinary, provoke joy from the simple taste of cold beer and hot French fries—what's wrong with that?

No one is here yet but I'm early. It's damp and windy, the iron gray sky promises crappy weather. It won't matter; we'll be in the van, probably singing.

JJ said the plan is to first head north, maybe Montreal, then Quebec, then west to Vancouver and British Columbia. Jeri mentioned she has family in Calgary but didn't plan to visit. Said, it's a town on the water where we could park the van for a while and maybe do some odd jobs. I didn't ask what kind of jobs and wonder now what they might be. Perhaps they make jewelry and other things, then sell them on the road or . . . Where else would they sell them, I can't imagine. Clearly, they've survived and prospered, proof they know how.

I wrap my arms in straitjacket style around my lightly clad chest. I'm too revved up to be still and begin walking backwards along the water's edge to keep watch. Nothing but sand until a figure appears atop the ramp and heads toward the beach. It's too far to see exactly who it is, but it looks like JJ, thin, dark hair. Maybe there's been a glitch, flat tire or sick person? Anything can put off a departure. He'll take me to where the van is parked. I run to meet him and see the dog: a man walking his dog. Not JJ. The man unleashes the animal and then sprints after the dog as it runs along the shore.

The incoming water undulates past the ridges of low tide only to recede further. I find a patch of semi-dry sand and sit. It's a little past eleven, more than an hour since I arrived.

My mother taught me how to tell time when I was little. That way at Sadie's, where a big clock adorned the kitchen wall, I'd be able to know when my mother would arrive from work to pick me up. One day she didn't show up at her usual time. I watched the clock fearing abandonment. When she arrived two hours later, my relief was so profound that it was almost worth the misery.

And now, too, I'm starting to feel the pull of fear, which no doubt will be relieved by their appearance. I don't care why they're late as long as they get here. But how long to wait: Till dark? Return tomorrow morning? The group has no idea where I live, so going back home to wait is out of the question. I try to think: Did they mention where they park over night? They never said.

By late afternoon the wind has picked up and small bits of gritty sand fly at my face as I pace back and forth near the ramp. Hack told me that the sandstorms in the desert could blind a guy. Well, it's not that bad here. A coin of milky sun tries to break through the gathering clouds. Taking out my phone I check to see if I have a text, but they don't have my number.

"Are you pondering your environment?" the man quips as his dog rushes ahead to the water.

And maybe I should; it'd be safer than the intrusive questions piling up in my head: How to reach them if not on the beach? Did the police pick them up as vagrants? Did the van breakdown? Or did they take my money and clothes and leave town? Did they play me? Earn my trust with a few days of cavorting together? JJ suggested he take the money and bag of clothing a day before departure, because, he said, they pack the van the night before. Still . . .

The clouds have won the contest, not a hint of sun to warm a body.

Dusk arrives with its false promise of home fires, but no one from the gang has appeared. My body is stiff with tension. Stupid. Stupid. I've been played. They took my money, and clothes, too, of course they did. It's how they manage. Odd jobs my ass. I begin to laugh, loud hearty shouts of laughter. The milk has been spilt; I'll not waste my tears, and head home to Hack, who's taken residence on the couch, it seems.

In what passes for a living room Hack is trying to read the label on a small vial of pills.

"Share, Hack, share," My hand is out.

"What?"

"Whatever you just popped, I want."

"Why give you stuff prescribed for me?" Even stoned he sounds perplexed.

"Because I know that you know that most of the shit you take isn't prescribed. Because I'm tense and upset, because I've had a can't-be-beat awful day, because why not?" I take the vial out of his hand, remove two pills, swallow them on my saliva, and wait nervously. Nothing. Then pace the room to aid the work of my nervous system. Isn't that where such pills go?

Hack tries to stand but falls back on the couch. Tries again, and unsteady, ambles to the kitchen, returns with two beers, hands me one. Imitating what I've seen Scotty do again and again, I twist off the cap, tilt back my head and guzzle down as much of the liquid as I can.

"Tastes best from the bottle."

"Why?" I ask not remotely caring.

"The kid at the base . . . could down a can without taking it from his mouth. After two cans the kid wobbles away . . . doing a hula dance . . . cracks us up. Very devoted to us. We love him. Comes every day . . . No one says why he's dead."

"Sad story." I sit in Scotty's chair and face Hack, whose eyes open and close, though maybe it's my eyes.

"Do you want to hear about my day?" I ask listening to my voice.

"Am I a priest?"

"Forget it."

"What?"

"I spent a windy day at the beach waiting for assholes to fly me to the moon."

"A riot."

"Yeah, funny, so funny, you might've heard me laughing like a loony-tune."

"Seeing you get high . . . makes me jealous, like watching someone eat ice cream for the first time."

"You aren't interested in my hard luck story. I lost money, your money, some clothing, too."

"Minor losses," he says more solemnly than most of his words.

"Well, I want to apologize for the money that I took from you and gave away."

"Bad, bad girl, twenty push-ups and twenty laps around the house."

I laugh, but it's a funny sound more like a croak. "Is that what you had to do?" The words are now a bit harder to push out, something to do with my breathing, or is it my tongue?

"I was the good—the very good soldier—ask anyone. Saluted my superiors, killed their enemies, not mine. Did I lose men? You fucking bet I did. But a good, good soldier was I, not on one tour, not two but three tours. How do you fucking like that?"

"I'm really hungry," I say from a distance and wait to hear if there's an echo. "I need . . . "

"Who wants my stories? Not me."

"It's just that I haven't eaten all day." Suddenly, my empty stomach feels excavated. I want something sweet; a piece of candy would be great.

13

Self-exiled in my room, gazing out the window at the dark unknown, not sure what Hack remembers of yesterday. Still hung over from the pills and beer, one thing is sure: drugs are not on my future agenda. During the night, pictures, colors, and sounds played in my head like a bad symphony. How I got to bed remains a mystery. Did Hack take me? Jesus! He was far from steady himself. Did my mother? Probably not or she would've gone on and on, and I'd recall that.

What is clear in my all-day sorrowful brain is the gang that never showed, their image as sharp as broken glass. It's going to take a while to erase them from up-front memory. That I even believed them shames me. The whole episode a result of Marla being gone, though how can I blame her for wanting something more, too? I can't.

I've tried to reach my sister all day, tell her about the pills I took yesterday and so on and so on, but she and Marcus may be away on one of their jaunts.

"Dinner, everyone," my mother calls as my phone rings.

"Marla, Jesus, finally, do you know how many ti—"

"I need you," Marla's tone frantic.

"What's wrong?"

"Everything. I don't know, can't be alone, hard to breathe, scary noises. I need you. Come now. You have to."

"Where's Marcus?"

"Florida, two days, working. Get Mom to drive you. Need you

here. Now. Can't do Mom. Not now. Say you're on the way. I don't want to die. Tessa?"

Her breathless urgency terrifies me. "I'm coming."

They're all sitting at the kitchen table. "Mom. Marla phoned."

"Oh. You should've told me. I . . ."

"I need to go there. Right now."

"What? Why?"

"Please drive me. Don't ask me anything more."

"Tell me," She stands, her fingers strong on my shoulders.

"She took some pill, I think, and it's having weird side effects. She's scared. She can't breathe. She can't be alone. Marcus is in Florida. That's all I know."

"Get your jacket. Sorry, guys, we'll be back soon."

We rush out to the car. Doors slam. Hands clasping the wheel, my mother drives quickly her lips pressed tight; neither of us speaks. What's there to say? Headlights cut a funnel of light along the dark route.

We park at the front door. "Mom, I'll phone you to pick me up. You can't come in. She wants just me."

"I'm going in."

"Please. Don't," I beg. "It'll make matters worse. I promise. Please. I need you to hear me. Please!"

She studies my no doubt alarmed face. "You tell Marla I'm out here and not leaving till I see her. Ten minutes, then I come in."

Before she can say another word, I bolt from the car.

Thank God, the door's ajar; the dog must be out. Inside, the place is lit up like a stage, lights everywhere. "Marla?"

"Bathroom. Tessa?"

Perched on the rim of the tub, her head bobbing, arms slung around her body, heels tapping the floor, her pupils as dilated as a cat's in the dark. How long has she been like this? All day?

I undo the wrap of her arms, help her stand and slide an arm around her waist. "It's going to be okay. Let's walk. Water will dilute whatever you've taken." Is that true? It was in a movie I saw. Did it help? I can't remember.

We shuffle slowly across to the kitchen alcove; her trembling body leans on me. Without letting go of her, I fill a glass with water. She takes only a sip.

"Tell me what you took, why is this happening," I say gruffly, suddenly furious at her.

"The green pill, then the blue, wanted . . . needed to feel fine . . . didn't, tried . . . Tessa, make it stop,"

"What?"

"The whoosh in my ears, so loud. Make it stop." Her voice childish, her face scrunched against whatever terror has her in its grip.

"Take another sip," I hold the glass near her lips, but she moves her head away. What if she's poisoned? Dying? Needs a hospital? I can't handle this; it's too scary. I've seen her stoned, but she's out of control. "Mom's in the car. Let me get her."

"Can't, no, she can't see me this way, she'll blame Marcus. Not his fault. Please. Keep her out, for now. Oh God, make it go away! The lights," she pleads. "They hurt."

I switch off the overhead, leave on the lamps. And continue to slowly circle her around a room so beautiful anyone would be envious, except none of that matters now.

※

It's been seven minutes. Three more, but she can't just sit here. Damn. That stupid girl, what is she taking now? Why isn't Marcus caring for her? What's going on inside? If she phones Scotty he'll tell her not to worry, Marla will be fine, let her be, just come back. If she phones Peter, he'll provide words of support. It's not enough. She wants someone to relieve her, to take over, to make it all easier. She dials Peter's number anyway.

"Hello," a groggy voice.

"Are you drunk?"

"Nina? No. You woke me. Am I dreaming?"

"I'm in front of where my oldest is staying. She's freaking out on some drug but doesn't want me to come in. Tessa is with her. I'm beside myself."

"For God's sake. Don't listen. Go in. Just go. I've handled a few too many soldiers on stuff. If she's jumping out of her skin stand behind her, wrap your arms around her as tight as you can, hold her still, tell her to breathe slowly, and reassure her softly. Don't let her sleep till some of it begins to wear off. If you need to call me when you're with her, pretend I'm a medic. I'm awake now. I love you, Nina."

She turns off the headlights, rushes to the front door pushes it open. Her daughters are circling a huge room. Marla's head bobs; her shoulders twitch. Without a word, she removes Tessa's arm from her sister's waist, and stands behind Marla, pulling her close. She holds her still, and speaks softly. "Baby, this will end. It's an episode. It won't last. It will get better soon. Do what I say. Breathe in slowly; now breathe out, slowly, slowly. Good, that's it."

With her arms wrapped around her first born she continues to coo, not sure what she's even saying, but doesn't stop. This is the child who used to grab her skirt to toddle alongside wherever she went, who drove her mad with constant requests: Momma, see this, watch that, play with me, dress up. The girl was a miniature director who ordered her what to do and how to be as soon as Nina arrived home from work. Exhausted she'd bargain with the child: give her a half hour to rest and then she'd play a game, and Marla would watch the clock. Now all she wants is that spunky girl back again, whatever it takes, though Lord she has no idea how to make it happen.

"Tessa, see if you can heat some water, find a tea bag, and bring one of her sweaters she's trembling. Look for the pills, too. We need to know what she took, especially if we end up in the ER." Marla's head falls back against her chest. "Don't close your eyes, honey, you can't sleep. Not yet. Do you hear me?"

Watching my sister, remembering the pills I took from Hack, I'm grateful I got away with temporary bodily trauma. Will never, ever take shit, I again swear to the universe.

Grateful as well that my mother's here and seems to know what to do, I find a box of teabags, but the stove looks nothing like any stove I've seen. I can't figure out how to use it. Tea will have to wait. In the bedroom, I grab Marla's hoodie off a chair. The sheets on the king-size bed are taut but pillows are strewn on the floor. Has Marla even slept since Marcus left? Outside the window, a navy blue sky obliterates the beach.

The pill bottles are on the bedside table where I first saw them. Labeled only morning and night with no other description. That bastard, Marcus, and take the bottles with me.

"Marla, what are the names of these pills?" I ask, holding out the bottles. "I can phone the ER and maybe get an antidote."

"Don't know, morning and night, just different colors. I took the greens last night, then later a few blue ones, I think."

"Shit," I say. "Mom, here's her hoodie."

"Place it over her shoulders,"

I do and notice Marla's tremors slow down a bit

"Sit with Tessa while I make some tea." My mother says, depositing Marla on the couch beside me.

My mother fiddles with the stove, which has buttons instead of normal knobs. How the rich live, I think. Clearly she, too, is giving up on the tea. Marla leans on me, her lips dry, cracked.

"You sleep here tonight, okay?" Her pleading, slurry voice annoys the crap out of me, and have to remind myself she's an addict. She's ill.

"No," my mother says with certainty. "You're coming home with us. Now. End of story."

"If Marcus calls, he'll freak if I'm not here."

"Call him, tell him you're with us." I say.

"I don't know how to reach him. He's in exhibit halls and whatever."

"Well, fuck Marcus," I say. "He'll find you if he needs to."

Hack sits alone at the kitchen table and watches my mother maneuver Marla into a chair.

"Tessa, make some tea, she's still cold."

"No . . . just hot water, no caffeine." We all look at Hack, not sure he's even talking to us. But he is.

I put water to boil. "What else, Hack?"

"Hey, girl, Marla, look at my handsome face."

Marla's head swings around toward him. Hack grabs her chin, and using thumb and index fingers squeezes the key-top of her nose. Hurt?" She nods.

"Got any Benadryl?"

"More pills?" My mother asks, but somehow Hack has us believing whatever he says. "Tessa check the medicine cabinet and the effective date."

"Fuck the date, just bring it here, girl." Hack isn't too steady himself and sways in his chair.

In the bathroom, I rummage quickly through the cabinet, and find a squashed packet of Benadryl.

The water is ready. I turn off the flame. "Now what," I ask Hack, the whole scene ludicrous. But I do as I'm told and bring a tablespoon and glass of hot water to the table.

Hack tries to dissolve two pills in a spoon of water, but the spoon and his fingers keep missing each other.

I take the spoon and dissolve the pills, blow to cool the water and kind of shove the spoon in Marla's mouth. "Swallow it." She does.

"Everything all right in there," Scotty calls from the living room, where the TV has never stopped going.

"Why don't you come see for yourself," I say. Hack throws me a weird look and lumbers out to the living room. "What now," my voice on the edge of hysteria.

Marla slides a cool hand down the side of my cheek. "We can't all be unhappy all of the time," her voice calmer, slurry, sleepy.

Gray light as unpromising as yesterday's memories leaks through the blinds. Even before I'm fully awake I know Marla's not in bed. Do I even want to get up? The phone reads past seven. My mother must be on her way to work. Where's Marla? Hoisting myself off the bed I slip on jeans and a sweatshirt and, hungry, head to the kitchen. Marla and my mother are at the table.

"Aren't you going to work?" I ask.

"Shortly. There might be cereal in the cabinet."

"Where's Hack?"

"Went back to the bungalow to get some things."

"Marla, what's up?" I ask.

"What's up?" My mother repeats. "This girl isn't going back to that place to get sick all over again."

It's about time, I don't say.

"Mom, I'm fine now. Please, let's not fight. You were great last night. I love you," Marla says. "But Marcus and me . . . we have something really good. He's about to photograph me for a themed portfolio. I'll be the centerpiece. Yesterday was a bad moment. It won't happen again. I learn from mistakes." Marla's eyes no longer wide and frightened are weary, her pale face worn.

Marla will get high again, of course she will, I don't say, because this is my mother's fight; I'm on her side. And busy myself emptying what's left of the cereal into a bowl, add what's left of the milk and hope it isn't rancid. Then stand near the counter to eat. Coffee will have to go down black.

"Marla the drugs will ruin your beauty along with your dream of modeling. Look at Hack, look at all the kids around here on stuff. It's horrid."

"I'm not those kids, I'm different. I'm stronger. I'm determined. I know what I'm doing. I have a future. I'm not going to fuck it."

My mother shakes her head, "How can I trust that? You need to be here with me at least for a while; it's the only thing that makes sense. Marcus can still photograph you; he can come here."

"Tessa, tell mom how great that house is. How generously I'm being taken care of . . . you saw . . . you were there . . . "

"Please, leave me out of this."

"Marla, honey, I know you blame me for not being able to give you all the things that Marcus provides, but—"

"No, Mom, I don't blame you at all for my life. I blame you for yours. You never did or do anything you really want to do. Everything is about the should-s: should marry Scotty because he has a house, should live the way Scotty wants because you have two kids. Haven't you heard: women don't need to be grateful anymore. All my life it was should this and should that. You do nothing that really satisfies you. So, Mom, you have it wrong. I don't blame you for me but I sure as shit don't want to end up living the life you live. I'm returning to Marcus. He'll be seriously worried if I'm not there. And here's the thing, I want to be there with him. I'm going now. I have to feed the dog."

I walk out of the kitchen, through the hallway to the bathroom. Close the door, turn on the hot shower full blast to heat the room, stare at my face in the mirror till steam erases my image. As water pounds against the plastic curtain all other sound disappears.

Driving slowly, more than exhausted she's worn thin; a slight push could topple her. She'll be late for work. So what? They won't fire her. They need her. Already short one kitchen person, only two of them working the busy cleanup while the wounded keep arriving, no shortage there. The wounded must be fed and dishes must be clean, ready. Why don't they hire someone at once? Do they expect her and . . .

She's angry, she is. Marla's words have taken up residence in her brain, irritating the crap out of her. She didn't welcome them; she doesn't. Of course, women needn't be grateful. Of course, the should-s needn't determine a life. But what if you've grown up poor and struggling in a house with parents who wanted her out sooner than soon. Yes, Scotty came into her life when her need was huge, and yes, she is grateful, how could she not be? How dare Marla judge her? Even without money, Marla was brought up with love, attention, confidence, and most of all expectations. Where the hell does she think her determination comes from?

Anyway, her first marriage wasn't about should-s. She was young and in love. Why didn't she say that? Why not defend her choice: because in truth the marriage was anchored in a need to get away from a desolate home life. Is that what Marla is doing? No, she's getting away from a desolate future. Young and ambitious and yes, needy; she wants to determine the next years. She gets that, of course she does. Lord knows she wants for Marla all that Marla wants for herself. Yet, last night's overdose happened and it scared her no end.

As usual, the parking lot is crowded but a space opens up almost immediately and she pulls in. Walking quickly toward the hospital, passing the lawn where she and Peter met, the question crosses her mind: Is Peter one of her should-s? No, of course not. He's tried to know her, really know her the way no one else has, and to so carefully cherish that knowledge. She senses his unspoken impatience for them to move in together, but aware of her equally silent message of not yet he doesn't push. Why not yet? What stops her?

14

Getting out of bed, dressing, why bother? There are already too many hours in the day. With classes on winter break I seriously need more diversions. How many books can I read? How many times can I walk the beach? Daytime TV rots the brain, which Hack doesn't seem to mind. My friends bore me. At least Raff kills a few hours working at the bike shop. Where in this bleak town could I do that? I tried to volunteer at the library; they didn't need me.

Hack on the couch, the TV going, is it ever not? "Hey, Hack, don't you realize daytime television rots the brain?"

"Doesn't matter."

"Yes, it does."

"Don't watch."

"I won't."

In the kitchen, there's coffee in the pot and I pour a cup. My mother left for work hours ago. Smearing jelly on a slice of bread, I stand at the counter. The coffee tastes bitter. Outside, the cold sky is too blue. It's been a while since I spoke to Marla; she hasn't called me either. Marcus is the only one she's interested in. What if he's not letting her be in touch? The thought infuriates me. Would Marla obey him? Maybe, if he threatens to take away her stuff. Looking at my phone for less than a second, I call her.

"Tessa, hi, wow, great, I was just going to call you. You heard me thinking. Meet me on the beach. So much to tell you, can't bear knowing without you knowing too. Twenty minutes. Need to see you."

With her speedy voice in my head, I leave and jog up the beach toward Marcus's house. She needs to see me? What's that about?

I wait a short distance away for her to walk out. She doesn't; she's late. A few more minutes of staring at the front door, I knock.

"Tessa! Has it already been twenty minutes? I have so much to do and I'm so disorganized. Has it already been twenty minutes?" She repeats. "Come in, come in."

"Are you alone?"

"Argo is roaming about."

"Where's Marcus?"

"Out getting supplies. Tessa, my love," Marla's arm wraps my waist. "So much to tell you," her voice loud, her expression animated, her hair streaked purple, which is attractive, and all of it fills me with sadness. The sister I love is changing in ways that I can't stop.

"So. What's going on?"

"Ta-da! Marcus and I are going to Florida where he'll photograph me in different costumes for the portfolio: jodhpurs with a crop in hand, a pilot with goggles, and lots of others." Her voice runs down as if she's lost the train of thought.

"Marcus found a theme," I say, and feel a spark of dread.

"To be young and on the run. Isn't that a fabulous theme?" Her body sways slightly. "We're not going to just work. We'll see a lot of plays. Marcus said some of the best ones on Broadway open there. Did you know that?"

"How would I know that," and hear my sullen tone. "But I'm envious."

"Don't be, I mean . . . yes . . . be envious because you need to want all that, too. Growing is more than height and weight." She laughs, too gleefully.

Even on stuff, my sister is more interesting than anyone I know. "Where will you live?"

"A villa at a Miami motel complex. Spend time with us. You're a senior. Fuck classes, right? Learn another way. Learn more. Definitely need you there."

"Yes, but . . . well we'll see," and don't say, why would I want to watch that man feed you drugs? "Are you still taking the stuff you crashed on?"

"Don't worry so much." Her mouth twitches, perhaps at the memory.

"You almost died."

"You're being melodramatic."

"Okay," I nearly sigh. "But answer me. Are you taking morning and night pills?"

"Of course. Why wouldn't I?"

"What would happen if you stopped?"

"Please . . .you sound like mom. I have to finish packing. Marcus is packed. Tomorrow, we're leaving tomorrow. Tessa, you have to come there. I'll text you info. Tell mom."

"Don't you want to take a jog first?" Didn't she want to meet on the beach?

"No time. Do need help packing. Marcus won't," she grabs my hand tugs me to the bedroom, the bed strewn with clothing, a half-packed bag on the floor.

"Marla, listen to me. You're high . . . "

"Of course I'm high, I'm joyful."

"But you're in danger, you're—"

"Stop. Don't bring me down."

"I'm just worried . . . and you'll be so far, and I'll miss you."

"And me, you. But it's not forever, right? Don't be concerned. I know exactly what I'm doing, and more important, I know why. So, please sister, just help me pack. Okay?"

"Okay." And try not to see her dry, chapped lips, which brings Hack to mind. Always stoned, yet not frantic like Marla. He's sleepy, unsteady, and itchy. Is that where Marla is headed? How will I know? She'll be far away.

At the small motel table near the window dusk begins to blur the outline of the adjacent complex. That's the thing about darkness, if she's watching, it comes on slowly, but turn away for even a few seconds and it's there, full blown, and time to go home. She runs her hand along the silky caftan, a present from Peter that she leaves at the motel. At home it would be viewed with suspicion; Tessa would have questions. Would Scotty?

Peter continues to search for a homier place. Yet this past month of meeting here has deepened their relationship, and this despite her worries about leaving Richie's place. How ironic, she thinks.

In the tiny alcove, Peter pours two glasses of red wine. "To us," he says as he always does, and sits across from her in a polo and sweatpants.

"Yes, to us."

"You sound far away."

"Our talk the other day about moving in together is using up a lot of space in my head. At work I forgot to bring the dirty towels to the autoclave. Then as I was rushing to the car, I remembered and ran back to finish the job."

"That's you, good at what you do, I'd say."

"You mean reliable."

"Yes, that too. But why the sad tone?"

"I'm afraid."

"Of me?" he says jokingly.

"That I'll somehow let you down, or else hurt people who love me. It's unfair."

"It is, of course, but . . . "

"Tessa's shock, Scotty's face, the misery that pursuing my happiness will bring them. Can you understand?"

"You deserve to be loved by me, deeply, without restraint. I need your presence, the promise of our future together. Believing that we'll manage to do this keeps me going." There's alarm in his voice.

"I'm not giving up on us, Peter."

"Good. I've bundled my hopes into one thought: finally being with you, full time."

"I know. It's what I want, too. Please trust me."

"Of course. I love you, Nina. We'll figure out a way."

But will she? Scotty, I'm leaving you because . . . what? I don't love you the way I love Peter? Scotty never promised her anything, but he's been there, every day of every week of every year. Is a person's presence enough? Marla, still in Miami would be surprised to see her mother sitting here. And Tessa? The girl already lost one father, who she no doubt can't remember, and now a stepfather too? It pains her to imagine Tessa's response, not because the girl's close to Scotty, but she'll feel betrayed by her mother as children can and do. Would Tessa even agree to live with her and Peter? One more unanswered question to plague her nights.

"Nina, please don't stay quiet, let me in."

"Sorry. I can't imagine Tessa would remain with Scotty," she hears herself say.

"Why don't I meet Tessa?"

"Oh, I don't know . . . "

"Why not?"

"She'll see you as an interloper who is taking her mother away from her."

"I can woo her."

"Tessa isn't easy to win over. It would take time, but, maybe, on second thought it might be the only way: tell them all I'm in a relationship. Then I can stop lying, at least that. I need to think on it more."

"I'm patient. Just never forget how much I want us to be together."

"How could I?"

15

There's coffee in the old pot, thank you Scotty. He's out back, but for how long? I grab the bowl of last night's popcorn, and take it into the bedroom. I can't leave for class until I hear back from Marla. She sent me so many-middle-of the night texts. Why? Every few minutes I call, leave a message or text her to contact me. No response. Unable to wait any longer I phone the motel, ask to be connected to Marcus's room. The phone rings and rings, they're both out. Maybe that's a good sign? Maybe they're busy working on her portfolio? Maybe that's why Marla called and texted during the night; my phone was off. It's never off. Why was it off last night? I can't remember. Why isn't she responding? The phone rings. "Marla?"

"No. It's Jacob from *The Daily* . . . " I click off.

TV voices reach me from the living room where Hack is or isn't watching.

The phone rings. Marla. Thank God, it's Marla.

"Hey. I called you a million times."

"Tess, girl, how you doing? Couldn't call before now, okay?" Marla's languid voice, low and slow, stoned

"Of course, it's okay. Where's Marcus?"

"Yeah, it's what I want to tell you. I don't like him anymore. I want to come home, but no money, need you to wire me cash, a place across the road. I'll text you where. Not to say anything to mom, want to surprise her. Okay, sister, nothing to mom? Say okay. Please."

"Where are you now?" I try to sound calm, but I'm terrified.

"Outside the motel, don't worry. I won't go back in his room, don't want to sleep in his bed just need to go home, Tess? Okay?" Marla clicks off.

Marcus, piece of scum I think, but it's not helpful. When Marla returns home she'll need rehab, and maybe—just maybe—after a while she'll be okay.

It doesn't take long for her text to come through with an address. How much would a plane ticket cost? Where did Marla think I'd get the money? I can't borrow from Hack again. I text Raff and ask him to meet me in the churchyard. He doesn't go in to work now till later in the day. Tell him the truth, I think. Around here drugs are less than shocking. He knows Marla, I'll explain her predicament, and maybe he'll lend me money for a plane ticket.

I try to reach Marla to let her know I received the address and that I'm working on it, but it goes to voicemail. I phone the motel room, just in case.

"Yes?" It's Marcus.

"Marla called, she wants to come home. What happened?"

"She abused her instructions. She's an addict. I don't know what she's on now, but it's more than pills. I can't use her as a model. Take her home, it's the only way."

"What! Listen asshole, don't leave her outside, don't abandon her, get her a room for shit-sake. You're the one who . . . "

He clicks off.

<hr />

At lunch break, Nina takes her muffin and coffee out to the hospital lawn. She sits in one of the chairs close to where she and Peter met. Nearby a patient is being visited by his wife or girlfriend. It's chilly out, but tolerable. Though she usually lunches with women from the cafeteria, she begged off today, saying what, she hardly remembers, her mind overwhelmed by her conversation with Peter yesterday, no different from other recent talks, all of which continue to unspool inside her.

Peter isn't a passing flirtation, sexual encounter, or someone that holds the promise of riches. Their relationship is one of love, admiration, affection, and for her, healing of so much in her life that came before. With him, the universe seems to have tilted in her direction, offering another chance. Doesn't she have a right to a more fulfilling life? Her father would say, where's that written?

Taking a sip of the too hot coffee, she puts the cup on the ground. Not hungry, she shoves the bagged muffin into her tote. Looking around as if something within view might offer an easier solution, she sees only the bare tree limbs and a scattering of leaves. Scotty always rakes leaves into neat piles out back, why, she never asked.

Scotty, I'm seeing another man. We're in a relationship. I didn't look for it, pursue it, and had no idea it could happen, but it has. It's not about anything that you've done. Which is true. He'll say little and look past her and won't reveal his hurt. They already live somewhat separate lives; they rarely share activities or even meals. He loves her in his way, she supposes, but his way is dour, skeptical. Yet Scotty is what he is, never promised surprise, just steady at the wheel. How can she blame him for that? She can't. Except her life with him is empty.

Her daughters are her world, their safety and happiness more important than her own. Marla with Marcus is struggling to start a career. Tessa is busy trying to understand the mélange of her own changing emotions. But would she come live with them? Peter's right, they'd have to meet first, of course they would. The thought gives her anxiety, though not as much as the lies and the guilt, which are becoming too heavy to carry. Enough, she thinks. Enough.

Nearby, she watches the man tenderly stroke the woman's hair, the small gesture that holds a lifetime.

She'll tell Peter today that she's decided to reveal their relationship to Tessa first, then Marla, and after that admit all to Scotty. Unexpectedly the plan excites her or maybe it's that rare moment when suddenly it all feels doable. She takes out her phone to call Louise. Someone beside herself needs to hear what's in her head.

Heading back from seeing Raff, I feel foolish, perhaps ashamed that I asked him for a loan. He laughed when I mentioned savings; he receives a pittance of salary at the bike shop. He did offer to try and borrow but wasn't sure from whom. I discouraged him. Marla would hate for her situation to become the town story, which it would.

The water is choppy as it moves closer to the shore; it pools and swirls at my feet, soaking my sneakers. Could I care less? Once not far from shore Marla and I were playing in the water. I stepped in a deep hole, the water rose quickly over my head. Marla tugged and tugged until my head rose above the water. She was only eight years old. She'd never leave me in danger. I'll find a way to get her home. I'll go with her to rehab. Leaving Marcus is a good thing, isn't it?

I head for the paved road to call my mother. She needs to know. She needs to help me help Marla, I can't do this alone. My sister will have to understand. The call goes to voicemail. Maybe she can't answer at work. But I have to talk to her. I phone the central number at the veteran's hospital, ask to be connected to the cafeteria, that my mother is there working overtime.

"Sorry, the cafeteria is closed. There is no one working there now."

I stare at the phone: Did my mother leave earlier than usual? I hurry toward the house; her car isn't there. Where is she? What's going on? Is she ill? Is she going for treatments but trying to spare me? Oh Christ, how would I know? Does Scotty know? Something in me is afraid to ask him. I leave a message on my mother's phone that it's an emergency, to call me.

As I reach the front door, the phone rings.

"What emergency?"

"Mom, where are you? I called work. The cafeteria is closed."

"What emergency," her tone sharp.

"Marla, she left Marcus. She's living on the street. She's in danger. Marcus said he doesn't know what she's on. But she wants to come home. We have to send her money to get here. Are you sick?"

"What?"

"What is it that you're not telling me?"

"I'm on my way home. Just stay put."

Nina pockets the phone, "Peter, I have to go right now."

"Why? You just got here."

"Bad news about Marla. She's on drugs, wants to come home. Is leaving Marcus. I need to deal with it. I'll see or call you tomorrow. I'm . . ."

"Baby, what can I do?"

"Can't think of a thing just now."

"Can I call you later?"

"Peter, let me call you. Please."

He grips her arm. "I love you."

"Yes. Me too."

She grabs her car keys, plants a quick kiss on Peter's stunned face, but she can't slow down, can't think about his feelings just now.

In the car, speeding toward home she castigates herself for not answering the phone when it rang. She won't think about Tessa's curiosity. Not yet, first things first, her daughter's in danger. The cold calmness of determination overtakes her. Money is the next quest. She'll do whatever she must to get the cash. Then she'll leave a paid plane ticket for Marla to pick up at the Miami airport.

She never did get to tell Peter her decision. It'll have to wait now.

16

The doors at JFK airport slide open to reveal crowds and white lights. It's the second time in three days that my mother and I have come here. The first time was to meet my sister, except Marla never picked up her ticket, which is mine now, and I'm aching to bring her home.

In uncomfortable silence we walk toward the security line where, thank God, my mother will have to leave me. "Tessa," she begins.

"Not now," I say curtly. If it's reassurance my mother wants, I can't give it. I'm too shocked and upset. Who is this Peter? Why has he become so important to her, perhaps more so than us? And what about Scotty; he cares about her. Doesn't that mean anything? I should've said that too, but anger knotted my throat.

For the last few days, I questioned her repeatedly about why she wasn't at work when I called? Where was she? What wasn't she telling me? Each time, she waved a dismissive hand, and droned on about one problem at a time.

Why didn't she come clean? Why wait until now in the car to tell me about her secret life? It didn't help at all. We spent yesterday arguing about who should go to pick up Marla, but she could've told me then about her adultery. Instead, she wanted only to explain why it should be her that went to Miami. Eventually I wore her down, insisting that Marla didn't even want her to know the situation.

The long security line takes forever. My mother stands there until I go through. Without a backward glance, I head to the gate area. One after another open-door shops appear along the way, restaurants galore, people everywhere. If I didn't expect some asshole to card me, I'd have a drink at one of the bars. Isn't that what people do if they've never flown before?

The constant loud announcements make thinking impossible. Directions to the Palm Villa Motel are in my bag, thank you Google. I left several explicit voicemails and texts for both Marla and Marcus that I was on the way, and for her to stay near the motel. But what if she's not there, or too stoned to travel? The plan is for us to immediately head back to the airport, board a plane to New York. Our return tickets securely tucked away. Will she survive the trip without drugs . . . *stop Tessa, just get there and find her.*

The area is crowded, the seats taken, people sit on floors, on suitcases. Beyond the large window, the planes take off, land, and roll toward gates. Men and women in orange jackets holding lighted wands move about the tarmac in a strange, silent dance.

The brief afternoon light is at it's brightest. Nina parks in a quiet spot outside town, facing the beach. Even after her tight-lipped, pale daughter passed through security, she was reluctant to leave the airport. Tessa's words in the car are knife-etched into her brain, permanent scars. How could she have allowed Marla to go live with Marcus? Didn't she realize that he fed Marla drugs, or was Nina too busy with her paramour to notice? Why didn't she check on Marla? Go see her, find out what was going on there? Did she even think about Marla?

Tessa's right; she'd failed her responsibilities. As a mother it was her duty to check on Marla. And why didn't she find out more about Marcus? There might've been a way, but she didn't even try. Despite her love and concern for her daughters, her mind was taken up with Peter, with her future. What kind of mother is that? No wonder she didn't defend herself to Tessa. How could she? What would she say? You're wrong, I did think about you both . . . but she didn't, not really, not enough. Oh Lord.

Once her daughters return home her focus will be entirely and razor sharp on Marla until she's out of danger. She'll find a rehab program somewhere, somehow. It will take time to nurse her back to health. She'll make sure Marla attends even if she has to take a leave from work and drive her there. Tessa will notice all that she's trying to do, to amend, of course she will, and maybe, just maybe, she can earn back the girl's respect. No more lies.

She and Peter will have to take a brief hiatus. Marla must come first. Seeing his distress will make it a million times harder to say so, maybe impossible. It's unfair that her situation will also punish Peter. He's done nothing but love her deeply. She takes out her phone and calls him.

Her head is still throbbing with Peter's sorrowful voice. She heads down to the beach. He pleaded against any hiatus, insisted they'd find a way to meet. She didn't argue, couldn't. Of course, she wants to be with him. Of course, she wishes Marla didn't need her. Of course, she wishes she was free to change her life, but she isn't, not at this moment. She said all that, but doubts he heard a word.

Striding back-and-forth across the wet sand to keep warm, too edgy to go home, a ghostly fog rises off the darkening water, obscuring the horizon. She waits for Tessa's call, her hand frozen around the phone. It's been hours. The plane already landed, she checked.

Tessa is supposed to phone as soon as she meets Marla. It's the plan they agreed on. What's going on? Call after call goes to voicemail. Why isn't Tessa picking up? Why isn't she responding to the texts? The waiting, it's punishing. She tries the motel room. It rings and rings, no one answers. She tries Marla's phone, no answer. Tess, where are you? Her plea lost in the ether. She won't—no, she won't—allow her imagination to go into full negative. She can't. She's hundreds of miles away. But this waiting, it's deranging. Maybe Tessa called Hack or Scotty? Maybe she's too angry to call

Nina? Even as she thinks this, she doesn't believe it. Still . . . her anxiety level barely containable, she heads back to the car, her aching fingers crossed. It should've been her who went to Miami.

17

Carrying my jacket and backpack, I walk through the upscale, colorful, and highly air-conditioned Miami airport. Wide windows reveal tall dark green-leaved palm trees, a blazing blue sky, and a parking lot filled with cars and taxis. Taking the escalator down to an exit, I step into the tropical heat, which warms my cold skin. Google said the motel is within walking distance of the airport.

The road cuts a long slice between beach and resorts. The calm, bright, blue water is a replica of the sky. It's weird how the resorts differ yet also look alike, most with pools abutting the road and glass-fronted lobby entrances. After about a half mile, I enter the huge grassy grounds of the Palm Villa Motel. Wide swaths of space separate each villa, which has its own patio bordered by blooming shrubs and tall palm trees. Chaises and a kiosk bar are steps away from a huge kidney-shaped pool. Across the road there's a strip of boardwalk with one shop after another.

Villa 117 is written in three-dimensional gold letters across a polished wooden door, with a shiny gold knob. I knock. Marcus opens the door, barefoot and tanned in Bermuda shorts and t-shirt.

"Marla . . . I've come . . . "

"I'm sorry Tessa, Marla's in the hospital she . . . "

"What? Why? Is she okay? What happened? Why didn't you—?"

"Stop a minute. I'll tell you."

I hate this man.

"I don't know what she was taking, but someone found her—I think yesterday—in the doorway of the next villa. She was out of it. The motel receptionist recognized her, contacted me and I called an ambulance. She's in St. Margaret's Hospital, about a quarter mile down the—"

"Fuck you," I begin to trace my way back to the road, and then jog toward the hospital. My breathing, the humidity, I'm gasping for air.

Rushing into the hospital lobby, which eerily resembles a resort, quiet reigns. Where do they keep the patients? Looking around for someone to help me, I notice a small square open window, behind which is a small office, a woman and a desk.

"My sister Marla Boyce was brought here yesterday. Please, I must see her now. Where's her room? I need . . . "

"The rooms are on the second floor. The nurses' station there will direct you. The stairs are behind you," she points to a closed door.

I rush up the steps, find myself in front of another desk. "I'm Marla Boyce's sister. Where is her room?"

The nurse checks something on her desk. "One of the sisters will be right with you." She speaks in a slow low drawl, which annoys me.

In a minute or two, a tall, thin middle-aged woman wearing a long gray skirt and white over-blouse escorts me to another office. What is the matter with these people, I just want to see Marla.

"I'm Sister Agnes. I'm so very sorry, so very sorry—"

"Oh no, no, no. Marla Boyce? She's very young, you must have . . . " I grab her arm, "You can't . . ." my voice an echo from a strange tunnel.

Gently, she disengages my hand. "I'm sorry. Marla over-dosed and aspirated on her vomit during the night. The doctors worked on her for quite awhile. They tried everything. There was nothing else the doctors could do. When I receive the toxicology report I can send . . .

Paralyzed with disbelief accompanied by a loud sound, like a gunshot that clogs my ears and smacks my chest. Sister's clear blue eyes watch me closely. What does she think I'll do? What can I do? Sister's hand clasps my shoulder as she instructs me how to breathe because apparently I've forgotten. And though I do as she says, the me that is me, that girl, is gone forever.

"Come." With her hand on my shoulder she gently leads me to the end of a hallway. She opens a door into a highly air-conditioned room with drawn blinds.

"Would you like to be alone with her?"

"No," I whisper, terrified.

On a bed, a sheet covers the body. Not my sister, I think. I've seen those movies where the dead person is misidentified. Slowly, the Sister moves aside the sheet to uncover the face Marla's face her beautiful haughty face. Slowly, then, I move aside the rest of the sheet to see a slim, nude, alabaster statue; round breasts flattened, nipples deflated; heart stopped. I place my lips lightly on my sister's cheek; it's cold; run my finger across her brow to lift away a strand of hair; imagine the large eyes behind the closed lids, the dark lashes still apparent, still long. I've seen my sister asleep; this isn't sleep.

Marla isn't here anymore. How is that possible? Still I wish to lie down beside her, but my feet remain on the ground, and what's really mysterious is the painting above the bed of a flower whose petals seem to be falling away.

Sister's arm gently cradles my waist the way Marla and I often embraced. She walks with me to the stairs, informs me about possible arrangements, cremation, her words parking somewhere in my nether brain. Then in a soft voice, Sister talks to me about grief.

Walking down the steps, I hold the railing tightly, falling is possible.

I bang at the door of Villa 117. Marcus opens it. I walk past him into the room. "Marla's dead." I say more to hear the truth of it than to inform him. "You killed her, you pervert. You made her an addict," my voice rising with each word. "I will go to the police, and report you," I shout furiously.

"I'm not about to listen to this shit." He walks out, slams the door.

My fury won't let go, I begin to scream, my arm sweeps clear the dresser top, tugs at the drapes but they won't give. I haul an unopened beer can at the mirror, which shatters, seven years horrid luck for him. Not enough. My voice cracks. I grab his camera off the table, stuff it in my backpack, flee into blueberry darkness, and phone my mother.

"Tessa?" my mother says.

I'm sobbing so loudly my mother's wails are but faint background.

18

The Miami sun beats down without mercy, the sky blinding white. It's been weeks, and I'm still not used to it. Too hot for people to bask, the beach is empty. I lug the heavy plastic bag to the water's edge; undo the polite twist that keeps the lips closed. Then aim the bag at the water and shake the ashes free. They rise and then begin slowly to settle. I find a rock and with the point of another carve Marla's name on it. Then bury the rock in the muddy sand where the tide will eventually move it into the water, perhaps sail it home across the ocean, my sister, the free spirit.

The remnants of my sister's ashes float atop the water like a tissue of dissipating fog. I re-read my mother's letter, sent c/o the general delivery post office.

My sweet girl, it's no use to come home. There's little here for you. That sounds harsh, but I fear if you return, you'll feel the need to care for me, and that's the last thing I want. You need not, must not feel any obligation to do so. I want a better life for you than any that can be achieved here. I'm broken, as I know Scotty told you, though I wish he hadn't. But in truth, except for you I don't care about much; I can't.

Marla found this town limiting, and I know that you do, too. It was wrong to trust Marcus. And I'll forever blame myself for doing so. Yet, I believed, I wanted to believe that his offer would help her future. And now I'm concerned for your future.

I've told Scotty everything. If I hadn't, then any kind gesture from him would only make me feel guiltier for my lies than I already am. I asked if he wanted me to leave. He said no, to stay. Lord knows where I'd go if he'd said yes. Scotty answered one of Peter's calls and told him that Marla died.

It was too late for Peter and I the moment we met. I see that now, and pray that someday you will experience deep, reliable love. Don't settle for less. Marla was right. Be wary of the should-s.

Hack asks after you daily; he's here most of the time now, which is good for Scotty. I don't want you to worry about me; there isn't anything that I want or need. Call home so that I'll know what you're doing and that you're okay.

You are now responsible for yourself, Tessa. You need to know that so you will take care to stay safe. If there's anything at all that I'm still sure of it's that you can achieve the life you want.

I love you deeply and forever and ever. Despite my unbowed grief about Marla, which I know we share, I am still always here for you, please, remember. My heart to you my beautiful, smart, wise daughter. Mom.

The evening brings no relief from the heat as I walk out of the diner without saying good-bye, though everyone here knows me. Someone calls Tessa, hey, but I don't wait. I've spent many a night here drinking coffee with the old Native American woman, and hold close only the old woman's words: "You manage without being prepared. That's your strength."

On the road leading out, palm leaves flap a farewell. The backpack is heavy but not nearly as heavy as the grief.

II.

19

Port Authority bus station, seedy, dirty, teeming with people, New York at its finest. After days of travel I can't believe I'm here. The return-trip a blur of varied voices, offerings, sights, and cars that drove me only so far before I boarded the Greyhound.

Weaving my way out of the station, images as insistent as a woodpecker stab at my brain: the dank basement of the seedy hotel where I bussed breakfast dishes for a week; the waiter who shared his motel bed with me during several horribly stormy days; the street of hotels where I squatted on a large towel 'borrowed' from the motel, the hot ground penetrating my jeans. The empty coffee cup with a hand-written sign asking to give what you can; the people dropping coins and bills into the cup, the weird attempts to talk to me, the utterances . . . such a young girl. I hated sitting there. But the busy foot traffic on Collins Avenue netted me enough money to leave Miami, a haven for drug use and drug rehab, signs at every corner, beckoning, walk in, immediate care. Signs I wouldn't have noticed before.

On Ninth Avenue, well-lit streets filled with restaurant smells tease the hunger I'm trying to ignore. Cars whizz past going further downtown. Everything reminds me of something and nothing is comfortable. One hot day when Marla and I came into the city she stepped into the cascading waters that danced around the rim of a building, calling me to join her. My adventurous sister! Was she already on more than weed?

I don't have enough money to pay for one night even at a sleazy hotel. Once upon a time, churches kept their doors open. I head uptown toward Times Square, where all the lonely people go after dark. I'm not lonely, just tired, hungry, and what else? Oh right, I'm not homeless either, not in the usual way.

On 45th Street and Broadway, I stop outside the now darkened ticket office where anyone can buy two tickets to any show for the price of one. A bargain. In a small alcove near two doors that will open in the morning, an aluminum bench snuggles up to a wall. Maybe I'll sit here a while and rest, then again falling asleep would be dangerous: goodbye phone, camera, best to move on. Survival is now my responsibility, my mother said as much.

I continue to walk with no real stopping place. The smell of hot dogs emanating from Papaya on 72nd Street is too much to ignore and I indulge, one frankfurter with mustard and relish, which I gobble down in no time, then ask for a cup of water. There's now two dollars and sixty-seven cents left in my pocket. It's strange to be poor in Manhattan where so many have so much. Not that I envy them, but tonight I resent their comforts.

A few streets away I bump into a bar with an unexpected open door pouring music and voices onto the sidewalk.

The crowd inside is three deep; the few tables occupied. My tiredness needs sleep, somewhere, anywhere but not a bench outdoors please. Desperation incites courage; I learned this in Miami. I skirt the crowd, stopping near a man old enough to not need sex to get through the night.

"Waiting for anyone in particular?" he asks.

He has a worn face and wears his hair long. But I like his merry eyes, which don't focus on my anatomy.

"Seems that way, but, no, I'm not. Actually, just arrived by bus from Florida, not the easiest trip, I have to admit," and shake my head.

"What's in Florida?"

"Family. Tessa," I say, holding out my hand. I know how to be charming.

"Frank." His hand warms mine for a second.

"Things got screwed. I didn't expect to arrive before tomorrow morning, when my new job begins. Do you know of anywhere I can crash for the night?"

"I'll put on my thinking cap. What are you drinking?"

"Any kind of beer is fine." I'd keel over with anything stronger.

The morning light wakes me. Cramped from the too-soft old couch, I stretch and walk quietly to the bathroom. Behind the closed bedroom door, Frank's still asleep. Good. I'm not in the mood for either small talk or anything edging on serious. I chose well, Frank was a gentleman.

Peering into a mirror, smoky with age, I remove several studs from my ear lobes then wash my face clean of makeup. The freckles all redheads must wear lend an air of innocence. I hold the wild, auburn hair away from my face, but, no, too tame, and it feels like a violation. Of what I'm not sure, but no makeup, no studs, that's enough alteration for an interview.

His bathroom isn't the cleanest, dirt line around the tub, soiled, damp towel puddled in the corner, still, I'm grateful to Frank for letting me crash on the couch. I told him I was really tired, which couldn't have been truer and fell asleep at once. Only when I woke did I take in the closet-sized apartment disheveled to the point of scary.

Taking a few things out of the backpack, stuffing them into my tote, I shake out the dress, and slip it on. I check for the camera. Still safe inside the zippered compartment, the camera Marcus cared for like a newborn, Marla said, the camera he promised would take marvelous pictures of her, enough for a portfolio, though he neglected to fill her in on the particulars of his generosity. The camera I intend to sell for needed cash.

On a paper napkin I write thank you and that I'll return to pick up my backpack later, then tiptoe out the door, close it ever so gently.

In a small Broadway coffee shop I join a few people at the counter where no one looks at anyone. It's as if there's a shared understanding of privacy, which is nothing like my hometown diner where any stranger is marked.

"Anything to eat?" The waitress, older than my mother, whom I don't want to think about, is already eyeing another customer's needs.

"Not really," I apologize. "Just coffee, black." My makeup free face in the adjacent mirror seems to belong to another person. Maybe that's a good sign.

The waitress places the coffee in front of me. It's black and hot and outside it's bleak and breezy though only September. It won't be long before it gets cold, and snows. Back home the snowbanks don't melt till spring. As kids, Marla and I used to stare at the many-layered, dirty snowbanks until castles and old men's faces revealed themselves.

That was then, where the future offered nothing more or different than what all those around us already had.

The fifteen-story building on Park Avenue is old, but its glory days are still on view in the large, mirrored lobby with its maroon-velvet chairs, and a doorman who calls up to announce my arrival. Though I phoned from Miami to set up the interview, I feared it wouldn't be real, but it is. Thank you, coffee shop Internet. It's a seventh-floor apartment. The elevator is temporarily out of service. Ignoring the service lift—a cage-like contraption that makes me nervous—I use the stairs.

On floor six I take out a small mirror and for the millionth time check my appearance. On the phone I lied, said I was twenty-four, old enough to have some experience, but young enough to be healthy and energetic. The job offered a decent stipend with free room and board for help to an eighty-year-old woman living alone, nursing experience not needed. I cross my fingers and hike up the last flight.

The bell chimes loudly. The door opens quickly.

"Hi I'm Tessa, we spoke on the phone a—"

"Of course. Come in. How was your trip?"

"Fine, thanks. I arrived yesterday."

I follow the tall, slim body to a living room heavy with furniture, mahogany breakfront, lamp tables, worn green velvet couch, and two wide-armed brown chairs where we sit. There's a formality about the woman's appearance, gray hair in a neat bun, ballet slippers beneath a long, dark skirt and beige blouse. Though gravity has had its way, the woman's face looks knowable.

"I'm Rhonda Steward. You can call me Rhonda. What's your last name again?" The voice is clearly confident; a woman who seems well cared for.

"Boyce."

"Where did you grow up?"

"Small town in Long Island."

"And you said your last job was assisting in a doctor's office, was that in—"

"No. It was in Florida," I lie.

"What did you do there exactly?"

"Mostly desk work, but when it was busy, I helped out the nurses. I learned a lot by watching, I guess."

"If I needed to have written reference . . ." Rhonda's eyes are steady, taking me in like a deep breath.

"I'm sure one of the people there would be able to give me a reference," I say with conviction, praying the woman won't dwell on it.

"I want someone to accompany me to doctor visits, to help me shop or open jar lids I can't maneuver anymore; in short, to be available. A housekeeper comes in once a week to clean. I can't anticipate the amount of hours of work a week, except to say that the schedule will vary day-to-day, every day, as my needs do. How does that sound?"

"Fine, totally fine."

"Do you have any questions for me?" her tone polite.

"Not at the moment," I say, eager to get on with this.

"Tell me something about your life."

Not nearly possible, I think. "I'd like to enroll in some courses, but first need to work for a while."

"So you plan to stay in Manhattan?"

"Yes."

"Why did you move here?"

"I'm interested in photography," I lie. "The city offers excellent courses."

"Is it a hobby or something you're serious about?"

"Serious." I lie again, because it's better than being aimless.

"Does that mean you'll be wandering about when I would need you?"

"No, of course not. I'm reliable." Crap, the interview is beginning to feel like an interrogation. "I was wondering . . . Would you be able to make a decision about the job some time today?" Rhonda looks taken aback.

"Is that important?"

"I'm staying with a friend who would like her boyfriend to move in and there's no space for all of us. And this would be a perfect situation for me." The last statement couldn't be truer.

"Well . . . I don't like making decisions quickly . . . Go take a peek at the room at the end of the hallway while I think about it."

Passing through a long hallway, I pray I didn't mess up by asking for the job so quickly. But with less than two dollars in my purse I can't wait around for that yes or no phone call. If this falls through, I need a plan for what's next, and decide I'll walk the busy streets to search out help-wanted signs. If I don't see any I'll go into stores, restaurants, whatever, wherever to ask for work, something will turn up, it's the city, it's New York; it has to.

At the end of the corridor, a door opens to a large room with a floor to ceiling window and a double bed high off the ground covered with a thick, yellow comforter. It's a room that belonged to someone special once, I'm certain. It couldn't seem more welcoming, and clearly a lot better than any room I ever slept in. A good start I'd say, if anyone asked, but who would ask?

The window overlooks adjacent buildings and in the distance a sliver of the East River. A pale-gray palette of clouds reminds me of the beach in winter, no seagulls here though. Well, that's done with now. People lose many things in a lifetime, houses, jobs, money and loved ones, but losing the past, why would I care?

Several abstract oil paintings hang on the wall and I take in the largest one. It's filled with broad-stroked Mexican colors, a design that could be a pattern for fabrics, except for the deep silvery whorls of water disappearing rapidly down a drain. Despite the bright colors, something about it chills me.

"How do you like the room," Rhonda startles me.

"Perfect." And I mean it.

"Let's try this out, shall we?" She hands me a set of keys. "Come, I'll show you the rest of the apartment. Most of the day I'm in my studio, working, and points to a closed door along the hallway.

We pass two bedrooms—one hers, one a guest room—and a library. Somehow, I don't think she'd mind if I borrowed a book. The kitchen, a large room lit by two tall windows, features a heavy wooden table with eight chairs, different from the scratched, glass-topped table at home with its dangerously chipped edges. A carafe of hot coffee rests on a white tiled trivet next to a loaf of bread. Is landing this job lucky or what?

I take the stairs down at a clip, and head to the West Side, the air tinged with a thin blue glow. On Broadway, homeless men and women sleep in doorways, their heads on shopping bags, or near laundry carts filled with stuff. They sleep as though dead, and I stop at the side of a woman to see if she's breathing; she is. Outside a bar, a young woman, stoned, looks at me with bleary eyes. I don't look away never will. How can I?

When Marla was high everything was hilarious to her, even pigeons feasting on a tipped-over garbage can. Why didn't it scare me more? Why didn't I tell the police about Marcus? Why was I such a coward? Questions that will never let go, and maybe that's a good thing though I can't think how.

I step into a nearby hallway quieter than the street, and call my mother. She'll want to hear about the job.

"Hi," Scotty answers. "You're mother's in bed."

"Can you ask her to take the phone, tell her I have news?"

"I'll see," but doesn't sound hopeful.

I wait, phone at my ear. I'm starving, but so relieved. A ninety-nine-cent hamburger and a soda will do. If I can get through one more night at Frank's, room and board will no longer be a worry. Rhonda wants me tomorrow at nine.

"Your mom can't come to the phone."

"Oh," I say, disappointed. "Is she sick?"

"I told you, your mother's broken, not interested in anything, taking pills."

"Did a doctor prescribe the pills?" I persist.

"Doctors cost money. I get them from the VA."

"Okay, thanks, tell her I'll call later," and click off. Since when does Scotty go to the VA? Never that I remember. Probably Hack is scoring stuff for her on the street. My mother on drugs! Jesus and Christ Almighty! Suddenly Marla's desperate voice, the last one I heard comes to mind with an ache of grief that stills me. Sister Agnes warned that grief was sneaky, could be roused by a memory, smell, picture even a word. Grief wanted to be absorbed a teaspoon at a sitting over great swaths of time, Sister said, and even then could rise up to tackle one's heart.

Through the thin bedroom wall Nina hears Scotty on the phone, hears him tell Tessa that she's in bed, broken, taking pills. She doesn't want Tessa to worry about her. The girl's going through her own hell of loss. A mother should be able to rise above her misery to help her daughter, but she doesn't have it in her to pretend any strength, a further blemish on her soul.

Her firstborn is dead, and she did nothing to keep her alive. If only she'd kept Marla away from Marcus, not allowed her to go to Florida, not listened to her pleas, forced Marcus to leave her be, then Marla would be alive. It's a waking nightmare of punishment for the lies and betrayal, perhaps, too for the crime of illicit happiness.

This morning Scotty told her the pill supply wasn't endless. He didn't need to spell out the rest. She isn't bringing in any money; he's doing what he can against expenses, the pill cost, etc. She said she'd stop taking them and she will. It won't matter, nothing does.

Since telling Scotty about Peter, he's become even more silent than usual. Though she was already grieving Marla's death, telling him was painful. She promised the affair was over, said if Peter called, she had no wish to speak to him, or to read any mail he might send, and left her phone in the living room. He said nothing, looked wary, and continues to do in her presence. Whatever trust he had in her is gone; she can't blame him.

In bed not to rest but to wait for numbness, which even the pills couldn't manage. Gratefully, she watches the eyelid of darkness close over the sky.

20

Exiting the cross-town bus at 79th Street, I head to Blondie's Sports Bar, where I met Frank. Besides Rhonda, he's the only other person in Manhattan I know, though I've been here almost six months. Thank the universe, Rhonda's been healthy, and pretty much my time is my own. Except for our walks near dusk, weather permitting. She uses a cane outdoors, and I keep at her pace. Some days we make it all the way to the East River, others not. It's weird how I look forward to these outings. We chat nonstop. She's friendly, warm, interesting, and knows so much. She's different from anyone else in my life.

She grew up in Philadelphia, said it was a big house, plenty to eat, maids and all that stuff. Had three much older brothers, who are dead now. Said she was overly sheltered, left her family as soon as she could in order to become herself. Said early struggle and push create a sort of welcome freeness. Did that make sense to me? I said I thought so, but actually I'm not sure, though I want to understand.

Thing is, she's easy to talk to. I told her I'd lied about my age. She said, no matter I'd clearly lived up to the lie. We laughed. I feel seen by her in ways that are different from how others have seen me. Maybe it's that she takes what I say seriously; or maybe it's that she really listens. When I told her about Marla's addiction, her death, the grief, she squeezed my hand. Said, one can barely explain loss.

Waiting for the light to change, the wind picks up, and litter and other street debris fly around. Music, drinks, crowd is what I need for an hour or so, unused as I am to Rhonda's peaceful abode. She spends hours in her studio where I haven't yet been invited. Back home the sounds of Scotty's drill, the toss of empty beer cans missing the trash, and of course the TV droning on about one war becoming two wars becoming never-ending.

Already there are fake Christmas wreaths in a few gritty apartment windows. Too much is expected from the holiday with too little take away. Last Christmas I remember Scotty's rough-hewn friends drunk and raucous, carrying on like Jesus himself would soon be visiting, my mother trying to cope. Marla and I loaded up with bottles of beer, drank them in the bedroom and couldn't stop laughing at nothing funny.

On the phone Hack said my mother hangs out in bed 24/7. It's so not like her. The woman would rarely sit still. If I needed a few days to visit her, Rhonda wouldn't object. But I can't handle going back there yet, Marla's presence not at my side, Marcus's house too close.

Blondie's is crowded and noisy and just what I need. It's a young, middle-aged, Black, white, and whatever crowd. It's the regulars that make a bar successful, Scotty would repeat, as if he dared anyone to dispute it.

Edging around the bar to look for Frank, a hand reaches out, tugs me in beside him. "Name's Mike."

I take in his coppery skin, large dark eyes with lashes so thick they invite picking. "You look more like Mohammed."

"That's my father. And you?" he asks matter-of-factly.

"I'm a runaway."

"Do you have a name?"

"Tessa."

"You alone?"

"Most of the time."

"Want a drink?"

"Bourbon on ice."

His slim torso weaves easily between people to catch the bartender's attention. Tall, dark, and handsome, I'd say, except Mike's not tall, barely a head above me.

Mike hands me the drink and steers me toward a space against one of the walls.

"So, tell me, is Mike your American name?"

"Yes, American Mike, born in Jackson Heights, Queens. Mom and Dad from Iran, they don't drink, take care of all of us. Mom cooks the most sumptuous meals, which made going overseas difficult. Do you need more information in order to talk to me?"

"Sorry. But I always need to know everything about beautiful men."

"Flattery is nice. And you? Born in a hospital or maybe a home birth in some cushy atmosphere where anything goes. Right?"

"Wrong. Born in a ward, payments for same still being dunned. More about you?"

"Just got out of the Army Rangers, not sure if I'm going back."

"You like Russian Roulette?"

He laughs a quick bark. "Depends on who has the gun. Kidding. Depends on which American enterprise offers me work. Your turn."

"New to town, new to job, no real story yet."

"You're beautiful, too." His eyes steady on me.

"Oh, that's what all the men say."

"I know a place that isn't so crowded, find a table to drink and chat."

"I don't think so. I mean believe me or not, I have a curfew. I'm taking care of an elderly woman and need to be back by nine."

"That's restrictive."

"So is life, sometimes."

"Do you always talk in quips?"

"Maybe, not sure, now that you ask. Let me think about it."

"I will. I'm getting another drink. Want one?"

"Not yet."

Two TV screens lend color to either side of the bar, a soccer game on one, basketball game on the other.

It's a few minutes to nine when we enter the building's warm lobby where after chatting nonstop for more than an hour there suddenly seems nothing to say. Is this a goodbye moment or simply goodnight?

"Want to give me your phone number?" such a serious voice.

"Only if you give me yours," I say, and we enter the numbers into our phones. He kisses my cheek and takes off.

Unlocking the apartment door, I see Rhonda on the couch, wearing an elegant maroon velvet lounger; she's reading. We exchange hellos.

Before reaching my room, she calls out, "Tessa, I have a favor to ask."

"Of course, what?"

"My son and grandson are arriving Friday night until Sunday evening. I would appreciate it if you stayed in during their visit."

"I can do that. No problem." But why, I don't ask, and close my bedroom door to think a bit more about Mike, about his interest in what I had to say, and I did say more than I would've expected to. But he talked a lot, too about his immigrant parents, his three brothers having a difficult time at their jobs since the planes hit the towers, that his non-Muslim friends seem edgy around him. I said idiot assholes should be ignored, and he smiled, sadly I thought. Will I see him again? No doubt!

Careful, Tessa. Sweet American Mike is an example of who I don't want to hook up with, tender in youth, with simple dreams. I know where the Mikes (like Raff) end up: in a small house, in a small community, with people too tired to care about anything larger. I've seen it, tasted it, know each of the flavors, vanilla sad, chocolate scared, strawberry depressed.

Rhonda watches the girl's lively step down the hallway, and wonders where Tessa spent the past hours, though not enough to ask. Except for their delightful walks, too much talk demands what she's no longer willing to give. Her need for comfort makes her selfish, perhaps even indifferent. She's fond of Tessa, cares about her more than she would've expected. The girl isn't a complainer or intrusive, and easily adjusts to the way Rhonda like things done. She works without much instruction, smart girl. From what she can gather, Tessa hasn't had lots in the way of material help yet has grown up with a sensitive nature.

She wishes her son Phillip had some of those attributes. She isn't looking forward to his visit. Phillip is like a Jack Russell dog constantly sniffing out how his aging mother will impinge on his busy life. Will it be sudden illness, memory loss, or God knows? He checks her out without saying a word. It's insensitive at the least and hateful as well. But he won't understand that till he's eighty, and maybe not then.

Like his late father he sees things through his own needs. Harold, too, was immersed in his work. He provided whatever she wanted but shared none of her interests, called painting her habit, and couldn't care less about her discontents. Albert, though, cared about all aspects of her.

How strange the life! Passing each other on Broadway, the rain had stopped, and his closed umbrella handle caught the strap of her bag and pulled it off her shoulder. Such an innocuous beginning, such a momentous aftermath!

Picking up the bag, he apologized, and heading in the same direction, they walked and chatted. He was a sculptor, she a painter. It was clear they found each other interesting, and they parted with a plan to meet at a museum exhibit. Was it the Impressionists? She forgets, only that they went out for a glass of wine after. And so it began, a long, but not long enough relationship. Pure Hollywood, she thinks now; only it was real.

She misses him still, though he's been gone six years: their delicious furtive meetings and brief vacations of exploration, checking into inns, hotels, and B&Bs, which he loved. In Mexico at the ruins near Merida they climbed to the top of the Warrior Temple, the view magnificent. In Italy, the hours spent visiting cultural sites followed by intimate nighttime dinners in narrow alley restaurants. They talked about everything. How flamboyant it all was, she was. How daring and adventurous they were together. Until recently, she continued to walk through the sculpture garden behind the UN building where two of his pieces reside. She favored the one of a child whose every muscle strained to leap heavenward.

Remembering those times pleases her, but memories also replay what's been and gone, and do little to relieve the present, except, perhaps, to provoke longing.

Had Albert asked her to, she would've left her marriage. But he wouldn't upend his large family. Shame on her, she supposes. If Harold suspected her affair, it didn't seem to trouble him. He never commented on her absences and she concluded he didn't mind. He never loved her, married to get the chore done with, and go on to get his various medical degrees. He never turned to her sexually; it was she who said she wanted a baby. He complied, technically, though as Phillip got older and showed his adoration, Harold enjoyed him immensely. Sometimes she has the urge to tell Phillip about Albert to shock him out of his properness. But he is her son and she can't hurt him. He idolized his father.

Hopefully, with Tessa present, Phillip won't bring up all the lovely retirement places he's discovered. Her intention is to live and die in this apartment, and Phillip will not change her mind, as long as she has one, that is. Her grandson's presence will be a consolation. She and Gregory spent many lovely summers together when he was a boy, his parents too busy to be anything but grateful. It boggles her mind now to remember the activities she could do then.

When Greg finishes his studies, he will be a wonderful doctor, better than his grandfather who found so many of his patients irritating. Greg told her that he's drawn to medical research. Maybe he'll find a cure for arthritic fingers or perhaps a pill to energize the body or at least reduce the awful fear of losing control of it. At times, the simple act of crossing Madison can be unnerving with all the bus and car traffic. Such insults, trivial as they may be, do make being old a chore. However, all is not lost; there's also the unexpected relief of no longer needing to be or do or meet the expectations of anyone, including her past self. And she can still paint.

She takes a sip of the cooling tea that contains a generous amount of scotch, which works its healing way into her limbs faster than any pain medicine, allowing her mind to wander free of care. When before was that ever true?

※

Peter puts down the phone, dazed by the unexpected voice of Nina's husband who curtly informed him that Nina was unavailable, grieving her dead daughter Marla, and then clicking off. Gave him no time to say or ask anything. Calling back isn't feasible. He couldn't care less about what her husband thinks of him, but making a pest of himself may somehow hurt Nina. She's suffering enough, of that he's certain.

Refilling the shot glass, still stunned, he stares into the darkness outside the window, and then eyes the diminishing liquid in the bottle. Maybe he should get drunk at a bar; it would be more social. Jesus, what can he do? How can he reach her? Think, Peter, think. He can feel the fingers of desperation creeping up his back.

Maybe it was wrong not to call before now. He wanted to give her time to deal with the needs of her daughter, time she asked for. He kept busy with the move to the sublet. But now, now, he can't let any more time elapse. She has to know he knows. He picks up the pad of blank paper on the table and prays her husband won't toss the letter.

Nina, dear one, I phoned; I heard; your husband told me about Marla. I can't even begin to imagine all that you're going through. You are my soul, which is in pain with your pain, which wants so much to find a way to siphon off some of all that you are feeling. I know. I know. It's not possible. Grief is one burden that can't be shared despite all of my love . . .

Nevertheless, I can't help but fantasize arriving at your house and in caveman style sweep you up, carry you far enough away so that no further distress can find you. Though your grief will travel with you, I would be there to hold you.

If you could manage even a brief meeting anywhere, I'll be there to console you. I'm not at the motel, couldn't stay there without you, too depressing. I accepted a friend's sublet in the city where I'm waiting for your return. I can't stop loving you, Peter.

He inserts the letter in an envelope, and clearly prints his new return address. Then pours another drink and hears the chug-chug of an overhead helicopter, which brings back skies that told a different tale, one he rarely allows himself to ponder. He once described a sandstorm to Nina: how sight changed in an instant, how sand waves rose higher than those in a stormy ocean. She listened, her green eyes intent on his face. He wants that again.

21

From the bedroom window I watch snow fall gently onto roofs and water towers.

There's a tap at the door.

"Yes, come in?"

"Hello, I'm Greg, Rhonda's grandson." He stands in the doorway, barefoot in jeans and crewneck sweater.

"Tessa, hi."

"I prepared breakfast. Granny suggested you might want to join us."

"Thank you," and I follow his long, sturdy back to the kitchen. I heard them arrive late last night, but stayed in my room.

"Take some food," Rhonda waves at the table arrayed with English muffins, scrambled eggs, and something I don't recognize that look like sardines but are larger. "Phillip, this is Tessa, I told you she . . . "

"Hello," Phillip says briskly. Short and stocky, with no resemblance to Rhonda's tall slim self. "Are you a nurse?"

"No, but I'm very capable and your mom is doing very well." Almost imperceptivity Rhonda nods her approval.

"What if there's an emergency?" Phillip asks.

"Dad, I'm sure Tessa has the phone numbers of Granny's doctors, and there's plenty of Urgent Care places around here."

"Someone of Grandma's age, things happen fast. You need to be Johnny on the spot. Right?"

"No, dad," the aspiring doctor replies. "Elderly people often respond well in emergencies, bodies gone through much become resilient, plus cells reproduce more slowly, slowing disease."

"Of course, you know better than me," Phillip allows. "But I don't want my mother to experience a fall where no one is around."

"But, darling, Tessa is here. She's around all the time," Rhonda says.

"I am," Tessa agrees, disliking Phillip at once.

"Eat something, Tessa," Rhonda says.

No one really expects me to converse, so I scoop scrambled eggs onto my plate along with an English muffin. I can feel Greg watching me. Let him feast.

"Greg, how's your dear mother?" Rhonda asks.

"Busy."

"With?"

"A thousand volunteer jobs, a million dates with who knows who. I rarely see her."

"But with your studies you're away so much of the time now."

"True, Granny, but after Christmas, I'll have off the entire month of January."

"That sounds like a treat."

"With all the snow, we may be stuck here," Greg, says, his eyes flick to me, and I allow a slight smile, and continue eating.

"We won't be stuck. We have snow tires. But I'll check the weather. If necessary, we'll leave earlier, if that's okay with you mother."

"It's probably prudent."

"The food was delicious, thank you. Rhonda I'll be in my room if you need me." I walk slowly through the hallway, knowing Greg is watching.

Typical rich boy who wears his sense of entitlement easily, I think. And why shouldn't he? What has ever been denied him? He's probably traveled half the world already, no doubt owns more clothes than he'll ever need, wouldn't know a maxed-out credit card if it bit him, and clearly runs around with . . . why am I working myself into disliking him?

My phone rings.

"Mike, hey."

"Can you steal away? Play in the snow. Or better yet, get warm in—"

"I'm grounded for the weekend."

"What bad thing did you do?"

"Never mind." I say, and feel an immediate sense of camaraderie.

"I continue my job hunt on Monday. What about a drink Monday night?"

"Can I phone you Sunday evening, let you know?"

"If you make seeing you too hard, I'll stop trying," Mike's voice deep, velvety.

"Message received. Good luck hunting."

Clearly, I'm not going out there again, unless Rhonda calls me; and settle in on the bed with a book from Rhonda's library.

"Tessa?" Greg gently pushes open the door, but doesn't come in. "My father's decided to leave late afternoon. Weather says the roads are bad. He doesn't want my mother alone in case the power goes off. I'm staying and will return by train tomorrow. If the snow doesn't put you off . . . would you like to have dinner somewhere close by?" His words offered in a rush.

Surprised, I almost say but we've just met. "I need to check with your grandmother."

"Already did. She seemed content to be rid of us. What do you say?"

"Why not?"

"Is six okay?"

"Of course." Dinner with the boss's grandson, now there's a slippery slope.

With Phillip gone home and Greg and Tessa out to dinner, the comfort of the couch is a sudden joy. The early darkness of winter enters the room to brighten the lamplight. Nothing new in the way of decoration has been added, so most everything within sight is at least half her age. Her eyes take in the paintings, photos, chairs, even the plants along the windowsill—all of it feels more dear to her now than it once did. What strange mood is this?

Perhaps it's the result of too many hours in her studio this week with little time to contemplate anything else. She must remember to place a second cushion on the studio chair. Her bottom aches, and her wrist, well, it aches, too. Nevertheless, she's determined to finish the triptych before . . . what? Death? Yes, but why burden the art with urgency? She's done showing her work, isn't she? Is the ego ever done? Even at eighty? Frightening to think not. It isn't death, however, that makes her work for hours; it's life. As long as work is there to get on with, her earthly being has purpose. Why else start a triptych, which will take forever to complete? When she drops the brushes in the cleaning fluid, she's done but only for today.

She'd like a drink and so she'll have one. Why not? In the kitchen she pours a scotch and water. Getting the ice tray out of the freezer, a painful spasm grabs at her spine and won't let go, a veritable knife in the back. She can't straighten up and hunched over, hobbles to sit in a kitchen chair. Then reminds herself that bodily insults come and go, and waits for the latter. Taking a few deep breaths, she fixes her sight on the scene outside the window: an unflattering smoggy coat of snow covers all. How she loved the New England college winters with their pristine, invigorating frost. Now winter offers the danger of slipping on ice, how unfair. Youth wasted on the young then age wasted on the body. Bummer.

She realized today at breakfast what it is about Tessa that grabbed her from the first day. Tessa reminds her of Magda, the feistiness against all odds. Traveling by herself from Hungry, Magda won her heart as soon as she came to live with them. Not yet eleven, burdened with a past, needing to learn English, Magda was adventurous, affectionate, cuddly, all that Phillip wasn't. Of course, he too was only a child and though she wanted Phillip to enjoy Magda, he mostly ignored her. Those early years of marriage, so sure she knew what she was doing when there was still everything to learn.

Slowly, she tries to stand. Yes, okay, then takes a few tentative steps, yes, still okay, the pain now an ache, the knife replaced by a fist. What in heavens name would she have done had this occurred outdoors? But she has Tessa now.

Taking her drink to the couch, she flips through the pages of a magazine, but her mind is on the upcoming visit to her son in a few weeks. Since his father died, Phillip picks her up Christmas morning to spend a day and night, and then drives her back the next day. Never does she have a good time there. His wife, bothered by life in ways that Rhonda doesn't understand, can't sit still. And Phillip's desire to push away the holiday in order to get back to the office oppresses them all. Why in the world do they even want her there? Certainly not for scintillating conversation, which in earlier years may have been just that, but now talk devolves into banalities that bore her even more than it must bore them. It's about duty, of course. Old mother shouldn't be left alone on Christmas. If only they knew how much she'd rather that—well, she could simply say no. But then Phillip would think she was hiding some illness, more proof she shouldn't be living on her own. Best to just go there.

The Italian restaurant is tiny with real logs crackling in a fireplace. It's as cozy as someone's living room. We're the only customers, no surprise.

"Red or white wine," Greg asks. "Or something else?"

"Red is good."

The waiter, a man in his seventies, who shouldn't be out tonight, smiles benevolently as he comes to the table. Greg orders the wine by its Italian name, which both impresses and discomforts me. The waiter leaves two menus on the table and walks slowly toward the kitchen. I decide he must be the owner.

"Have you been here before?"

"I've taken Granny here a few times. She doesn't like going too far from home."

The flickering candle on the table brightens and darkens his face but obscures his expressions, which is slightly disconcerting.

"Lately Granny doesn't converse as much, have you noticed?" Greg asks.

"We don't talk much during the day, but chat a lot during our early evening walks, which aim to reach the East River. Sometimes we get there. She's very knowledgeable, philosophical too. They mean a lot to me, the walks, to her, too, I think."

"I'm happy she has you with her."

"What you said at breakfast . . . that the elderly don't need quick care, is that true?"

"Not entirely. I wanted my father to stop badgering her. What I said about cells not reproducing fast, that's true. I do worry about her, though. She was always such a doer and now seems content to be still. You know, she's a wonderful artist, has had many exhibits. Is she working?"

"She's in her studio several hours a day."

The waiter pours the wine. We both order pasta.

Greg lifts his glass, "So glad to meet you," he says with exaggerated formality.

"And I you," my glass lifted as well.

"Tell me something about you. Are you an only child or one of many?"

"It's just me now. My sister died recently."

"I'm so sorry."

"Yes, me too. Very."

"Do you want to say more about it?"

"I don't, it's too raw." My honesty surprises me. "Do you have siblings?"

"An only child, pampered and spoiled as you would expect."

"You're right, I would expect that. You must be close to your parents, then."

He shrugs. "Mother is always busy, which I don't understand, and well . . . Dad is brilliant in business, and I admire him but . . . families . . . you know how it goes. What about you? Granny said you grew up on Long Island. What was it like?"

"Small town that didn't fit my personality, so I left."

"I'd like to live in a small town where there'd be a sense of community, unlike Connecticut."

I decide to allow him his vision.

"Is that where you went to college?" he asks.

"I quit school in my senior year to move to the city and get a job." An edge of challenge creeps into my tone, as if daring him to either show disapproval or admire my grit. Neither is evident as he tops off both our glasses.

"I never went rogue the way most of my college classmates did," he confides.

"So, you learned something?"

"Probably." He smiles.

"You must have plans for your next few weeks."

"Freedom. Some studying, sleep late and do whatever."

"Hmm, sound like good choices."

"Would you like to suggest a more interesting way to spend the time?"

"Oh no. Freedom is about not following anyone else's idea of what you ought to do. My sister believed in getting rid of the should-s. You know, should do this or that instead of tapping into what it is that feels right."

"Smart woman," he says.

"She was."

As we hurry back through a wind of sleety pellets, neither of us speaks. Rhonda asleep, the apartment silent, we whisper. "I leave before noon tomorrow, can we exchange phone numbers?" We do.

He gives my shoulder a quick squeeze, and disappears down the hallway to his room.

Alone, I want another drink, and tiptoe to the kitchen, find an open bottle of white wine in the fridge, pour a few inches into a glass, and take it to my room.

22

The busy Broadway supermarket aisles are brightly lit and filled with products that the grocery back home wouldn't know to carry. What for? Who there could afford them? Truly no one I can think of. Here, an array of dips and sauces from other countries fill several shelves. Though Rhonda needs only a few things, I traipse the well-peopled aisles, pick up snippets of all manner of conversation, but hear nothing about the food on display.

At the register, the cashier asks if I'm doing anything for the upcoming holidays. I say I have no special plans. Sounding quite pleased she announces she'll be off work for the week between Christmas and New Years. I wish her a good holiday, and decide to call my mother, who also used to take off the holiday week.

Again, I duck into a building hallway to avoid the traffic-noisy street and phone her. Hack answers.

"Hey Tess. I think to call you then the thought disappears like time. What's happening," he asks in his slow druggy tone.

"Come visit me and see?"

"That's further than the one-mile radius I never venture past."

"Why's that?"

"I'd be obliged to mingle with the suffering masses of which I'm already a member."

"My mother still hasn't gone back to work?"

"So the story is told."

"How is she?"

"Where is she, maybe nowhere I can say."

"You're scaring me."

"I see what I see, my problem."

"Why do you have her phone?"

"It's in the living room."

"Can you bring it to my mother. Now?"

"I'm walking."

The cold hallway penetrates, and I huddle in a corner.

"Tessa," her voice, barely audible.

"Mom? I've tried to reach you several times."

"I heard."

"How are you?"

"I don't know, lovey. Tired, mostly."

"Are you taking too many pills?"

"I'm stopping them."

"Okay. Good. When do you think you'll go back to work?"

"Can't think past the next hour."

"Should I come visit," which I don't mean.

"No, baby, not yet. I'm still so out of it. Best if you wait awhile. You take care of yourself is all I want. Promise?"

"Yes, okay, I will, don't worry about me. I have a fine job. I'll call on Christmas. Love you."

"Love you more."

For a moment Nina continues to stare at the silent phone as if that will keep Tessa's sweet voice in her ear. No, it's best if Tessa doesn't visit. She couldn't muster either the energy or enthusiasm that Tessa deserves. The least she can do is to spare her daughter . . .

Scotty opens the bedroom door, stands in the doorway.

"What is it?"

"It would be good for everyone if you'd get out of bed," and leaves the door ajar. Is this a coded message of concern? Or is getting out of bed a step toward getting out of the house to go to work? She doesn't blame him. He's carrying all of the expenses. But how to explain that she's in a strange land of loss without a map. And even if she could explain he wouldn't understand. She doesn't blame him for that either. Marla is hers; the loss is personal. She once saw a movie about a hospitalized woman having a breakdown. She cries and screams and bangs at the door to be let out. When the nurse opens the door to let her out, she refuses to go.

Okay, she'll try to leave the bed for a while each day.

23

Heading to meet Mike at the bar, snow piled along curbs. The snow has interfered with my walks with Rhonda. To my surprise, now and then she comes out of her studio to have lunch with me.

It's impossible to ignore the holiday season. Shops shout their wares from tinsel-filled windows. Christmas trees line the street. People lug packages, their expressions frazzled, tired, maybe even exasperated. How to survive the holiday remains an open question.

I'm sure that Greg's Christmas will be postcard perfect, a candle in every window, rooms scented in cinnamon and nutmeg with small tables garnished with dishes of nuts and candies. A majestic tree dressed in white lights will stand across from the . . . Is that what I want, the picture-perfect? What I want is just once to be part of what something is supposed to be.

I remember one Christmas when we were little and my mother was out of work, can't remember why, and Louise brought food to the house. Scotty would remind us to turn off the light as we left a room. Windows were encased in plastic to keep out the wind, but it didn't. Heat was rationed, but that wasn't new. Marla and I wore jackets indoors and complained. Scotty said we should be glad to have a roof over our heads. My mother added that we also had each other. True, true, true!

Santa rings a tiny bell near a collection dish filled with bills and coins. Does Santa have a job after Christmas? If not, will the money go into his coffer? Should anyone blame him?

Entering the crowded bar, Mike sees me and waves. He's snagged us a table. He looks cozy in his green flannel shirt.

"Any luck job-hunting," I ask taking a seat.

"No. I'm thinking of joining the coast guard." He doesn't sound serious.

"Uniforms attract you?"

"It's not about uniforms. It's about post 9/11 life: Who's going to hire a Muslim veteran who knows how to shoot? Then again Muslim, Brown, African American, Black, this land is crazy racist." His earnest tone unlocks a desire to comfort him.

"You're more than right about the racism, but no one finds work quickly these days."

"Quickly, I've been hoofing it for months. I get home and smoke some weed or hash to forget about the lack of success, so I can do it again the next day."

"Go to school, Mike, that's where being a veteran will help. You could become a nurse, teacher, a . . . "

"A teacher, yes. I'd want that, but I need to bring money home now. My brothers are also out of work."

"Of course, I understand," is all I say, unwilling to hear the details of a reality I know too well, and which brings Raff to mind. He wanted to become a pilot. His family said it would take too long to pull in any money, that it's better not to reach too high if he wants to succeed, which is how Scotty thinks too. Not my mother though . . . she wanted us to reach high, just me now. Go away, sadness.

"Hey, come back, I didn't mean to depress you," he says no doubt reading my sorrowful face. "Why the weekend curfew?"

"Rhonda's son and grandson visited. Her son wants her safe in a nursing home. Having me there is her excuse not to have to consider it."

"That would mean your job?"

"Yeah, then what?"

"Come live at my house. Always space for one more cousin."

"You have cousins there?"

"Most of the time but not the same ones."

"It must be nice to have a full house," the wistful tone surprises me.

"You don't?"

"Not anymore, not since my sister died."

"Death," he repeats and shakes his head sadly. "Saying sorry doesn't work, I know. I lost a buddy I loved, though I only knew him a year. But someone you've grown up with, that you share genes with, who is as much a part of you as your name, man, I can't even imagine."

"Are we drinking tonight or what?" too close to tears.

He heads to the bar, already he doesn't need to ask what I drink. Already, I accept that he's allowed to know one more thing about me.

People are in a holiday mood, calling out to each other, cheering new arrivals. Marla would get into the spirit easily; she'd speak to strangers. She was always more daring than me. Why, I wonder?

Mike navigates the crowd, holding aloft two drinks.

"Make a toast, Tessa."

"Can't think . . . "

"Doubtful." He lifts his glass, "To a very merry night."

"Amen." He laughs, erasing his serious expression.

Holding my hand, he leads me down a dark path through Riverside Park toward the Hudson River. We've both had a few drinks, and the late December cold feels forgiving.

"Where are we headed, Mike?"

"Worried?"

"Isn't this far from where Rhonda lives? You know I have to be—"

"It's only eight, Cinderella, you still have an hour. I want to show you the Marina."

We hurry through a short smelly tunnel, pass a homeless wino who lifts his bottle in a salute, which Mike returns, and exit onto a road parallel to the West Side Highway. Cars zip by, headlights briefly illuminate the darkness.

"You're quiet. It worries me," he says.

"Am I really such a talker?"

"Constant. Opinionated, too."

I laugh.

The marina isn't far and we're soon leaning over a railing, watching boats of all sizes and shapes rock in the water. In the distance, a necklace of lights glitters off the George Washington Bridge. I tell him about the beach near where I lived, about the constant lap of water and seagull cries, which were the best things about living there. After Marla died, the only things, I don't say.

"Now that's a houseboat I'd like to live on for a month or two," and points to a long, wide yacht.

"Hmm," I say, mesmerized by a peacefulness that seems to insist on itself.

"Would you like that?"

"Not sure." I will sleep with him. It's inevitable.

"That surprises me."

"Why?"

"You take risks, you spoke to me."

"My sister was the daring one, too bad she chose drugs."

"Maybe dissatisfaction makes someone itch to find out whatever."

"That's true."

"I'm about to kiss you. More than once."

In the apartment, Rhonda's awake on the couch sipping a drink, the TV on, the volume low.

"Hi. Do you need anything before I turn in?"

"No, dear, sleep well."

Closing the bedroom door gently, and without switching on the light, I sit on the bed and replay the last hours. Mike smoked a joint at the Marina, which annoyed me. But everyone smokes weed. Raff carried a small bag . . .

A gentle tap on the door, "Are you in bed, dear?"

"No, come in." I switch on the lamp, and pray Rhonda isn't feeling ill.

"Are you doing anything special Christmas Day?" She stands in the doorway, her eyes reading me.

"It's just another day."

"I agree Tessa, but no one else does. I had a thought. Phillip arrives early Christmas morning to drive me to his house for the day and then home the next day. I don't have it in me to travel alone. But if you were to accompany me, well . . . we could take the train to and from Westport, and I needn't stay the night. And, Tessa, I would so much rather come home. But you think about it. Let me know. Good night, dear."

"Good night."

Well, that's a surprise. Of course I'll go with her, though it does bring up—

My phone rings. Scotty? Jesus! The man never calls me. Is it my mother? "Hi?" I say.

"You ought to come visit Nina for the holiday. She's getting out of bed."

"That's good news, but I'm working. I can't just leave."

"Sure you can. It's your mother. You only have one."

"I'm committed to escorting the woman I care for to her son's house."

"See you on Christmas Day," he says as if he hadn't heard me, "and clicks off.

With his voice in my head, I lay back on the bed. Why did he call? It doesn't make sense. If she's out of bed, that's good, isn't it? I spoke to her the other day; she doesn't want me to visit. Probably has no idea that Scotty called me. What isn't he saying? Is he upset or frightened, but of what? I should call my mother or Hack, but I don't have it in me now to do either. It can wait a day.

24

Penn Station is a holiday mob scene. I link Rhonda's arm to keep her from being jostled and falling. She, however, doesn't complain about any of it. With her cane, she treads carefully. We wait in front of the crowded information board for the gate to be listed.

She opens the leather purse, with its extravagant gold clasp, and hands me a twenty-dollar bill, indicating with her chin the nearby redcap. "Give it to him. He'll take us to the gate before it's listed."

It's as she says. We follow the redcap to an elevator that takes us down to the platform to await the train.

"I'm impressed," and wonder, is this privilege or age?

"I used to do a lot of coming and going," she says as if reading my mind.

"Voila," Rhonda whispers, as we find two seats on the train.

I stow the shopping bag of gifts in the upper compartment. Rhonda asked me to pick up a few small things. Tokens, she called them. For Greg, argyle socks; for Phillip, a pair of gloves; for Martha, a silk scarf. Looking for a suitable gift for her I feared that any art book I chose would be too simplistic for her, and settled on a biography of Diane Arbus, someone Marla mentioned. She unwrapped it this morning, exclaiming that Arbus is one of her favorites. And gave me an envelope with fifty dollars, and one of her small paintings: tiny figures, arms outstretched, walking toward an endless aqua horizon.

I didn't follow up Scotty's call and feel a bit guilty. Too late now. I push aside the guilt to wonder how Phillip will respond to me, the uninvited guest. Rhonda must've told him the change of plans.

"The holiday always brings Magda to mind," Rhonda says as if musing to herself."

"Magda?"

"Years ago, I cared for a Hungarian foster child. Christmas was very hard for her, though she was in relative comfort here. Later, when she was able to speak better English, she explained how being so far away during the holidays felt especially impossible. She missed her family all the time, but at Christmas she missed her town as well where the holidays came alive with an all-encompassing celebration."

Surprised by this bit of information, not sure how to respond, I ask only if the girl's family were able to visit her.

"No. Her mother was very ill, and her father was doing his best to care for younger siblings, which is why she was fostered out. I rarely talk about Magda, though I've never forgotten her. She was amazing. She died when she was nearly thirteen of the same blood disease that took her mother."

"How terrible and sad. My room was her room, wasn't it?"

"Why do you say that?"

"The moment I walked in I felt someone special had lived there."

"Yes," she says, but nothing more.

Phillip's shiny black Lexus waits for us in the lot below the outdoor train platform. With barely a nod in my direction, he helps his mother into the front seat. I climb in the back. A few bits of boring conversation exchanged between them then silence prevails. It's only a short ride thank goodness before we enter a circular driveway framed with landscaped hedges and bushes on a piece of land I can't see the edges of. The car stops in front of a sprawling three-story, pristine white house.

We step carefully over the skin of icy puddles that lead to the front door, opened now by a tiny, thin, almost bird-like woman with shoulder-length steel gray hair, her small chin lost over a long neck. Rhonda introduces me to her daughter-in-law, Martha. In the large vestibule Phillip takes our coats and packages. We follow Martha into a high-ceiling dining room. A long table covered in a white linen cloth is set for eight. White tapered candles in beautiful brass holders are ready to be lit; berries and poinsettia leaves are strewn across the cloth. And where is Greg, I wouldn't dare ask?

"Are you expecting other guests," Rhonda says.

"You never know who might drop in. What can I get you both to drink?" Martha seems to want something to do.

"Scotch and water for me," Rhonda says.

Bourbon with ice, I don't say. "White wine would be great. Thank you." The sooner the better, I pray. Despite the warmth of the décor, the house feels cold, or maybe it's Martha and Phillip, who haven't kissed Rhonda hello or shaken my hand or even said Merry Christmas.

"Happy Noel to everyone and welcome." Greg appears in the dining room doorway. He seems uncomfortable, but maybe that's me. He taps my elbow. "Let me show you the tree."

I feel eyes on me. "Greg, it's rude to walk away," I whisper when we're out of earshot.

"Don't worry." Barefoot in well-creased khakis and a blazer, he walks ahead, but I stand still.

"Rhonda came all the way out here . . . "

"Oh, she isn't bothered. You don't know her. She isn't half as proper as you think."

"What do you mean?"

"Not now. Come to the den and have some very well-laced eggnog."

"Where's the tree?"

"Behind you, in the corner of the living room."

It was as I imagined, tall, majestic but with royal blue lights; no tinsel, of course not, tinsel is the cheap decoration. Silver and gold wrapped presents are neatly stacked beneath it.

"My den," he says, pushing open a door into a wood-paneled room with a large desk, leather couch, two leather chairs, a TV, and spanning one wall, shelves filled with books. A glass bowl of eggnog sits on a driftwood table in front of the couch. He fills a glass and hands it to me. I sip at it politely; it's malted-thick and goes down like sludge.

"Did you know I was coming?"

"My mother mentioned it. I'm not a fan of this day with all it's phony-baloney."

"Haven't heard that expression in a long time."

"I thought it was original." He drops onto the couch. "Come sit."

"Greg. I'm not comfortable being with you in your den while Rhonda and your parents are out there thinking whatever." I refuse to be his distraction from the phony-baloney.

He stares past me for a moment. "Okay, let's go back."

We enter the living room together, where late afternoon sun still brightens the very white walls. Two long windows overlook a spacious lawn that slopes down toward a distant road. I sit next to Rhonda on a velour couch, which is so soft I want to pet it.

Martha perches on the edge of a tall, winged chair and begins to distribute presents with little fanfare. My head is suddenly spacey, my sight a tad blurry. The last time I felt this way I had the flu, more likely now it's the abundance of whiskey in the eggnog aided by the wine I now sip. After giving the others their gifts, Martha hands me a small package, which both surprises and embarrasses me. Do I have to open it now? Of course I do. Everyone else has done so. Inside is a small, square satin sachet pillow, which smells of lavender. "Thank you, it's lovely," I say to no one in particular and can't seem to summon even a smile. This is the way it is, I think, well-off people always have something in a drawer for the unexpected guest.

Phillip hovers about his mother. What is he looking for? Why is he obsessed with moving Rhonda to a nursing home? Once in a while, he casts a baleful eye at me. Assessing me as well, I suppose; do I look drunk?

Greg is quiet, looks comfortable. Why not? He's used to it all. Did he really expect me to hang out in the den with him?

A woman in a maid's outfit arrives to announce that the meal is ready. Where was she hidden? Are there more servants as well?

Obediently, we traipse into the dining room. Martha has organized the seating, placing me across from Greg and between Rhonda and Phillip. We take our seats. Phillip says nothing to me, which I can't take personally since he says nothing much to anyone. The array of silverware at each setting remains a puzzle. I've never felt this self-conscious about eating.

In Christmases past, Scotty's bar buddies would arrive, bringing their own bottles and ready to offer a stream of loud talk about who knows what. The TV would be going with no one watching. My mother would be running in and out with plates that were quickly emptied. For that one day, Scotty would jack up the heat. Under the small fake tree on the coffee table would be one or two presents for Marla and me. There was singing, joke telling, teasing. Faces would redden with drink and no one would leave until the day wore down. Today will be different there, I'm sure. No tree, maybe a guest or two will drop by. My sister's absence would squeeze my heart to pain if—

Rhonda's gentle nudge interrupts my thoughts. Everyone's head is bowed as Martha recites, "Thank you, Lord, for all we have." *Indeed*, I think, *for you have much.*

Phillip serves after-dinner drinks in the living room. Martha sits in her wing chair, and mentions the new supermarket that's being rebuilt, describing the fire last year that decimated an entire area. I nod, try to look interested. Greg continues to top his wine glass and mine. Talk remains scarce, Martha and Rhonda the only ones who try to fill the silences. I've never been in a situation in which time passing felt so exhausting; no wonder Rhonda would rather not stay overnight.

As dusk enters the room, Martha gets up to switch on the lamps, saying that except for the recent snow, so inconvenient, it's been a fairly mild winter. Yes, we all agree. And I can't stand another minute of this. Perhaps it's my expression, my silence or body language, but Rhonda announces we must leave, that we do have a train to catch. Greg says he'll drive us to the station. He's had quite a bit to drink, but it's a short ride, I think, and I'd much rather it be him than Phillip, who I've become allergic to.

It takes forever to get our coats on and pack up Rhonda's presents. Martha helps with all of it no doubt glad to see the last of us.

Mild winter or not, it's freezing outdoors. Rhonda fumbles to put something in her purse and in what seems like a split-second slips on a patch of ice, her bag of gifts flung into the driveway. I quickly kneel beside her, so does Greg.

"Granny, don't move until we know what hurts."

Rhonda looks stunned but she manages to sit and take a few deep breaths. Gingerly she straightens the leg still caught beneath her. "I'm okay, I think. Greg, help me up."

"No, Greg," Phillip says, alarmed. "Don't touch her. I'll call an ambulance."

"Don't you dare," Rhonda says in no uncertain terms.

Martha stands in the doorway, as if waiting for instructions.

I'm still kneeling at Rhonda's side, trying to clear my head, unsure if Phillip is right or not. "Rhonda, what hurts," I ask gently.

She looks directly into my face. "I've hurt my fanny, for sure, but it's my ankle that feels sprained. I'm positive no bones are broken. Now if you guys can help me up, you'll see I'm okay."

Phillip and Greg look at each other. "Okay, granny, let's go." He places his hands beneath her armpits, and Phillip very gently slips an arm around Rhonda's waist and helps her to stand.

"Yes, it's my ankle, not broken just sprained, but I can't put weight on it."

"Listen, Granny, stay here. I'll keep the ankle raised and ice it and, if necessary, wrap it. It'll probably take a few days before you can walk on it. What do you say?" Greg, though tipsy, sounds quite professional. Convincing as well.

"What about an X-ray," Phillip asks, but no one responds.

When Rhonda agrees, I realize the pain must be much worse than she's admitted. It's clear she's not able to walk without help. Poor Rhonda, I think. What if I have to stay here with her? Holy horror. Yet, I don't like leaving her alone with this crew. If I do stay . . .

"Tessa, you go on back to the apartment, and then come get me when I'm ready to return in a few days?" Still held upright by Greg and Phillip, I try to read her face.

"Are you sure?" I ask with hope in my heart.

"Yes, I am. "

"I'll phone you daily. If there's anything you need, clothing, whatever, I'll bring it right up."

"I don't know," Phillip draws out the words. "It's better if the girl stays to help watch over mother's recovery."

"Actually, Phillip, I prefer not to leave the apartment empty with all of my work there. If I knew I'd be away, I would've stored certain pieces. Tessa, will you be all right alone?"

"Of course," and I want to hug her.

"There's cash in my bedroom dresser drawer, take what you need to buy food. Not to worry, everything will go on as it usually does." Rhonda offers a weak smile. "Greg, I need some aspirin. At once."

I watch, as she's half-carried into the house. Should I follow; should I remain out here?

"Tessa, I'll be right back," Greg says. "The car door's unlocked."

Waiting in the car as the last remnants of sunset stain the sky, I'm sad, a feeling that's been lurking all day. It's the house, the opulence, and the finery—it increased my sense of being an outsider.

"Granny's resting, she'll be fine." He slides into the driver's seat. "If you like I can take you back to the city."

"With much appreciation, no thanks. You've had a lot to drink, and my life is worth more than my time."

"You're pretty outspoken."

"So I've heard."

"Refreshing."

In the apartment I slip off my shoes and sit on the couch. Other people's homes don't usually affect me one way or another. Today, though, it was as if I'd entered a Fifth Avenue shop window to engage with mannequins. Poor Rhonda. At least Greg will be there, and he does love her. I take out my phone and call my mother.

"Hi Tessa," my mother's low tone.

"Merry Christmas."

"And to you, sweet pea."

"How did your day go?" I ask, not wanting to talk about mine.

"Rico and another of Scotty's friends came by. Louise was here for a short while; Hack said little." Her reluctant voice tells me more than I wish to know.

"Mom, Scotty phoned yesterday to say I should visit. Do you know why?"

"Not the faintest . . . he barely talks to me."

"Do you need me there?"

"No. I'm doing okay. How are you doing?"

"Still living with that lovely elderly lady." I know this isn't what she wants for me, a caretaker in someone's house. "Mom as soon as I save enough money, I plan to take a few courses."

"Good."

"Are you still on those pills?"

"I stopped."

"Is that okay?"

"Hack's in the kitchen. Want me to get him?"

"No. Tell him I said Merry Christmas."

She sighs. "Okay, sweet girl. Please take care, really good care."

"I will. Love you, Mom."

"Love you more."

Why doesn't Scotty talk to her? He's being an asshole. Maybe she doesn't want his attention; maybe anything he'd say would depress her further. Maybe he wants me there because he's too angry to take care of her? I don't know, it's between them.

I switch on the TV news. Mike says the wars will never end. He's probably with his family. Do Muslims celebrate Christmas? I switch off the TV and text him:

"Hi. How's the holiday?"

Christmas all day, Peter laments silently. He stretches his arms across the top of the couch like Jesus in the photo his mother touched each morning, a shrine of sorts. Maybe she thought doing so would induce sobriety. The last time he saw her, when? Three years already, she looked older, but the Jesus photo looked the same. He stayed two days, couldn't watch her drink morning, noon, etc.

He eyes the bottle on the table. Own it, he's drinking like his mother's son. It could detonate his ulcer. His Marine buddies insist that a man needs several stiff drinks to help the medicine go down. Does he miss their camaraderie? A little. Two buddies out west he's sometimes in touch with aren't doing as well as he'd like to hear: divorce, depression, so forth and so on. He has some nasty dreams, too, but he's not stalked by daytime nightmares. Sure, he startles if a balloon bursts, who wouldn't? Then again, he never bought into the whole deal the way they did.

But he did buy in to Nina, didn't he? She's responsible for the burning heat of pain inside him. How can she ignore him like this? Not a word from her, doesn't he matter to her? Didn't he? She declared her love as often as he did, right? Did he read her all wrong? Was he only a pleasant interruption in her dull life? If she'd tell him that, well, he'd be badly wounded, but wounds heal, or you die. He saw that up front. So, what besides booze does a man do? Go out and get laid, he thinks. Punish her. Christ, she lost her daughter; she's hurting plenty. Does he know that? Does he know anything except the unacceptable silence?

By now she must've received his last letter. Will she read it? She'll read it; he can feel it. Or is it the booze talking, sending him false hope along with Nina images, aching and beautiful, terrible, wonderful, but to what end? Say she does read his missives. Say they meet for old times sake, a meal, a walk, a talk. Then what? She returns to her husband? How will that change anything? It will. It will. He believes that and he believes in little. Their feelings for each other are too deep to be erased by time or tragedy. He can't prove it, but he knows he's right. If he doesn't hold on to that, what does he have?

On the round wheel of a table that once held yards of cable wire is his glass, now empty. The cable guys let him have the table with a wave and a smile, glad to see him roll the heavy wooden piece out of their way. Moving it into this apartment was a bitch, but he persevered. Though chipped in places, the table serves him well: his TV dinner now cooling on its surface. Big Man's Meal: meatloaf, mashed potatoes, and green beans. Nina loved the potatoes he grilled outdoors, baked till the skin singed and smelled burnt-ready. Cooking for her was a trip. She wasn't used to being served. Before even tasting, she'd say it's great. He'd laugh. Then she'd laugh. They read each other so well. Did they ever fight? Not really, not in the usual sense where love can turn to hate in a flash. Their struggles were about reassurance: him trying to help absolve her guilt, she unable to shake it off.

Out the window, it's dark, traffic quiet for Manhattan, people exhausted by their holiday cheer. Yesterday, walking down Broadway and back on Amsterdam Avenue, wanting to become more familiar with the neighborhood, he actually felt the city around him, it's aura of indifference, and yet opening space to let him in. Unlike his California environs where nature is the first call of day, and absent such wandering souls as he.

Even if he went out to a bar, other people's revelry would only deepen the aloneness. Go on, Peter, finish off what's left in the bottle. It's Christmas, everyone's allowed a treat or three.

25

White winter light leaks through the blinds. Rolling to the edge of the bed, I slip out. Mike in sleep looks boyish, hair falling across his forehead, arms hugging a pillow. There's nothing boyish about his passion, though. His hard stomach, whisky scented breath, and eager hands traveling my body like a blind man needing to know the terrain. Two hungry people wanting to feed our souls, and we did. Not sorry about that, not sorry at all. I've slept with Raff and two others in Miami; their hunger was selfish, demanding. With Mike it was as if our bodies couldn't wait to reassure each other.

I think of returning to bed, cuddling up to the experience for a few more lovely, entangled hours, except that would be dangerous, and head for the coffee machine instead.

The kitchen is cold. I look around for a thermostat. Nothing. Rhonda would know, but I've conveniently put her out of mind. Hot liquid will have to do, and I fill the machine with water and her French Roast coffee. In Marcus's kitchen, Marla served my first cup of French Roast, and insisted I take some home. The next morning, I brewed the coffee in Scotty's old pot. He tasted it, said it reminded him of something he didn't like.

"Hey Cherry Blossom," are you planning breakfast for two?" He strides in bare-chested wearing skimpy undershorts over long, thin legs, his arms more muscular than they look in clothing. He stands with legs hip length apart, welcoming my gaze, taking me in as well. Suddenly, I'm self-conscious in the t-shirt that barely covers my ass.

"After breakfast, let's take another little nap," he says in his velvety voice.

Turning back to the coffee machine, I busy myself with mugs and stuff.

"It was a great night," he says.

"Coffee in a minute or two. How about you make some eggs?"

"Why the rush?" His warm hands massage my shoulders. "Are you a woman who doesn't like to talk in the mornings?"

"Yeah." It's happening too quickly; I don't want to care this much.

"But morning's almost gone, it's after eleven."

"Is there something in particular you want me to say?"

"Thanks for coming over in that freezing cold, considering I had to take two trains to get here, or I enjoyed your company last night."

"Of course, I enjoyed last night. How about the eggs?"

"Tessa, what the fuck's bugging you?"

"Mike, can we just be best friends?"

"What?"

"I want your friendship."

"What does that mean? No sex?" He sounds insulted.

"I didn't say that."

"I don't have sex with my friends."

"Mike, I didn't mean to . . . I just . . . "

"What did you mean?"

That he's my danger man who will lead me back to the life I'm running from. The coffee drips down so slowly, it will never fill.

"What's this about Tessa?" His hands on my shoulders turn me to face him.

"I can't become seriously involved, or be obligated to anyone at this point in my life. I'm trying to figure out next steps."

"You mean you don't love me," his tone overly sarcastic.

"Mike, I'm sorry if I hurt your feelings."

"Yeah. Got it. Been there."

"Been where?"

"Muslim boyfriend not—"

"Oh shit. No, no, Mike, oh shit nothing like that I swear."

"Then what?"

"I could easily fall in love with you and then there'd be no next steps."

"Why not?"

"It's not explainable."

"Try." He commands.

"We can see each other, and share whatever but . . . "

"You want me to help you not to feel deeply for me? I can't do that. I wouldn't know how. I'll see you around."

Let him walk out, my brain warns. "Mike, wait, don't leave," the desperation apparent in my voice.

"Why not?" He challenges, standing in military posture, ridiculous in undershorts.

The emptiness would swallow me, I don't say. "Stay, we'll talk. We'll . . . I don't know, figure it out . . . "

"Don't mess with me, Tessa." His stern expression is a cold fist in my gut.

"I'm not. I won't." And hug him long, fiercely.

"Promise?" his voice muffled in my hair.

"Yes." I step away.

"Yes, what," he asks playfully, in drill sergeant tone.

"You figure it out." The coffee pot is full.

I look out the window to catch sight of Mike as he leaves the building, but it's too dark. The day went by so quickly, so wonderfully. Mike taught me how to use the camera I stole from Marcus, which he said was a smart move when I explained why. He's a good teacher and would be one if life allowed. He's patient, precise, though he smokes too much weed or is it hash? Neither of us spoke much about our families. He did mention how his father had stared mutely at anti-Muslim graffiti on the side of their building. Certain kinds of anger are too close to grief for words, I didn't say, but eager to use my new knowledge, offered to photograph the graffiti.

We took the subway to Jackson Heights, the area crowded with people, shops and buildings. I photographed not only the racist graffiti, but also the street itself, and several windows featuring old, sad Christmas wreaths. I insisted we couldn't leave the racist shit up there, that we needed spray paint. Our adventure to locate an open hardware store a day after Christmas didn't pan out, but in a 99 Cents Store we bought thick markers and scribbled over the horrid words, which I took a photo of as well.

I like the feel of a camera it's heft, the promise of its lens. Choosing a scene, homing in, and focusing to capture the moment feels important, as if doing so has consequence, matters. When before have I done anything like that? Strange to remember now that when Rhonda interviewed me, she asked if I was serious about photography. I said, yes, sure that I was lying. Is there a hidden self that knows things ahead of our brains? I must listen closely to what else it might be trying to tell me.

Back at the apartment, Mike wrapped my shivering self in a blanket. Body heat, he advised, pulling me into the bedroom. In the lamp-lit room, we made love again, watching each other in a way we hadn't last night. I wouldn't let him stay over again, too nervous that for some reason Rhonda or her son could suddenly appear.

With both of us free the next few days, Mike wants to show me the city I don't yet know, counting off on his fingers places he seemed anxious to share: it will be glorious, he promises. Of course it will. And that's still my problem. I don't want us to become a couple. But the holiday week will end, and individual needs will take precedence, which will reinforce separateness. He'll begin his job-hunting again. I'll be busy with chores or visits to Rhonda. Damn. I forgot to call her. It's almost nine but I dial the house number Greg gave me and pray Phillip won't answer.

"Hello," Greg says.

"Hi, it's Tessa. How's Rhonda?"

"She's doing fine, in bed, dozing."

"Tell her I called, that all is well here, and I'll phone tomorrow."

"Will do. So . . . how goes it being there by your lonesome?"

"Not so bad."

"How did you spend the day?"

"Let's see. A few hours with a friend, then back at Rhonda's, drank hot chocolate and read my novel."

"What are you reading?"

I think quickly through the latest books I've read. I say, "Jane Austen," which seems appropriate, though at the moment I'm reading a mystery.

"Why is every woman I've met so taken with her?"

"Every woman?" I tease.

"A bit of exaggeration."

"Austen advises men of their flaws so politely, nary a curse word passes her mouth."

He laughs.

"Do you like reading her?" I ask.

"She bores me. Anyway, I'm mostly studying medical texts. Are there other authors that you like to read?"

"Is this a test?"

"Sounds like it, sorry."

"Don't forget to tell—"

"Tessa, I'm off all month. Can we have dinner one evening?"

"Sounds good."

"I want to be here the next few days to watch over Granny, but maybe when I drive her back to the city?"

"It's a plan."

"Goodnight," he says softly.

"You, too."

What is it about that boy that leaves me nervous? Having been at his house didn't help. Is it simply the difference between our lives? An old memory surfaces: some do-gooder from a fairy-tale area of the city came to our middle school and chose several of us to ride a bus to a Broadway show. Afterward we were escorted to a Fifth Avenue Department Store to browse, but "not touch." I overheard the do-gooder whisper to the salesman, "We need to watch them."

I gave the gloves I'd pocketed to my mother, said I'd found them. Is theft my mode of resistance?

Rhonda opens her eyes, sees Greg's note on the bed table that Tessa phoned. She's been dosing on and off all day, unusual for her. But the anti-inflammatories and aspirins that Greg seems to feed her hourly, maybe not quite, must be the reason. There's a TV in her room, but she hasn't switched it on. Doesn't mind being alone with her thoughts.

The bed comfortable, her leg on pillows, her mind roams. She toys with the idea of a brief late spring vacation in Italy with Tessa. Then the cool hand of reality reminds her it's best to respond to an idea as it arises, not bank it for later use, which at her age can't be counted on. The future now is all in a day. It's a truth that doesn't frighten her. It may even be a relief. To worry, or think, or wonder only about what is and not about what may or may not be, there's the relief.

Phillip's brief visit this morning comes to mind. He asked how she was, said he was going to the office, and that Greg would be here. She assured him she was fine. He continued to stand there, lost in thought, perhaps? She asked, "What is it, Phillip?" What if she'd been alone and fallen, he wanted to know. Of course she's had these thoughts herself, but again reassured him that Tessa is in the apartment most of the time, that his worrying was unnecessary. He said nothing more, but looked at her as if—what? She couldn't read his expression. Then he left for the office. What is it about her son that can't be mollified? She doesn't know him, not really, not the way she ought to, the way a mother should, the way she'd like to. Sadly, it's too late to change that.

Too late, she turns the words over in her mind. *Too late for what else*, she wonders. Is it time to make a list? She can't think how or even what. Her yearnings have been replaced by daily satisfactions, smaller in scale than those that are now memories. Sometimes

Albert would pat her head ask how far her thoughts had just traveled. She'd laugh because he caught her being elsewhere. Is that what she did to Phillip too, leave him while there, and miss his moment again and again? She must have, and, yes, it saddens her, but can she still retrieve something of what was lost?

Well, now for sure she won't be able to sleep without a drink. Greg said it's best not to drink till she's steadier on her feet. She misses her tea and scotch. Yes, home is where she does as she pleases, and in a few days will be there. Now, using more willpower than leg power, she hoists herself off the bed, reaches for the crutch, which Greg magically procured, and walk-hops to the living room.

"Granny? What . . . "

"Can't sleep, not tired enough. Where's your mom?"

"In her room watching TV, I guess. Dad won't be home till near midnight. Are you in pain?"

"No."

"Do you want a pill to help you sleep?"

"Not at all, just a drink, and if it doesn't disturb, I'll sit here for awhile."

"You're incorrigible."

Still that, she thinks. Thank God.

Nina walks up the driveway. Snow melts in the rutted holes. She's glad to have Christmas day behind her. Louise popped in but didn't stay long, though long enough to offer her a few Saturday hours at the diner. She's not ready to meet and greet people and said as much. She can't stay home forever. Scotty's resentment grows to fill any room in which they're together. She understands, money is needed to help with expenses.

The flag on the mailbox is up. She takes out bills and flyers and a letter from Peter. Near the road where the trash awaits pickup, she drops the envelope in the bin and pockets the rest of the mail. The pale winter sun begins its retreat, darkening the beach and water.

A sudden chill goes through her. She huddles inside her coat, and then reaches in the bin to retrieve the envelope. It opens easily, the page unfolds in her hand. The driveway is silent. A few seagulls float in the air looking to perch.

From the first words, his voice comes alive in her head. She reads what he offers, returns the letter to the envelope, and drops it in the trash then walks back to the house.

In bed later, tired, she can't sleep. She shouldn't have read his letter. Again, last night she had the dream and woke up crying: she's running toward Marla, arms outstretched, and then wakes before reaching her. Not seeing Peter is the necessary punishment for her crime. Didn't she learn from her father that anything stolen must be paid for, even happiness?

She gets out of bed and opens the window a few inches, cold air rushes in, and she shuts it again. Scotty views open windows in winter akin to sin. One of those pills might help her sleep, but she has none, gave what was left to Hack. It's the letter; she shouldn't have read it. Slipping into her robe, she pads across the cold floors to the living room, where TV's flickering light brightens Hack, slumped on the couch. Asleep or awake, she can't decide. On the screen, an elephant crushes a floor of jungle foliage, as dense clusters of leaves perspire under a low canopy, the dampness palpable.

"Not the desert," Hack says, startling her.

"You're awake?" She sits in Scotty's well-worn chair. "I couldn't sleep."

"Hot milk," he says, offering her a lopsided smile.

"I need something stronger."

"Bad shit makes you feel good," but offers no further aid.

Clearly, he no longer has any of her pills left.

"What's keeping you awake?" he asks, surprising her.

"I read a letter I shouldn't have."

"Peter."

The name in his mouth shocks her.

He sways a little as he sits up straighter.

"I shouldn't have read it."

"Maybe."

"What?"

"How I see it, when I can see it . . . ignoring the call wounds you forever. The dead man is the enemy, okay to leave, but what if there's a breath. See?"

"I'm trying."

"Yeah."

"That it would've been worse if I hadn't read the letter?"

"If you say so," his eyes open and close against sleep.

"Was it Scotty who told you about Peter?" Does it matter?

"I heard you tell all."

"Are you angry that I hurt your brother?"

"Wish you hadn't, but the man is durable as leather, otherwise I'd be dead."

"Could you be a bit more explicit?"

"He took care of me after the apocalypse, couldn't do it for himself."

A bitter sadness fills her.

"Let's have another beer." He stretches out on the couch.

Obediently, she goes to the kitchen and takes three cold ones out of the fridge. He seems asleep when she returns, and she leaves one on the table. Death and dying are familiar to Hack, the ones he killed, those trying to kill him, and he's found his escape, not one open to her. She leaves the TV on; if he wakes in the night, there'll be some light.

26

I stretch awake, content after the last few days with Mike. Rhonda's eager to return home. We talked on the phone a few times and twice yesterday. She said her ankle is healing. But last night she sounded weary, probably she's had it with being there. Reluctantly, I get out of bed; it's cold, of course it is. I keep forgetting to ask Rhonda where the thermostat is hidden. It's not yet seven, but I plan my day: shower, breakfast, and then search online for—my phone rings. Who calls this early? "Hello," I accuse.

"Sorry to phone at this hour. Granny had a mild stroke. We're in New Haven Hospital now."

"Oh Jesus! What happened? How is she?"

"Can't really chat now. Looks like her left side has been affected, but she wasn't confused. We're waiting now for test results."

"I'll be on the next train." Rhonda must be frightened; I am.

"Tessa, it'd be better if you didn't come just now. My father's very upset, my mother as well. We need to wait here to see what's what."

"Of course. Will you call me when you know more?"

"Yes. I'd better go."

I stare out the bedroom window. Tell myself not to go to the dark side. Mild stroke, Greg said. Will she come home? Will she have to go to rehab? Will she recover? Will she need a trained nurse? Will she need me anymore? Where would I go? Not home. The pain of defeat would sink me. Tessa, stop, Rhonda's feisty, strong of mind and body, she could recover enough to need only what I'll be able to provide. I remind myself, Greg did say mild. Oh Rhonda, you didn't want this, I know. I'm upset for both of us.

But something more doesn't sit right. It's being told not to come to the hospital. Caretakers not allowed until family has digested, discussed, and decided what to share with outsiders. Rhonda would want me there, I'm sure. Why didn't I say that to Greg instead of agreeing immediately? What if Rhonda dies? I didn't get to Marla in time. Anyway, who says I have to be obedient?

⊗

Relieved to see them leave the room if only for a while. They didn't fuss, they hovered, mainly Phillip. Martha stood at the foot of the bed her expression a cross between despair and confusion. Greg sat in a chair staring at her. What the promising doctor thinks, she didn't ask, both for an unexpected lack of curiosity, and because it's too soon to know anything but their worries.

The bed jacked up to a good angle, her head supported by several soft pillows, she's comfortable. The nurse switched off the unnecessary overhead florescent, allowing silky, pearl-white afternoon light to leak through the blind slats.

Colors soothe her. On the adjacent blank wall, she imagines painting a huge complicated maze of many colors with an exit if one can find it. Usually illness, even death, whether one's own or another's arrive at the most inconvenient times. It was so when cancer's sneaky hand took Albert from her. But he's gone now and except for the triptych, much of the work she began is completed, the canvases distributed among several galleries and museums.

Last night's tremors to her body—will there be more? It seems no one can say, or they're trying to spare her. She doesn't mind being spared. Besides she's never been good at guessing. An image of a jar of jellybeans comes to mind, but where was it? Yes. She filled the jar for Magda and Phillip to guess the number of jellybeans. The closest guess would win a prize. What was the prize? No idea.

Her eyes track the line of plastic tubing as it travels from the vein in her hand up to two IV bags that hang off a tree, like inverted birds. She wiggles her right foot but can't do so with her left. So, it's true, a piece of her is immovable. What does she think of that? She won't, not yet. However, she isn't inclined to put in the herculean energy it would take to overcome incapacity if that is even possible. What's the point? She'd only improve a little, and still not be able to get around. So, what then is left to her? Except for the comfort of evening tea laced with scotch, life would occur outside her windows.

Entering the hospital lobby the memory of Marla alone in that small, cold room accompanies me. I ask and I'm told to go to floor four, room 432, and take the elevator up. The buzz of low voices, clicking machines, and medicinal odors follows me through the long fluorescently lit hallway. Rhonda's room is large, with a wide window, alcove, and several padded chairs; it resembles a studio. On the sill, there is a tall, green vase filled with yellow, red, and pink roses, their meaty petals open.

Rhonda's alone, thank heaven, her eyes closed. I move a chair to the bedside, whisper, "Rhonda, its Tessa."

Her eyes open.

"Your family wanted me to wait, but I had to come see you," I whisper. "Everything in the apartment is fine. Don't worry about anything. Is there . . . "

The door opens. "Tessa!" Greg exclaims. "When did you get . . . "

"Just now. I had to see Rhonda. I'm sorry if it upsets you or your—"

"It's okay." He pulls up a chair beside mine and takes Rhonda's hand. "Granny, I know you will understand everything I'm about to say. I've studied the MRI and CAT scans with the radiologist. You had a blood clot that went to the brain in a region that affects movement, basically your left side, and—"

"Greg, where did you disappear—" Phillip sees me, shakes his head, and leans over his mother as I scoot away. "Mother it's me," Phillip says loudly.

"Dad, she can hear well don't shout, it's annoying."

"Rhonda, I'll see you again soon. If there's anything you need, someone will let me know." Caught where I shouldn't be, I can't leave fast enough, but won't scuttle away like a bug hit by a sudden light. "Greg, can you step into the hall with me?"

"What's up?" he asks, following me out, looking tired.

"I would like to pick up Rhonda's mail, but don't have a key. I'm not sure now is the time to rummage in her purse." In truth, I have an extra key, but that's not the point.

"I'll rummage and tell her what I'm doing. I'll meet you in the lobby."

I don't wait for an elevator.

Spotless with many plants on display the area could pass for a hotel lobby. Several people sit in the plush chairs. Avoiding faces, I sink into one and stare out the plate glass window.

A mistake, I think, *coming here, though Rhonda didn't mind, and wasn't she my reason?* So pale and not given a chance to utter a word before the family descended, and what could she say then? With one side paralyzed she'll need a wheelchair. I could handle that, but could I lift her to the bathroom or into bed? She told her family I was experienced; but Rhonda was only repeating what I'd said during our initial interview. Whatever Phillip thought about me before, he thinks even less now. His dismissive headshake felt horrid. Yet, I may have to deal with him after Greg leaves.

Greg slips into the next chair and hands me the key, then searches the room as if some secret lurks there.

"Did something more happen?" my alarm apparent.

"Everything you heard me tell Granny is accurate, but she's old, recovery will be slow and bumpy. Granny will refuse to go to a rehab facility afraid she'd be stuck there."

"Which, she'd hate, I agree, but can she stay in the hospital for weeks?"

He shakes his head. "Not a chance. My mother doesn't want to nurse Granny at the house. My father insists on supervised care. In a few weeks I'll receive my hospital match and who knows where that'll be. At any rate, I'll be gone and what I think won't have much effect."

Jesus! He's been reading my thoughts.

"I hate the idea of my parents forcing her into a skilled nursing home, even if it's for her own good. But I don't see how she can return to the apartment anytime soon. It would be too dangerous. Sorry to dump this on you . . . "

But he has; and I should respond but not sure how.

"What about a stay in a rehab facility not attached to a nursing home? There must be some."

"There are but they'd only be for two or three weeks, not enough time for Granny to improve."

"But, maybe, as a start to her recovery?"

"My father is too focused on supervised care to hear me. He adored my grandfather, who had a heart attack in the room where he sometimes slept after seeing patients. My father claims that if grandfather hadn't been alone, if anyone had been there to check on him, he would've gotten medical treatment and not died. But he was alone and found dead the next morning. He fears the same for Granny."

My dislike of Phillip goes down an eighth of a notch, though my anxiety rises.

"So much will depend on how hard Granny works to get better."

"Why wouldn't she?"

"Because she's smart enough to know that some level of paralysis will remain no matter how hard she works. And the possibility of another stroke is real. And I think she understands that, too."

"What can I do to help her?"

He shakes his head, "Too soon to know. Let me drive you to the train."

He's quiet in the car.

"Hard to be at the mercy of others," I muse aloud, thinking how Rhonda never seemed old to me.

"It is."

"You love your Granny."

He nods. "I lived with her during many summers at their lake house in New Hampshire. Except for the days Granny had business in Manhattan she'd ask me each morning what I wanted to do and make it happen: canoeing, bike riding, treasure hunting. She was younger then and determined to treat me differently than my parents. Not that they mistreated me, but they made sure I'd follow the path they set out for me. Granny wanted me to be freer. So . . . I don't know . . . " He winds down.

"You didn't want to be a doctor?"

"I think I did, I do, but when I entered my teens, Granny told me that I needed to do something rebellious, perhaps dangerous. I never figured out how to do that."

As the station comes into view, the early evening air is gray and misty. A busted streetlamp completes the desolate scene.

As the train pulls out my phone beeps a text from Mike: "Call me!" I do.

"I've been trying to reach you. Meet me for a drink."

"What? Why?"

"I had your film developed. The photos are great. Don't you want to see them?"

"That was so sweet of you."

"It was. Also, I got a job."

"Tell me."

"I will."

He sounds jolly. I need jolly.

The bar is crowded as usual. Mike waits at a table. Before I can settle into a chair he slides a manila envelope toward me his eyes bright, too bright.

"Open it," he orders.

In the envelope are a bunch of enlarged photographs. I take one out. It's the shot of the racist graffiti. How real it looks! But it is real, and others can see that reality. A shiver of something unrecognizable moves through me. Mike's face looks happy, pleased with his surprise, or high on something? Probably just celebrating getting a job, I think, I hope."

"Going to get us drinks," he says, as I slide the photo back in the envelope. Later, I'll study each one of them.

Mike places two beers on the table and lifts his bottle. "To your upcoming career."

"Really. You think so? I mean . . . "

"I do think so. You have an eye. Take a course or something," he's slurring, but only a bit.

"I will," I say, surprising myself. "Tell me about the new job."

"Yeah, well . . . not much to brag about."

"Just share."

"Security guard at a warehouse, midnight to 7 a.m. Uniform included, no gun of course, and eighteen dollars an hour."

I hear his disappointment. "It's just till you figure out something more to your liking."

"I'll be bored, but eighteen an hour is hard to ignore."

"On my insomniac nights I'll offer myself as company."

"Well that sugars the deal."

"Mike, the job is only temporary."

"Right. After Bush leaves office and the wars end Muslims will no longer be in everyone's bad dream. And I'll be free to be me. So where were you, what's happening?"

"It's the woman I work for, Rhonda," and fill him in on both the particulars and my undecided future."

"That's shitty news. Will you get paid while she's away?"

"I don't know." And just like that I have an idea.

Back at the apartment I spread the photos across the kitchen table, like a deck of cards, then walk around and study each one from different angles. Shots of the racist graffiti include a piece of looming wall that looks menacing. How did I do that? I don't know; that's the problem. Spontaneity is fine, but making a shot come out the way I see and feel will need schooling. Take a course, Mike said. I

160

don't have that kind of money. Too chicken to rob a bank, I leave the photos on the table and head to bed.

<hr />

Alone in the darkening kitchen—Scotty working the bar, Hack watching TV, dinner cooked, eaten, dishes washed, dried, put away—she heads to bed. This is her work now, the way she earns her keep, the way she appeases Scotty if she even does. Going out, finding a job, dealing with people, no, she can't, not yet, maybe not ever, but surely not yet. Of course she's depressed, no secret to her. That's the thing about depression, nothing matters not really, not in ways they did before. Sometimes she tries to conjure up scenes that did matter but even they are not available to her, not in felt ways, only as pictures on a wall of the past.

Switching off the bedroom lamp, Tessa's earlier call comes to mind. Of course, it's sad that the woman is in the hospital, but the depth of her daughter's upset isn't warranted. The woman isn't her mother, not even family. Tessa needs to learn how to apportion her reactions or she'll be left with too much sorrow to bear. Though Tessa would visit if invited, she doesn't want her daughter to see her depressed, and isn't capable of pretending otherwise. Was she ever capable? Yes, while seeing Peter her life in this house was all pretenses.

Except for the TV's distant voices, which somehow soothe Hack to sleep, the house is quiet. In a while Scotty's loud, raspy coughing will come through the thin wall of the girl's room. He gave up cigarettes two years ago, but the coughing has gotten worse. As soon as he lies down it begins to interrupt his sleep and hers and Hack's as well. This morning, surprising herself and him, she offered to go with him to the VA hospital to have it checked out. At first he didn't respond, then chuckled derisively as if to say the suggestion was mainly to benefit her; his response another reminder of the emptiness burying her, but too slowly.

The blaring radio in Rico's pick-up truck comes through the closed windows. The front door bangs open then shut. Scotty lumbers into the bedroom, switches on the lamp. He's drunk, unusual, the smell of whiskey intense.

"What do you want?" she whispers.

"It's my bedroom, isn't it?"

"Of course. But you've been sleeping in the girl's room."

"Which you like," he says with amusement. "Tonight, I'll bed down here."

Warily she watches him begin to undress, unsure if he means to stay or is being drunk-ornery. She turns away. It's been a while since they slept together. Before Peter he would sometimes be affectionate in bed. Now, she doesn't want his affection. Once he's asleep she'll slip out to the girl's room.

He switches off the lamp, climbs in beside her, and begins to cough, another sleepless night.

27

While morning light streams in and the coffee perks, I take a few more turns around the table to study the photos. They are interesting. Somehow, I'd managed to capture what I'd want others to see. But it's simply the luck of firsts.

Taking a mug of coffee to the living room, I sit on the couch, stare into space and wonder anew if I've given enough thought to what I'm about to do. Again I remind myself desperation incites courage, and pick up the phone, press the numbers of the landline. It rings a few times. Am I calling too early?

"Yes?" It's Phillip's stentorian voice.

"Hello Mr. Steward, It's Tessa," my voice childish to my ears. "With your permission, I'd like to visit Rhonda every day she's in the hospital to make sure she gets whatever she needs, perhaps read to her if she'd like," all said too quickly. An eternity of silent seconds passes before he speaks.

"Not the worst idea," he muses aloud. "I do have to go into my office. What hours were you . . ."

"Twelve to five, or whatever you—"

"Very good," he interrupts. "Start today then?"

"Of course. I'd be glad to fill you in at the end of each . . ."

"We'll see. I'll be visiting her as well, evenings, so, yes good. Today. Thanks." He clicks off.

As exhausted as if I'd run a half-marathon, I remain sitting. Well that's that, I think. My stipend will continue, though who knows for how long. Still, it gives me some leeway to figure out what ifs. Besides, spending time with Rhonda is no chore.

Exiting the train at New Haven, I walk toward the hospital. My tote bag is heavy with two books, mail that looks personal, a pad to jot down chores Rhonda might want done. *What if she doesn't want visitors or can't talk, or . . . Tessa, stop.*

Palatial houses are hidden behind trees and hedges. Secrecy among the wealthy seems more like fear of the envious than modesty. I wouldn't want to live on these too quiet narrow streets with no one outdoors. It's not a decision I'll have to make.

Another late winter day without sun, crummy, my mother would say. On the phone I told her about Rhonda, careful not to mention the shakiness of my job. Her voice so low, almost stilted, it was difficult not only to hear her but also to know how to respond. It isn't fair that I have to worry about her when I have so much else to deal with.

The hospital is a white brick building that covers several acres, and nothing like the small hotel-like structure where Marla died. Would a hospital like this have made a difference? No, no, don't do this, and walk across the bustling lobby to the elevator.

The afternoon light is rationed through half-closed blinds. A silence that signals gravity is interrupted only by the repetitive click of a blood pressure machine near her bed, which is propped to almost a sitting position. On the sill the flowers have begun to droop.

Rhonda's eyes are closed, her skin waxy and pale, but it's her hair which surprises. I've only seen it pulled into a bun, now unbound it reaches past her shoulders, some strands pewter dark against the white pillow. Though covered with a blanket, I sense her frailty. I sit in the chair near the bed and take her hand the way Greg did. Her eyes open.

"Rhonda, hi. It's me."

"I know, dear," her voice hoarse, as if some instrument had invaded her throat.

"You can talk," I say, relieved.

"I haven't met anyone I care to engage with, until you."

"I called your son, asked if it was okay to spend time here with you. He said it was fine. I don't think he likes me."

"Not sure what it would mean if he did."

"I won't tire you. If you need something I'll get it, or find someone to help. I brought you mail that looked personal, also books to read aloud if you want, all of which can stay in the tote. I'm capable of sitting silently."

Rhonda squeezes my hand. "You must have a thousand questions."

"I do, but they don't need answering just now."

The door opens and a young woman steps in. "Hi, Ms. Stewart. I'm Janet, your occupational therapist."

"Thank you, but no, not now."

"Okay, I'll return at another time." She closes the door behind her.

"I'm not interested in relearning anything," she says more to herself. "Tell me a little of what you've been doing, and don't worry if my eyes close. I'm filled with a thousand tiny pills that refuse energy."

"The strangest thing happened on Christmas Day. My friend Mike . . . " I tell her about learning to use a camera, taking photos, and though I believe they're good I've no idea how I'd managed to do what I'd done.

"Was it fun?"

"Fantastic."

"Describe one." She moves her hand from under mine and places it beneath the blanket. Is she cold? Should I tell someone? I'm new at this, but she's waiting for an answer.

"I took a shot of a Christmas wreath on a grimy building window, but when developed it showed a toddler almost in shadow looking out at me."

"Do you know about the International Institute of Photography?" She coughs and I worry she shouldn't talk at all.

"No."

"Photography students need models. In exchange you can sometimes audit a class."

"Really?" But the word model brings the unwelcome memory of Marcus asking Marla to model. "I'll check it out." I will.

"Tell me how your mother is doing," her whispery voice invites me to do the talking as her eyes close.

"She's still quite depressed. Before my sister died, we had a bad fight. I was so angry at her . . . " surprised to be saying this I don't know how to go on.

"What happened . . . if you want to say?"

"She was having an affair that none of us knew about, sneaking around and pretending she was working late. Only in the car to drop me off at the airport did she admit the relationship, which she said was ended." Suddenly, I'm ashamed to be sharing a story, which isn't mine to tell.

"I'm sorry her news upset you, but not sorry your mother had an affair."

"What?"

"In my fifties I met a man. We fell in love and saw each other for many years until, to my deep sorrow, he died."

"Your son, your husband, did they . . . ?"

"Phillip never knew. I'm positive. My husband may have suspected but didn't care enough to pursue it. Anyway, the point is that one shouldn't have to live out a life with the wrong person. I'm grateful that I didn't."

Her admission disturbs me, though it doesn't alter my high regard for her. But then, she's not my mother. Still . . .

"Tessa, dear, I'm falling asleep. You needn't stay to watch me. Leave the bag on the chair. Come tomorrow."

I touch my fingers to my lips then to her forehead. "Tomorrow."

The room has grown darker, but switching on a light feels intrusive.

The door in the room closes gently. Sweet Tessa, she thinks, young and unknowing of all to still be revealed, reversed, or left untended.

There seems no way to transfer one's experiences to another. The delicious food is only known when tasted. She's not sorry she shared Alfred with Tessa. Since her stroke, he's been lodged in her mind. What did he think about during his last weeks? Was it death and dying or life and living, she wonders? He did think about it, of course, Alfred would. Did his fertile mind search for meaning not only cause? An artist, yes, but he was a bit of a philosopher as well. Now, all of his knowledge, ambitions, talents, conclusions, and fears are gone with him. Perhaps it's death's last laugh at our constant striving.

Her wandering mind . . . a bit morbid. Maybe not, maybe there's a reason that's not yet clear to her. She believes death sends a message of its near arrival, not in words or even illness itself, something more delicate, lacy, a miasma, not a warning; a shadow that moves out of reach if she tries to touch it.

She'll continue to shoo off the therapists, continue to say not now. For *now* is the time left to her. It's comfort she craves, no disturbance in body or mind, please.

Anxious to catch the next train and get to my computer I see Greg walking toward the hospital. Does he see me? He isn't waving. Maybe it isn't proper to wave from afar, what do I know. To avoid him straight on, I'd have to turn and walk the other way. That would be stupid. I wave.

"Tessa, hi, leaving?"

"Rhonda wanted to sleep. Did your father—"

"He said you would be visiting Granny while in hospital. Since she's asleep, how about getting some coffee?"

"Thing is, I need to get back to the city and if I miss the next train, the one after will be more than an hour and a local to boot."

"Understood. Let me walk you to the station."

"Rhonda never appeared fragile to me before now," I say.

"It's going to be difficult for her to climb back to her before self."

"Is there something more medicine can do?" The station isn't far, but the cold wind bites.

"Watch her vital signs, medicate her if one or two of those begin to fail, keep her comfortable. Physical therapy if she can manage it. Not too much else."

"I guess your Granny's illness has upended your free time plans?"

"Not really. I'm just studying, a doctor's lot. I like talking to you, you know," he says, as if surprised by his words."

"Of course you do."

He laughs.

"Why?"

"You're interesting."

"That's so banal."

"Sharp as a steak knife."

"A bit closer to my essence."

He laughs again.

We both know the train is due in the station momentarily.

"Our dinner date, still on, right?" he calls as I rush off.

Before taking off my jacket, I find my laptop, enter Google, search "Institute of Photography" then close my eyes. Please universe, I pray, let it still exist. It exists! I click on the link. There's a website with a phone number, too late now to phone, tomorrow, first thing.

Excited and needing to share, I call Mike. He'll love the modeling for course idea. He doesn't answer. Then remember he works the night shift, and I leave a message to call when he can.

Maybe I'll bring a few photos to the hospital to show Rhonda. If she seems too tired, I won't push it, of course I won't, but she'll love that I followed up on her suggestion. Too hyper to read, my thoughts leap from possibility to possibility, all too close to fantasy to count on. Back home windy nights like this would rattle every window; here the place is silent.

Peter considers his face in the mirror, the perpetual frown of his mouth. Shave off the short beard? Why not his hair as well? Restlessness spurs him to do something, anything, but really not this.

Already dark out, he takes a can of beer from the fridge, some ham and cheese and bread, slaps on some mustard, adds a few chips and takes it all to the living room where he sets it on the table. He's so not hungry. This morning, he called the Taxi garage, said he decided not to take the job, though he'd been the one who sought it. The thought of driving people around depresses him. Who wants to hear their hard luck stories? But how much longer can he dip into the savings before having to find some work?

He takes a long slug of beer. Stares out the window at an identical building across the street, some windows shuttered, others not. People there probably wondering about their lives same as him.

The nothingness of everything drives him crazy. One possible solution, maybe, the one he's been skirting for months: return to California, to his cabin, do some carpentry again. It'll keep him busy and who knows may offer a cure of sorts, except he'll be there without her. Is he really making a decision or playing with the idea?

He grabs a sheet of paper and a pen:

Nina, you need to know that living here without you is driving me out of my head. I'm not enjoying a thing. I would bet an arm you aren't either. How stupid it is to be apart. There's just no real reason anymore. At least I can't find one.

You're only staying there out of guilt and grief. The grief will follow you as I've said before, but I will be with you, and it will become more bearable. I know I'm right. The guilt, well, what can I say? How do I erase another's guilt, your guilt? Don't know. Why spend the rest of your years without my love, without expressing your own? Think about it; please think about it.

I don't know how to make sure that you read this. I might be bold and drop the letter at your door. I no longer care about causing havoc at your house. Your husband needs to understand that you're there on only borrowed time, borrowed from me, and I'm calling in my loan.

I can't stand being here alone anymore. Sooner than later, I'm going to return to California, to my cabin, to that place I told you about where all possibilities exist without consequence. Come with me, Nina. Let's make a life.

I love you, Peter.

He folds the letter into an envelope, decides it sounds too desperate, but he is desperate. Anyway, it's too soon after the last one to send it; he'll wait a bit before mailing.

He takes a bite of the sandwich, which tastes like straw. Christ, he's falling apart. It's not PTSD; it's a broken heart, folks.

28

When daylight comes through the window I get out of bed and traipse to the kitchen. Two eggs remain in the otherwise empty fridge. I'll stop in the market on the way back from seeing Rhonda. Still too early to call the institute, I notice a message on my phone, probably Mike, calling when he was done with work.

"Calling this . . . I know . . . " static, blurry male voice; I turn up the volume, listen again. The static is louder, I can't make out words, stupid cell phones. I check the number, area code 203, Connecticut? Greg? I press call back; it rings and rings, then goes to voicemail. It's Greg.

"Hi, it's Tessa. I received a garbled phone message, was it you?" Why would he call that early? I need coffee. There's enough in the bag for two cups, thank goodness. The phone rings.

"Hello."

"Tessa, Greg, I need . . . " His voice garbled as if in a tunnel or elevator, words drop away, leave blank spaces."

"Is everything okay?" but of course it's not.

"Granny passed, she . . . " his words blur.

"Passed?" That's not part of my lingo. Is it a code word, is he trying to tell me something he can't say out loud.

"Last night, she . . . "

"Where are you? I can barely make out what you're saying." But already I'm frantic.

"Talk . . . later."

I'm holding the bag of coffee as well as the dead phone and set them both on the table, sit in one of the chairs. Passed? What a stupid term. Marla died, not passed. Passed to where, how, why? Passed to nevermore, if Greg had put it that way, it would be clear, I admonish him in my head.

The phone rings. "Hello."

"It's Greg, I'm outside the hospital. Can you hear me better?"

"Yes, thank you so much for calling back." But it doesn't sound like him. "What happened, oh my God, what happened?" and try to muffle the near hysteria in my voice.

"Granny had another more serious stroke around eleven last night. They worked on her, tried to revive her, but she passed. None of us were there. She was alone. That's terrible," his voice up an octave, trying for control.

I want to tell him not to bother, but remain silent as he tries to pull himself together.

"I know you cared about Granny," and the words open a basket of sorrow in me.

"Yes," I whisper. "Very much, very much. I can't believe she died. Is there anything I can do?" though I know there's nothing his family would want from me.

"Not sure, Tessa. I have to get back to my parents. We'll talk soon."

Holding the edge of the table my limbs leaden, my chest tight, swallowing not possible, I must breathe, in and out, like Sister Agnes taught. It's not happening. I stand up. Standing might make it easier, but easier to what? I have no idea. Yesterday, just yesterday, she told me about her lover, about the Institute, about tomorrow when she expected me to visit again. Hours ago, only hours ago, she was alive and now she's not? How can that be?

I realize I'm keening, my arms tight around my waist as if the pain were in my stomach, and try to stop, but I can't stay still, the truth too heavy to bear. Marla gone, Rhonda gone. How to fill the empty spaces? It can't be done; I know; I remember: these losses are moth holes bitten out of life.

Maybe call my mother? No, I can't offer her news of another death. Who can I call? Is my life so unpeopled? Mike, he will listen . . . Instead, I walk through the apartment. Nothing has changed, except nothing seems the same. Rhonda's bedroom too bright, I pull the blinds shut, the room darkens as it does for sleep. I touch nothing, tiptoe out. Remember how in my fury I left Marcus's motel room a shambles. Now my sadness wants only to protect all that Rhonda loved.

At her studio, I stop. I've never been inside. I open the door, the presence of her absence as real as the smell of paint. Four windows drape the room in light and shadow. There's a worn, cushioned armchair, a small table covered with jars, brushes, and a smeared palette of color. This is where her spirit will come to linger; I'm sure of that, but not yet, it's too soon.

Propped against two of the walls are canvases in vivid colors. A few are abstract designs, others depict whole scenes, and one appears to be a self-portrait: A woman her hair in a bun sits in front of a rain-streaked window, in the distance a sunrise.

A piece of the triptych she was working on remains on an easel. A huge pale-blue wing of a headless bird covers the surface; embedded in the wing are miniature scenes: green cars on a city street, gray pebbles on sand, a log cabin amidst dense trees, two stick figures holding hands, ascending steps. Are the figures she and her lover? Are the scenes clues to her lived life?

Marla's short life left no clues. But I know where she was headed, and I know what she intended to achieve: a portfolio of photographs. Now I have the camera.

29

"Uh-huh, I say," only half listening to Hack's gibberish on the phone.

". . . . at the VA, why do it over?"

"Do what over?"

"Talk, talk, talk about fucking desert of fuckups. See?"

"They want you to attend group therapy?"

"Big difference between a fuckup and fuck-off."

"Where's my mother?"

"Nature's call."

"Hack, therapy might help."

"What?"

"I said, therapy might help . . . "

"Help what?"

"Never mind."

"Here, it's Tessa."

"Hi honey."

"Mom, how are you?"

"Okay."

"What are you doing?"

"Right now?"

"In general." Why am I calling?

"Nothing, really. Do you have more news?"

"Well, you already know about Rhonda and that I'm apartment sitting and . . . "

"You'll need another job?"

"No kidding."

"Sweet pea, do you mind if we talk later?"

"Yeah, sure. Bye."

Well, that took up no time and did nothing to lift my spirits. Clearly, she, too, could use some therapy. Haven't I learned yet that home isn't helpful?

It's debilitating, babysitting Rhonda's apartment with nothing to do while the men work to empty the walls around me. For the past week they've arrived from different art galleries to sort, pack and remove her paintings. They work quietly, too quietly. It's as if silence is building on silence to thicken the air.

Phillip asked me to remain in the apartment while they're here, and continues to pay my stipend, thank the Buddha. He hasn't yet given me a date to vacate. Though he tells me little, sooner than later the apartment will be sold.

So strange, even eerie living here without Rhonda being somewhere; I miss her. Not even a funeral to attend. Greg said her ashes will be buried in a family plot, and a private memorial will be held at a later date. So, no rite of passage I didn't say, not wanting to sound critical while he's in mourning. He's barely mentioned how he's dealing with her death.

When my grandmother died, everyone came to the house after the funeral, drinks all around, some tears shed. My mother was doing her best to hold it together. After the guests left, she told us stories from her childhood, talked about her mother's life. Though sad, she was nothing like the way she's been since Marla died. I guess I should stay in better touch. It's clear she isn't doing well.

Peering down at the cold, empty streets of Park Avenue, February looms with menace. My search for work and a cheap place to live can't be put off. Clearly, my photography future has no future. Auditing a course, modeling, and at the same time holding down a job or two won't be doable. The jobs will be dead-end, no different from the ones people work back home. They have to take what they can get, and now, so do I.

Maybe Mike could cheer me, though when we last met he was sullen and far from his usual self. I told him about Rhonda's death, and that I had to quickly figure out next steps. Expecting his hand to squeeze mine with encouragement, or maybe toss me a few supportive words, he barely acknowledged what I'd said. He seemed out of it. I didn't probe, my mood too despairing to check in on his. I phone him.

"What's up?" His voice is sleepy, slurry, otherworldly. Hack's voice!

"Are you okay?"

"What?"

"Did I wake you?"

"What?"

"Are you on something?"

"What?"

"Stop with what-s, you heard me."

"Tessa, don't, okay?"

"Just answer."

"A pull of hash. Weaker than the shit over there, which lasts a lifetime, depending on the length of that."

"Mike. I hate it. All of it, you know that."

"Sorry to upset you. I need a lift to get through nights so long and boring I'm ready to retire from living. Anyway, I haven't slept enough yet and . . . "

"Good, do it—sleep I mean."

"If you say so my Tessa."

"Bye, Mike," and click off. I was awful to him, but . . .

"Excuse me miss, we're done, I need a signature." The worker holds out an invoice in his thickly gloved hand. I lean it against the blank wall and sign with the pen he hands me.

"Everything went okay?"

"No problem, miss."

They ferry out one large crate after another, careful not to scrape the walls. Then they're gone. But I'm still here, alone. Tomorrow more workers will come. Again, I'll sit here and wonder when and how to start the rest of my life.

Leaving the apartment this morning, Peter slid the letter to Nina in his jacket pocket, the one he'd set aside to mail at a later date, He'd decided to drop it off at her house. Instead, he'd walked down to Greenwich Village, visited two bars, one restaurant and a crappy movie. The letter still in his pocket, he drops it in the first mailbox he passes, then finds a bench in nearby Washington Square Park, and sits.

Students from the neighboring college pass by, noisy, undaunted by the cold, interested only in each other, offering him not even a glance. A shabbily dressed man sits down on the bench beside him, though empty benches abound. Ragged jeans apparent beneath a thin fraying jacket, and bare feet in scuffed moccasins. No doubt Peter will be hit for a handout. That's okay, he doesn't mind, but, please, no sob story about being homeless with terminal cancer, all of which is so possible in this rich city of great divisions. But getting up and walking away feels too mean. Who knows when that could be him, except he'd shoot himself first.

"Got the time, mister?" The man looks at him with the bluest of eyes embedded in a thin, bony, weatherworn face that could be any age.

"Four ten."

"You sound down, man."

Peter shrugs.

"A woman, right?"

"Peter shrugs again.

"You look well kept, what else can it be?"

Peter chuckles. "You read fortunes too?"

"No way. No such thing. Today is it. World could blow up tomorrow. I wouldn't care."

"That bad?"

"Could always be worse is what the guys over there used to say."

"Are you a vet?" Peter asks.

"You see a uniform? Yeah, I guess that's what some call me. But I call myself carefree."

"You're kidding?"

"Buy me a drink. I'll explain."

Finally, what he expected. "Listen, I already had a few, but you fill yourself up," Peter takes a ten out of his wallet, hands it to the guy, who takes it with an almost shy smile.

"You bought, I'll talk," he says.

"About?"

"How to be carefree though still alive. First, give up all expectations. Second, don't look in the mirror. Third, drink booze every day. Fourth, don't read the papers or watch the news. And fifth, bury the memories. Thanks for the bill."

He walks away slowly, doesn't turn to wave, a slim figure disappearing in the early winter dusk. What was that if not a message to get his shit together and quickly, find a friend, his sixth-grade teacher used to say. He'll phone Richie, make a date to get together, tell Richie he's returning to California, no better way to cement a decision.

30

Getting off the bus I open the umbrella, glad the bar isn't far. It's the kind of rain that promises not to end. The sky low with clouds so dark the stars may never shine through. Mike has to be at work in a short while, but upset with myself after our phone call yesterday, I want to make amends. That stoner voice kills me. At least no one is feeding Mike pills. Of course, his boring job gets him down, but it's good he has one.

While housesitting I've searched for work online. Everywhere I called the jobs were already filled. One guy reminded me it's not a good time to look for work, recommended checking out store windows for a want ad.

The bar isn't crowded. Mike's not here yet so I grab us a table. Maybe I should consider walking along Broadway to look for want ads. I will if I have to. Mike comes in soaked. "Haven't you heard of umbrellas?"

"Hello to you, too. I'm going to dry off then get some beers."

Well, that wasn't the best opening. Beer will help. Help what? Mike? Myself? My mother? Oh God, the dreary day is seeping into my soul.

"Here you go," he places two bottles on the table.

"Thanks. I apologize for my bitchy tone on the phone yesterday."

"Apology accepted."

"Is that all you're going to say."

"Yep."

"It's just that . . . "

"I know, your sister. Tragedy. That's not me, okay?"

His large eyes seem wild, an animal looking to flee. "Did you catch some sleep?"

"Some. On the train here I stared back at the people watching me. Is it my face or what?"

"Mike how awful."

"I should reenlist. Everything taken care of plus a handful of buddies, plus whatever happens will happen. Hey, easier than trying to make it out here, whatever 'out here' means," and offers me a weird smile. "Say, right? Right? Anyway, if I don't reenlist, I'll have to find a room somewhere. Home is too crowded, noisy, too in my face. Tessa, hey, you listening?"

"You're pretty jazzed up."

"I am, how else to get through the night?"

"I'm going to have to find a place to live too. Rhonda's apartment will be sold quickly, I'm sure."

"Perfect! We'll move in together, cheaper, cozier, definitely wise. Yes?" He raises his bottle to toast.

"Something to think about," I chirp, knowing he's a bit out of it. Even if he wasn't, it's a dangerous path, but why say no now? If all else fails, I'm not going back home to live, so . . . We clink bottles, his nearly empty; I haven't taken a sip.

"Want another?" he asks, already headed to the bar.

"No, thanks." In addition to stuff did he have a few drinks? Because he's here but not here, and where else he might be scares me. More people have come into the bar. Maybe the rain did stop. The buzz of voices blends into the background music; both TVs have been switched on to an impolite volume. I sip my beer, unable to disrupt the messy thoughts crowding my mind.

Mike returns with two bottles for himself, two bags of chips, and tosses me one.

"Thanks, my favorite bad food," a flash memory of Marla in Central Park stuffing herself with chips and chocolate.

"Deep in thought?" he says.

"About you."

"I like that."

"What did you take before meeting me?"

"You're lovely, but, please, stay out of my head."

"I need to know."

"Know what? Did I smoke a joint? Did I eat lunch? Did I prepare a clean shirt for work, know what Tessa?"

"If you're seriously on stuff."

"Seriously?" He laughs; it's a harsh sound. "You have no clue what we did over there during the long hours of down time. We played cards, hours of cards, we napped, hours in our cots, and yet there were so many hours left that we wanted to turn into good time, so we drank and toked and snorted and shared fantasies, really wild ones that made us laugh or feel nostalgic or sometimes sex crazy. But, always, we could take another sip, drag, or snort. That's what we did when we weren't killing or being killed."

"Don't make simple what's complicated."

"You know, babe, this isn't good for me, the negative probing, especially before I enter that security cage for eight fucking hours."

"Seven hours and talking about it is good for you, and it's not negative that I'm concerned."

"Tessa, I'm in no mood to understand my bad habits. Talk to me about good stuff, like you taking more photos."

"That dream's unlikely to happen."

"Why?"

"I'll have to work full time with no time for classes, etc."

"Bummer. Walk me to the station so your face is the last good one I see."

It's not raining, but the damp cold is uncomfortable. I watch him descend into the subway maw, the dark clouds still apparent. Headlights sweep across slick streets. I walk uptown. Moving in with Mike . . . what a strange thought, unexpected. It doesn't have to be a contract for life, or be monogamous. We don't . . . Tessa, stop, not a good idea; too dangerous, it's bound to send the wrong message. Somehow, I'll find a cheap place of my own, maybe a room in someone's apartment.

I pass a small, dimly lit deli, the gate already half pulled across the front door, but the owner lets me in. A loaf of bread, box of pasta and can of tomato sauce: *my dinner*, I think with satisfaction.

"Wait," the doorman says. "Something for you," an envelope. "From the grandson. He has a key, but left a while ago."

"Thank you. Goodnight." I want to open the envelope at once but wait till I'm in the apartment. An index card on which Greg has written: *Sorry I missed you, had to pick up something in the apartment. Have news to share. Will try to come by tomorrow or the day after.*

What did he pick up, I wonder? What news, his residency? Why do I need to know where he's going? Why not call to tell me? Must be about the apartment, it's been sold. Why should I wait here to hear bad news? I won't. Tomorrow, after the workers leave, I'll look for another place to live. I take the bag of food to the kitchen.

31

I exit the barely lit train station at Longwood Avenue, which according to Google is in the South Bronx. The streets are filled with small shops with open doors and gated windows. People walk every which way, children in tow. Two elderly men sit on milk cartons in front of a bodega, playing dominoes. No one seems aimless. Car horns beep, trucks rattle past, neon lights wink in bar windows. The bustle pleases me. So different from where I grew up, where only summer filled streets with people, mainly tourists. Scotty called summer people interlopers, but Marla loved the busyness. She accused Scotty of being provincial. After summer the hush arrived, and we all waited, but for what?

I ask a woman if she can help me and show her the address. She points to an old brick building covered with chalk marks and colorful graffiti. Entering the dark hallway, though not dark enough to hide the cracked walls I smell fried food and old fruit, and pray the apartment I'm to see will be more winning.

The ad read first floor, ring super's bell. I walk up well-worn steps to the first floor of three apartments, none with numbers or names. I suppose people know where they live, markings superfluous.

I press the bell of one apartment. It doesn't ring. I knock at the door. "Who's there?"

"Hello. I'm looking for the super, I'm . . . "

"The basement."

"Isn't this the first floor?"

"Second."

Returning to the entry hallway, I see a door to what must be the basement and open it. Too nervous to descend the steps, call down, "Hello." Nothing. Then again call down: "Hello. Is anyone there?"

"Yes, what do you want?" a woman's voice.

"I'm here to see the apartment for rent."

"I'm coming up. Stay there."

I wait near the door, which opens in a few minutes to a woman wider and taller than me, perhaps her late thirties.

"Hello, I'm the super's wife, Teri. Come, I'll show you."

Holding a shaky railing, I follow her down the flight of steps to a dingy area with a cement floor and a plasterboard wall that cuts across the room. "I didn't know it was a basement apartment."

"There are two apartments down here. One we live in, the other for rent. Nice place, you'll see."

The woman, Teri, seems friendly and would probably make a good neighbor.

"Just you and your husband," I venture.

"If only. Four children."

I laugh. "Is this also considered the first floor?"

"Yes."

"So where is the boiler and other things."

"Behind the wall is the cellar with the boiler and things."

"I see."

She unlocks a dark green, metal door with no markings, walks in ahead and switches on an overhead light. "It's a furnished studio."

"Yes, the ad said as much, and it's only for one, me." The white walls are newly painted; two small windows a bit below street level offer scant light. In one corner are a sink, low fridge and oven on a tiled square of floor. Behind a curtained alcove is a small bathroom with a shower. There's also a flowered couch, rocking chair, and round table to eat on. "A bed? I ask.

"The couch pulls out to a bed."

I walk around the room a few times as Teri watches.

"Thank you for showing it to me. I'll call you soon and let you know my decision."

"Fine."

Once more out on the street, I head to the subway. The apartment is the cheapest one I could find online. Of course, cheap is cheap and it is the cellar even if they call it first floor. What did I expect for that money? On the other hand, I'd only need to pack my personal effects to move in.

On the train I revisit the studio in my head, inspect it anew, the walls smooth and clean, no awful smell inside except that of new paint. The place is close to a subway station, *that's a good thing*, I tell myself. Jesus, I don't know. If I take too much time to decide, the studio could be snatched away. Cheap rentals are more than scarce.

Should I call Mike to meet for a drink? He'll think I'm crazy moving into a cellar when together we could probably afford a larger space. I'll do one more online search tomorrow. If nothing better appears, I'll phone Teri and rent the damn studio, then begin my job search.

In my large, comfortable bedroom, sleep seems impossible, my brain fueled by too many fears to sort. Take the Bronx studio or move in with Mike, who will happily bring me a cup of coffee in bed? What's wrong with that? I could still look for a place of my own; I'd tell him as much, a message sent. He wouldn't argue, wouldn't believe me either. My laptop waits and I urge myself off the bed.

After more than two unsuccessful hours online, I decide to take the Bronx studio. I'll let Teri know and will drop off a month's security to keep her from renting it. I'll stay here till the apartment is sold. *There*, I think, *one problem solved, or*—

The doorbell rings. But no one buzzed me from the lobby, must be Greg. Christ, I'm not dressed. Pulling on a sweater that nearly reaches my knees, I head to the door. "Who is it?"

"It's Greg."

"Okay," and stare down at my bare shins. What the hell, and open the door, "Hi, just about to brew coffee, want some?"

"Indeed." He follows me to the kitchen.

"The workers finished crating the paintings yesterday." I'm as nervous as if I'm about to be issued a summons, which isn't far fetched. Instead of a court date, it'll be a move out date. As a kid, when something bad was clearly about to happen, I'd hide, not possible now.

I open the bag of coffee, dip in the measuring spoon, count out a few, pour water in the reservoir, all of it done slowly, needing to think, except my mind blanks. As the coffee begins to drip, I stand guard as if it might not do what it always does. Greg watches but says nothing.

I place two mugs on the table and send him a silent message to sit, but he doesn't obey. And continues to watch me move about the kitchen. Perhaps my semi-clad body has silenced him.

"Sorry, have nothing to go with the coffee, bare pantry," I say inanely, then sit at the table. He sits across from me, his expression far from doleful is somewhat smug, as if he's about to admit to a successful crime.

"So what have you come to tell me," I blurt out ridiculously.

"Too much to fit on an index card. My hospital match is at Lenox Hill in Manhattan. I'm so pleased, so are my parents. Granny would be too."

"That's great. I'm happy for you."

"I'll rotate through every medical department, which will give me an idea in which field to do my fellowship."

"Sounds wonderful." Is it possible he's here just to share his news?

"Tessa, I want to celebrate with you. We had a dinner planned but couldn't keep it. What about tonight? Can we have dinner?"

"Aren't you on your way back to . . . "

"I need to spend the day at Lenox Hill for administrative stuff. The residency begins in a few days, so dinner tonight, say yes."

"Yes," I say, confused by my quick response.

"I have to go now. How is 7:30?"

"Fine," and walk him to the door.

I drop onto the couch, power on the TV, stare at the muted screen of talking heads that are no doubt discussing foreclosures, job losses, and plant closings, which I don't want to hear. Did Greg come just to ask me out to dinner? Does he have any idea of what's next for me? Or is he too self-involved?

Our table is on the second floor in a room with wrap-around windows that overlooks the city.

"I hope you like French food?"

"Of course." I've never eaten French food and pray the menu will also be in English.

The waiter asks what we'd like to drink.

"Is it all right if I order a wonderful wine that I think you'll like?"

"Please do." I wish he'd order my food as well.

Greg pronounces the French name admirably.

"How did it go at Lenox Hill?"

"Boring, paperwork, quick tour, and so on. Until I get to work, real work I won't know what it feels like."

"You sound excited."

"I can't believe that I've reached my residency. It wasn't long ago that Granny and I were discussing my going into medical research. The idea of research is a real possibility."

"Rhonda," I say wistfully. "Without her presence the apartment feels cavernous."

"I miss her too."

"Do your parents have thoughts about which field—?"

"Not really, I have my medical degree, they've achieved their goal, if you know what I mean."

But how would I know? No one ever laid out expectations for me other than the hope I'd do better than they had.

The waiter reappears with the wine and pours a smidgen in my glass. I taste, smile, nod, and think, hurry and pour in more. Two menus are placed on the table. To my relief beneath the French are English translations. Greg studies his menu, his expression concentrated. Would I call him handsome? Except for his mother's small jutting chin the rest of his facial bone structure is strong. He has the kind of light blonde hair that won't show the gray. None of my boyfriends had blue eyes. I wonder about his ancestry; there's nothing ethnic in his appearance. Mike, go away, I command.

"Do you know what you want?" Greg asks.

"In a minute." And locate a fish dish that no doubt will be prepared in a way I haven't tasted before. New experiences are what I collect. "I've decided on a fish dish."

"Good choice. I'm going to go with the beef."

As if on cue the waiter returns and takes the order.

"A toast to your success," I raise my glass.

"Thank you."

"Will you work directly with patients?"

"Of course."

"Is that what you're most looking forward to?"

"I don't know."

"That's an honest answer. It's quite something to pledge to heal the sick."

"It is, and I will . . . that is, to the best of my ability. I'm still learning."

"Thank heavens you know that," I joke.

He laughs; it's a shy sound as if he fears waking someone? "So, Tessa, what's keeping you busy?"

"This and that." Outside the window Manhattan lights glisten majestically.

"I know you've been caretaking the apartment, but . . . "

Caretaking: the word upsets me. "I won't be doing that much longer.

Hasn't the apartment been sold?"

"I have no idea."

His cluelessness pisses me off. "Didn't your father tell you it's on the market?"

"Is that what he told you?"

"He hasn't told me anything, which is why I'm asking."

"You sound annoyed."

"Not knowing when I'll be asked to move upends my plans."

"What plans?"

Tell him, even if it's not exactly true, "Pursuing photography. However—"

"That sounds fascinating."

"Why?" I want to know.

"I've never known a photographer."

Is that the only reason? I don't ask, and feel I've given away a secret. "Everything is on hold till I know where I'll be living. I'm sure you can understand," and try to sound earnest but fail.

"My father wants to have lunch with me tomorrow. Perhaps it's about Granny's apartment. Tessa, as soon as I know anything, I'll tell you."

"Okay, thanks." I've spoiled the evening, if not for him than for me.

Greg rides up in the elevator with me. I don't ask him in. Ironic given it's his family's place.

"I'm going to kiss you," he announces, waits a beat to see my response, then pulls me close, holds me tight and finds my lips. He doesn't try for another or anything more. So polite, I think.

"Call you after I see my father. I'll let you know what he says."

"Thanks." At least he didn't forget.

Still in my jacket, I stand at the window, trying to arrange my thoughts, but they crash into each other. Did he really not know about the sale of the apartment? Could he be so devious? Does he have the faintest idea we're in a recession, finding a place almost impossible? Is he unable to empathize with the distress of others? If so he's in the wrong profession. What is it that I wanted him to say? I'll be sorry to see you go? I'll find you wherever you move? Is there something I can do to help?

Why am I angry? He did his best to please me. I didn't even thank him for dinner. I'm tired, probably a bit drunk as well, which is why it's Mike I want to snuggle up with. Thank goodness he works nights.

32

Greg is on the way up. It's early; he won't stay. He has to be at the hospital. It will be a short visit. What does that mean? I open the door before he can knock. He walks past me to sit on the couch. Again, I sense his excitement.

"I had lunch with my father yesterday. They're giving me Granny's apartment."

"What?"

"My residency is in New York. They're giving me the place as a gift. How great is that?"

"So, they're not going to sell?" I sound like an idiot.

"Anyway, father believes the real estate market is bad for selling just now. That's how he thinks, Tessa."

"How great for you," I say.

"Don't you get it?"

I shake my head.

You can stay here."

"As what?" A caretaker, I don't say.

"A roommate."

"I can't share a mortgage or the monthly fees of this place."

"My parents plan to pay maintenance for the first two years. There's no mortgage. You can . . . I don't know, buy food, whatever."

"You're inviting me to live here with you, rent-free?"

"Why not? Keep the room you have. I'll move into granny's room in a week or two. Besides I won't be around that much. I'll be pulling many all-nighters, plus hours studying at their library."

"Greg, I'm overwhelmed."

"That's okay," he sounds a bit embarrassed.

"Do your parents know that you're asking me to stay?"

"Doesn't matter, the place is mine, I can do what I want."

"God, Greg, its such a generous offer. I need to think about it."

"Why?"

"Can't you understand?"

"Not really."

"Its just . . . look . . . I don't know what to say yet. I'm going to visit my mother tomorrow for a few days," a decision I'm making as the words leave my mouth. "As soon as I return, I'll let you know my thoughts." I want him to go, now. I need to live with this information. Alone.

"If that's what you'd like," and sounds disappointed. He's offering me a gift that I refuse to accept.

"Greg, I will think seriously about your generous proposal."

"Okay. I'm due at the hospital. Call me when you get back."

"Of course," I walk him to the door, unsure if we're to kiss. We don't.

Alone, now, I'm unable to process the last minutes. Why didn't I jump at the offer? I try to think, but only questions arise. Why does Greg even want a roommate? Why me? It can't be love, we don't know each other well enough. Is it out of some noble gesture: Do something to help the poor waif? I hope to hell not. If I accept, would I feel too indebted? Obligated? A kept woman? For heaven's sake, he's Rhonda's grandson, not a dangerous stranger. So what is my problem? It just feels too easy; life doesn't fall this way. No doubt my mother will be as wary as I am. It's too close to the rainbow that Marcus offered Marla. Where did that leave her?

I phone my mother; she doesn't pick up. I leave a message: "Coming tomorrow for short visit, no need to meet me at the station. I'll take a taxi."

I don't know if I'm excited or frightened, but focusing feels impossible. I grab my jacket, take the elevator down, and walk to Lexington Avenue to look for a coffee shop. I find one, go in and sit at the counter, dazed. The place is empty, quiet. Outside the large window a mackerel sky gathers to darken the already dimly lit shop.

"Hi, welcome. Can I get you the royal plate?"

"What's that?"

"Waffles topped with scrambled eggs and bacon, two sausages on the side and whatever bread suits your fancy."

"That's a lot of food." Short, wiry and bald, he looks elfin.

"Food nourishes. Without it, we're vacant," his tone serious.

"Okay, but I might not be able to finish all of it."

"One royal," he calls out. "May I say something?"

"About food?" I wonder if I need to end this conversation.

"Your pleasure is blocked."

"Excuse me?"

"When thoughts pile up on the brain, they feel heavy. When you say them out loud, you name them label them, look at them, they lose weight. It's the stranger that safely receives the story."

Is he clairvoyant, nuts or just playing with me, but he sounds so earnest. Anyway, what's the big secret? I say a friend is offering me a rent-free apartment as his roommate and I'm not sure to accept or not.

He nods.

Recalling childhood fairy tales, I expect he'll now disappear in a puff of smoke. "No comment?" I ask.

"I'm here only to lighten and nourish." He picks up the royal plate on the shelf behind him, places it in front of me and moves to the end of the counter. Nothing this morning feels real.

Entering the apartment with a doggie bag of food, I remember I'll be gone the next few days, and stuff it in the big freezer. The intercom buzzes "Do I know a Mike?" the doorman asks in a tone that wishes I didn't.

"Yes, send him up. Thank you." Oh Jesus, what? I wonder.

I open the door to a bleary-eyed Mike, his unzipped jacket wide-open, wind-blown hair, swaying a bit and wearing a weird grin. "Were you in a fight?"

"Do I have to stand in the doorway?" He walks in and without taking off his jacket plops on the couch. "I quit or maybe I was fired. Good fucking riddance. Who the fuck do they think they are? Do you have a drink?"

"No."

"Are you just saying that?" he accuses.

"No, Mike. Tell me what happened?"

"Nothing to tell. The boss guy never liked me. He watches me with suspicion. His brother was the one who hired me. They're both unsavory. God knows what's in the crates that fill the warehouse. Last night, the boss guy said, 'Hey, what's the difference between a Haji and a terrorist?' I told him to fuck off or I'd break his neck and walked out. Should've slugged him right then. He yells after me not to come back, ever." Mike stares at me, waiting for a resurrecting word.

"Racist, idiot jerkoff," I say in truth. "Anyway, being fired frees you to look for something better."

"Yeah. Too bad you don't even have a beer." His eyes close, his head falls back against the couch.

I shake his shoulder. "Mike, don't fall asleep here. Go home."

"Yeah, okay, but I'm wasted . . ." his slurry words bite at my brain. Failing his attempt to get up off the couch, he falls back, stretches out closes his eyes. Shit! Mike, you're breaking my heart. I can't sit here and watch him. Ten minutes, and if he's still asleep, I'll water his face like a plant. That'll wake him. But a few minutes later, he hoists himself up, takes off his jacket leaves it on the couch. "Need a shower. Here, now, don't stop me."

I stand there unable to process the scene. Soon the noise of the shower comes through the silent rooms, and in a few minutes stops abruptly. Mike walks into the living room, a towel around his waist, looking a bit sheepish but more steady on his feet, or is that what I'm hoping?

"I'll make coffee."

He returns to the bathroom.

While coffee perks I spread generous globs of peanut butter on a few slices of bread, remembering the elf's words, lighten and nourish, then put the plate on the table.

Dressed and barefoot, he pads into the kitchen, his hair still wet, and takes a seat. "Thanks."

Filling two mugs, I sit across from him. "Do you want to talk about which junk you ingested?"

"Not really. But you seem determined to know. Are you going to take notes?"

"Definitely."

He smiles, lighting up his beautiful face. "I smoked some hash and weed, but mainly I drank. I didn't take stuff because I had none left. Am I more acceptable now, drunk but not stoned?"

"You're such a shit, Mike. Coming here instead of going home to sleep it off, what did you hope I'd do?"

"What friends are supposed to do, what I'd do for you, pretty lady." And I know he means it.

"I don't understand what it is you thought . . . "

"Let me tell you about Corporal Ben Booth, my buddy, my friend, even darker than me, always at my side. The guys called us clones. Ben only ever talked about the future and the paths he'd follow to get what he wanted, inspiring man. He had a girlfriend who wrote him ten-page love letters every day, that's devotion. He could never finish telling a joke. He'd crack up right before the punch line his laugh so infectious we'd all crack up. A month before he was to go home, he was blown to bits, literally. I called his girlfriend in shit-hole New Mexico and swore to her I'd never forget Ben no matter how many years passed. I haven't. I say hi to Ben every day. It's what friends do."

"Sad, but I don't understand how that—"

"Smile at my approach. Never reject."

"I let you in," I say miserably.

"A shelter would let me in, too."

"Mike, I'm sorry if I failed..."

194

"Don't be so hard on yourself. I'm glad you let me in." that smile again.

"Can you promise not to take stuff and die?"

"No."

"Why?"

"I don't make promises I can't keep."

For a minute or two I watch him devour the peanut butter sandwich. I can hear him thinking that he doesn't want to leave. Thing is, I don't want him to.

We decide to walk to Penn Station. I don't care what the doorman thought on seeing us leave the building together. Still high from a glorious night, my mind refuses worry. It's a temporary peace, I know, but it feels good.

This morning while I was still in bed Mike went out and brought back donuts and two containers of coffee. Just what I imagined he'd do. Not only does he know the whiskey I drink, he now knows how I like my coffee. Encroachment, I can feel it.

"Did you take your camera?" his eyes a bit red-rimmed.

"Yes. You once said camera are weapons."

"You shoot to capture, right? Over there everyone took pictures during down time. You'd be talking to someone he'd be framing a shot. It could be annoying. I told a buddy it was a waste of time. The images would never leave his head probably would need a shrink to get rid of them. He said I shoot to capture instead of kill."

We cross the Central Park viaduct to the west side; buses and cars pass, rush hour still on. It's cold we walk at a clip the silence compatible.

Penn station arrives too soon. We kiss. Neither of us says anything as I step onto the grimy escalator, which rumbles down to darkness. Why am I suddenly sad?

Waiting for the train doors to close, Mike in my head, my mother comes to mind. She told us our father was her mistake. He was handsome, sweet, and generous, the man that she wanted.

Love was all, and she refused to take his drug habit seriously, told herself it was the temporary result of the club life they led, that once they settled, his habit would disappear or at least be manageable. It didn't. It wasn't. It was a story she told not once but once a year. Her intention wasn't to explain; she was educating us. I listened. So did Marla. I don't know what my sister thought. But I'm afraid to make the same mistake.

Staring out the window, nothing has changed: still one long strip of nowhere filled with look-alike small houses, malls, and gas stations. At Freeport, where the hands of the tower clock always remain at nine, the train stalls. What's my hurry? I'm not heading anywhere I haven't been before.

No taxis at the station, of course not, its winter. The locals don't count.

Heading through town toward the beach road I feel outside of what I'm seeing. The diner, bank, church, and schoolyard, always background, now sit oddly, as if I were walking backwards. How is that possible? I've not been gone that long.

On the beach road, there's nothing but scrub, sand, sky. The wind picks up as it always does as I near the water; the cries of the seagulls as familiar as tears.

Reaching the house, which looks shabbier, I call out, "Hello."

My mother opens the door. I swallow something close to a sob. I haven't seen her since leaving for Miami, since before Marla died. Angry, then, did I even say good-by at the airport?

"I'm here," is all I can manage and hug her unexpectedly bony body.

"Sweet girl, come in."

"Hey, the real Tessa." Hack gives me a weak hug. I kiss his cheek, surprising us both. But words are difficult amidst the sudden swell of emotion clogging my throat.

The kitchen seems in disarray, paint greying, table more chipped, cabinet doors ajar. Never before were dirty dishes allowed to pile in the sink.

"A beer?" Hack offers. I nod. He walks unsteadily toward the fridge, takes out several, sets them on the table and we sit. Mike and Hack would like each other, I think. My mother's hand covers mine. She seems frail.

"Big city girl," Hack nods.

"Small town always."

"No, you're not," my mother says to my surprise.

"Look who's here," Scotty grabs a beer from the table, twists off the cap, flips it in the sink and leans against the wall.

I'd rather be alone with my mother, but that'll have to wait.

Hack pushes back his chair, and for a moment I think he might fall, but he doesn't. He takes out a dish from the fridge. "Tuna casserole for dinner," and shoves it in the oven.

"Great."

Scotty doesn't say a word to me, probably pissed that I didn't come at Christmas. Or maybe he believes I kept my mother's secret. It doesn't matter; he doesn't matter, I remind myself.

"So, fess up?" Hack says.

"It's good living there. So many people, you wouldn't believe, even after dark. Stores stay open forever, restaurants too. I've eaten French food and Italian food."

"Who with?" my mother's voice low.

"The grandson of the woman I worked for."

"Dicey," Scotty mumbles.

"Wasn't," I say, annoyed, though I'd thought so too. "Hack, did you clear out your bungalow?"

"Knew there was something I had to do."

Our words ebb and flow, mostly from Hack, but the atmosphere feels heavy, as if my presence makes everyone uncomfortable.

"Mom, want to take a walk on the beach. It's not that dark yet."

"Maybe tomorrow, honey. Too tired now. You go."

"I think I will, a short walk. Need a peek at the water."

"Casserole getting hot," Hack says.

"I hear you."

Closing the front door, I take a deep breath. Leaving is rude, but I had to get out. So odd, it doesn't feel like home, not even like the one I wanted to flee. It just feels distant, separate. Scotty's indifference expectable, but my mother too seems absent. What's going on with her?

Near the dunes, I step out of my shoes and traipse across the soft, cold sand to the water's edge. It's low tide, muddy, and remember the silly mud-fights Marla and I had, laughing till it hurt. Her ashes may be scattered on another beach, but her presence here as tangible as her voice in my head. Pointing to the horizon she'd say it's out there, all of it.

As the sky darkens, gulls begin to gather on the big rock further out in the water. It's still too early for stars.

"Food smells delicious," I say closing the door.

Hack begins to spoon gobs of casserole into each plate.

"Tastes great, Hack," I say. It does.

"I'm beaming," He makes a funny face. I laugh.

My mother, quiet, picks at the food, Scotty silent as usual. "So, Scotty the shed built yet?" I ask just to say something.

"Still clearing."

It doesn't take long to finish eating. "I'll clean up," I say to no one's objection.

On the way to the bedroom, I pass Hack asleep on the couch. A cot for Scotty is set up for him during my visit. I hear him out back. My mother sleeps alone, but at whose request? In bed, my hand slides across the space that was Marla's.

Winter-white beach light enters the shade-less bedroom window. Soon my mother will knock at the door, say time to get up. *No more*, I think, and slip out of bed, dress quickly in the cold room.

No one is in the kitchen, coffee in the pot. Even with plastic covering the windows, the wind comes through. I pour two cups, take them to my mother's room, and peek in. She's in bed, awake.

"Morning," I say.

She sits up, takes the cup from my hand. "That's sweet, thanks." I perch on the edge of the bed.

"I've never been so tired," she admits.

"You're not eating, not going out, not seeing friends, and I don't notice any traffic between you and Scotty."

"Sweet Tessa, too observant. I don't like you seeing me this way."

"What way?"

"Emotionally drained."

"That doesn't have to be. Are you taking medicine?"

"Done with trying to feel better."

"Mom! That's awful."

"It's hard for you to understand, but I've been there and back too many times to find the energy again."

"It scares me when you talk like this. Yes, Marla is gone, nothing could be worse, but it sure as shit doesn't help her for you to go under. And it really doesn't help me." It also pisses me off, I don't say. Mothers are supposed to be protective; she always was.

"I'm sorry, Tessa."

"For what?"

"Not worrying enough about you and Marla as I should have." Her eyes fill.

"Please get dressed. Take a walk with me on the beach or driveway, things I need to discuss with you. I want your input."

"It'll take a little while to get ready," her voice whispery.

"Okay," and take my untouched coffee to the kitchen. I sit at the table and wait. Hack is still asleep, more likely passed out.

"The driveway," she says, wrapped in an old coat now too big for her. "I'll pick up the mail. Box must be full," offering a destination. "So many bills," she mumbles.

We walk up the rutty, dirt road her gait slow. I need to pace myself not to get ahead of her.

"Did you ever think about maybe talking to someone, a therapist?" and resent having to ask, not my job.

"I know the reasons for my feelings."

"But talking about them—venting—that's a good thing."

"You should vent now before I get too tired. Are you in trouble? Money?"

"Greg, the grandson I mentioned . . . " I tell her about his offer, my confusion, my wish to take a photography course, my only other option a room in a basement.

"Do you know him well?"

"Actually, no. We went out to dinner a few times and shared grief over his grandmother's death. He's a doctor at a nearby hospital. It's his apartment; his parents gave it to him, a gift, can you imagine."

"Tessa, if you can't make up your mind or have such hesitation about accepting the offer, it's probably best to walk away from it."

"I wish you could see the apartment," I surprise myself saying. "It's lovely, big, centrally located, and here's the thing, it would be rent-free. I'd only need a part time job, which means I'd have time to take a photography course, and Greg said he wouldn't be home much, that he'd be at the hospital many nights," and wonder who I'm trying to convince.

My mother is silent. I want more from her.

The flag on the mailbox is up. She takes out handfuls of flyers and what looks to be bills. Two envelopes drift to the ground, which I pick up. One is from the VA the other from Peter. I hand her both and she tosses the flyers and Peter's letter in the trash bin, slips the rest in her pocket.

"Of course, I'd rather you be in a beautiful apartment than a basement," she suddenly says. "But, yes, the offer worries me, and you need to say more about your reluctance."

"I'm unsure what's behind it. What if anything would Greg want or expect from me if I accept, I'm—"

"Tessa, only he can answer these questions. You must put these to him in no uncertain terms plus a few more. You need to make it clear that you'd be a roommate, not a mistress. You need to make sure he understands what you're saying."

"Maybe he doesn't know the difference." Do I believe that?

"Tell him you can't accept the offer without his commitment to clear guidelines. Tell him what he must not expect. Be specific, get answers you can believe and count on. It's the only way to trust the situation. Anything less, anything too murky, don't accept. Let's go back, I'm cold."

"I can do that. I will explain the terms," I say more to myself. "Mom, you've helped me."

She nods. "I'm going in, need some hot coffee."

"I can make eggs for you?"

"No eggs, thanks. Are you coming in?"

"A jog on the beach first."

I walk her to the front door and once she's inside, go up the driveway, dip into the trash and pluck out Peter's letter, which I slip in my jacket pocket, then head down to the beach. I'm prepared to talk seriously with Greg. I'll be crystal clear about what being a roommate means and doesn't mean. He needs to be as well. I'm anxious now to get back. The biting cold wind is weirdly stimulating.

Jogging in the opposite direction of Marcus's beach house, which wasn't his, I remember that Marla left clothes and other stuff there when she went to Florida. No doubt he got rid of everything when he moved out. I will never stop hating that man.

When I get back to the house Hack's on the couch, finishing a beer, TV going about who cares what. I plop down beside him. He says my mother's in the bedroom.

"I'm worried about my mother."

"Falling below the life line."

"Hack! What does that mean?"

"Had to hurry each one to the medical tent for . . . "

"Hack, my mother, not your buddies."

"Too painful for some to go on."

"You go on."

"Mucho aids."

"Maybe she ought to be on an antidepressant," I wonder aloud, though the pills she was taking did upset me.

"Your mother tossed her pills. I rescued them."

"It's hard to see her this way, Hack."

"Over there we had dogs, something real to love. It isn't here," he says. "Want a beer?"

"No," and watch him walk to the kitchen for a refill, his balance in question. He's right, though, no love or warmth in these rooms, and I head to my mother's bedroom. "Are you asleep?"

"Just resting."

Once more I perch on the side of the bed. "Mom, I want . . . I need to go back and speak to Greg, discuss what we talked about."

"Absolutely. You should, don't wait."

"It's hard to leave when you're so depressed." You've always been so strong, I don't say.

"Honey, I have to go through what I must."

"You've already been to hell. Isn't it time to come back?"

"I knew if you visited you'd be upset. It's why I didn't want you to come. There's nothing here for you."

"You're here."

"Oh Tessa," her sad voice an ache.

"This afternoon you and I are going to the diner for lunch. Louise will be there, she always is."

"I don't know . . . "

"You need to get out of this dead-end place. Tell Louise you'll work the Saturday lunch shift she once offered. Do it for me. Please."

"I don't know that I can."

"Mom, you're all the family I have. I don't want to be an orphan. Please," I say, and leave ahead of tears. Hers or mine?

Tessa's words hang in the air, heavy and needful. They gnaw at her innards. She hears the front door close, and out the window sees Tessa walk toward the beach. Her daughter is asking that she be if not hopeful than at least a responsible mother. Except loss and grief and guilt can't be tossed off like a too hot blanket. It doesn't work that way. Oh Lord.

Pregnant with Tessa, she remembers going back home to ask her parents for shelter. Her mother's face tightened with anger. She scolded Nina for being careless, said she should've taken better precaution. Said she should never have married that addict. Said it was a small house with little room for added troubles. Still her mother took her and Marla in and saw her through the birth of Tessa, but made it clear they needed back their space. Who sends away their own child?

Tessa doesn't want shelter; she's asking for something much simpler. But pulling yourself together for another—is it even possible? Okay, she'll try. She'll work at the diner, an hour or two at the most. It'll relieve Tessa; she'll have a bit of earnings to give Scotty. She has no use for money. What for? Two good deeds, at least that.

Slipping out of bed, she sits a moment, her feet on the cold floor and listens for his whereabouts. A heavy walker, Scotty slams doors, drawers and cabinets. Years ago, she decided beneath his quiet manner lived a sleeping volcano. Someday he will explode, and now, it could very well be at her. Peter once said he'd met men like Scotty in the Marines, quiet, withholding, and upstanding, who were able to kill too easily. Scotty, too, fought in a war; did he kill easily? He never said.

<hr/>

Walking along the empty beach, camera strap over my shoulder, my mother's depression tugs at me. It's a gray day with a sheet-white sky, the tide inching up onto the sand. My mother's right, there's nothing here for me. She can visit me in the city, though the thought feels unreal. Will she get better is the question? What if she doesn't?

Trudging the sand back to the road that leads to the church-yard, I pass Kevin's house. The large black mourning bow still on the door a bit weathered now. It's wide, satiny streamers touch the ground with tattered ends. I hold the camera at the distance Mike suggested and snap. A few feet past the house is a large, frayed at the edges, bold-print marine recruitment poster wrapped around a lamppost with a smashed overhead light; I take a shot of that as well, then head toward Raff's place, a bit guilty for not responding to the few texts he sent me. He felt so far away; the least I can do now is say hello.

From the churchyard I can see Raff's house. The drawn shades and lack of light inside keep me from knocking. I'll wait here, maybe he'll come out. A convention of pigeons settles near my bench, their feathery iridescence on display as they peck for crumbs between cracks in the ground, their indifference amazing, ignoring everything around them, including me. I aim the camera, take a shot and imagine the last three images superimposed into one photo. Can that even be done?

"Oh, Jesus and Mary," Raff says seeing me. "What the—Are you okay? Weren't you gone, gone for good? Terrible about Marla. Really shitty, no words."

"Thanks. Yeah, bad stuff, wanted to say hello to my old friend. Sorry I didn't answer your texts. How are you?"

"Like . . . no different from when you last saw me."

"Okay. How's the job?"

"Weird. Quiet. Not sure why they need me there. I fix a few bikes, but no one comes in. I think the owner just wants company. It's boring, Tess."

"Sounds it. Maybe go for something else?"

"Yeah, but not till the summer. I mean now there's nothing."

"Right."

"Listen I can't hang out. I'm late. My mom, she's bad in the morning, it's arthritis, and I help her get ready. She opens the hardware store. Can we have a beer after work? I have some good smokes."

"Do you do a lot of that?"

"Hey, it helps the boredom. So, what about later?"

My mom isn't doing well either. If I can leave her, I'll text you. What happened, a fight?" I point at his missing two teeth.

"Wish. Decay, infection, abscess, they had to come out. I'm saving up to get them replaced. Then, again, once I join up, the army can replace them." He leans over, musses my hair, and kisses my cheek. "Still a pretty girl," then lopes off, and disappears around the bend in the road.

Okay, that was a downer. He looked awful. Poor Raff, none of it is his fault. What did I expect? I walk the road slowly to kill more time before returning to pick up my mother for lunch. In the near distance I see the grey brick school building with its locked doors to keep out drug dealers. Waste of effort then and now, the dealers wait outside, easy to locate. An unbidden memory floats into view: kindergarten, show-and-tell. My name is called; I have nothing to show. I stand silently near the teacher's desk for what feels like forever as flames of shame heat my cheeks.

My mother pulls the coat tighter around her as we head into town. Her silence echoed by the quiet road. Does she resent the outing, which she's clearly doing for my sake?

"Mom, I don't want to *make* you do what your really don't want to."

"It's okay for me to get out, to walk. You've brought your camera?"

"I recently learned how to use it. But there's so much about taking photos I don't know. Mike, a guy I've been seeing on and off, really sweet, an ex-army ranger, taught me how. I never told you that I stole the camera from Marcus's room in Miami. Does that upset you?"

"What upsets me, what I'll never get over, is ever letting her go with Marcus."

"She would've gone with or without your permission." Is that true?

"I don't know that."

"Do you talk about her to Scotty?"

"Since telling him about Peter, we barely talk. He's not forgiven me and may never. But he won't discuss that either. At least Hack is friendly."

"Did Hack ever try to get clean or . . . "

"I've tried; Scotty has too. But he always says, what for—a dead end job?"

"He's got a point," I mumble, thinking of Raff.

The town with its long quiet street shivers in the cold. It's a town asleep, with its shuttered shops that may or may not open in summer. At the door of the diner, my mother hesitates.

"What is it?"

"It's been so long, Tessa. I haven't returned Louise's calls and . . . "

"Mom, she's your friend, she understands. Come," I push open the door. The little bell tingles.

"Oh my God, it's you," Louise grabs my mother's hand. "I'm not going to ask how you are, just happy you're here. It's your doing, Tessa, isn't it, getting her out? Good for you, Tess honey."

"Great to see you. I like your new hair style," I say.

"Makes me look younger, I'm told. But who cares? I'll rustle up whatever you want, then join you. Coffee, first?"

"Yes, thanks."

We're the only customers and slip into a wooden booth near the window. In the distance, small look-alike houses remind me of Lego pieces. Across the road, a few houses double as offices, three with real-estate signs. "Mom, there are gates on the windows, why?"

"There've been some robberies."

"What could they possibly steal?" I wonder aloud.

"Laptops, mostly," Louise says, serving the coffee. Do you need menus?"

"I'll have a ham and cheese sandwich," my mother says.

"Same for me," and watch Louise hurry away.

Other than her lost ponytail, Louise hasn't changed a bit. My mother, however, is thinner, her face paler, and in her expression now a wish not to be here, but to be where? "Mom, some day not too far away, come visit me in the city. We'll go places, and you'll see the apartment."

My mother nods a few times but remains silent.

Louise places paper plates with our sandwiches on the table and slides in beside me.

"Tessa, what's it like there?" as if Manhattan is a thousand miles away.

"It's good, alive, busy. Hey, when did you two last see each other?"

206

"At Christmas, right, Nina?"

"Yes."

"I couldn't stay long. Matt was pissed at me for leaving him alone with his family, mind you. They are many." Louise watches my mother. They're old friends. Louise must know much.

"My mom is thinking of helping out here on Saturday's." A faint smile crosses my mother's face. But if I don't speak up, she won't.

"Great. Saturday, that's when people actually come in. It'll get busier as the weather warms."

As Louise describes Saturday lunch shift, my mind wanders to Mike who will appreciate the photos I took this morning, then to Greg who probably wouldn't, but do I know that? Then to Raff who can't fucking afford to replace his teeth!

Hack and my mother stand shoulder to shoulder in front of the house. It's cold but they're not wearing coats, my mother's frailty on display. We're all make-believe joyful at my imminent departure. Should I ask Scotty to join the family photo, decide no. Setting up the shot their brave stance sends a shiver of sadness through me. "Smile," I say, and promise to send home a print.

"Stay in touch," Hack calls as I head up the driveway.

"Do good, stay safe," my mother waves.

"Phone me," I call back.

Marshmallow clouds parry with the sun as I walk the road to the train station. A sense of déjà vu tugs at me; it's the memory of the road out of Miami, the old woman's words urging me forward. Now my mother's words do so as well. Marla said getting out is taking the first step. I've already done that, haven't I?

III.

33

In a cubby with the curtain pulled closed around us, Molly Kirsch, who everyone calls Kirsch, has posed me on a stool. Wearing a stern expression, she fiddles with a battery of lights that go on and off at her touch.

"Tessa, give me a Joan of Arc look." She focuses her deep-set penetrating eyes in my direction.

"Excuse me?"

"Joan. A saint. Look saintly."

"I can't imagine how."

"Turn semi-profile, chin slightly elevated and stare into the distance. Yes. Good. Hold. Hold. No, no, relax. The light, it's still not right. Relax a minute," her tall wiry-thin body moves easily between stands of klieg spots. I watch her head of thick, unruly dark hair appear and disappear behind cameras. With her, the readjustment of lights can take a while.

"Something not right . . . can't get used to indoor lighting," Kirsch mumbles, moving two of the klieg spots here and there, and settling them in two corners. "Okay. Place your hands on your thighs, relax."

"I doubt if Joan was relaxed," I say, and get a faint smile.

"Ready, don't move. Okay, no talk. All right St. Joan again. Hold. Done."

She shuts off the hot lights and begins fiddling with the cameras. "Are you eligible yet to audit a course?"

"Today is the end of my second week of modeling. I can start a class on Monday. I'm leaning to the one on Craft."

"Take the one on lights."

"Why?"

"I teach it."

"I thought you were a student."

"I am. I want to learn to do portraits. I've only done action stuff."

"Action?"

"War photographer."

"Oh Jesus," I mutter, can't get away from these vets.

"What?"

"But I don't even know the different elements of a camera."

"Easy. I'll show you.

"Why lighting course?"

"Photography isn't possible without proper indoor or outdoor lighting."

"Not possible?"

"The angle of falling light depends on where you stand, yes? It also determines the way you view what's in front of you. A photographer must be able to observe more than she sees."

Heading up Sixth Avenue, I forego the bus, though it's beginning to snow, too propelled by the day's excitement. After our session Kirsch spent an hour teaching me, just me, the various parts of a camera and how they work. She's patient and thorough, and focused on what she needed me to understand. It was surprising to learn how many more ways I could manipulate a shot, how to zoom, how to angle. I asked her if three images could appear in one photo. She said yes, that images can be triple exposed, blurred or be edged half out of a shot, and added that she takes her students to the dark room to learn developing.

I think I'm a little in love with her, or maybe it's awe, but no doubt I'll take her class. What she said about observing makes me think about what I want others to see: Contrasts, yes; between lies and reality; Wall Street and eviction notices; luxury buildings and hovels; posh hotels and shelters; faces of pain and faces of indifference. Photos that can show and tell.

With spirits high I head to the bar, remembering Greg's response a few days ago, the relief it brought. He said it would be wonderful to have me as a roommate. He said he understood my reservations, would respect my guidelines of privacy and whatever else I propose if it will make me feel safe.

Mike's not at the bar, waiting. Unusual. To my surprise, Frank is perched on a barstool his eyes glued to the TV. It's been a while. I tap his shoulder. "Hi, how are you?"

"My goodness, Tessa, was sure the big city had swallowed you up."

"Even if it had for a while, it couldn't keep me."

"Very believable. Can I buy you a drink?"

"I'm to meet my friend, Mike, but he isn't . . . Yes, bourbon on the rocks, please."

Frank hails the bartender and orders my drink.

"And you," I ask. "What's keeping you busy?"

"This and that," and shrugs his oversized shoulders. "How's the job, Tessa?"

"So much has changed, that job is done and I'm about to look for part time work because..."

"Do you need a lot of money?"

"No. Why?"

"I manage a small trucking firm, open 24-7 and the weekend person stopped showing up."

"Because it's a terrible job?"

"Maybe. Young people don't like working on weekends."

"What would I do?"

"Take down phone information. Can you read maps?"

"I can."

"It's a six-hour job. Twenty an hour in cash, but it begins early, six in the morning till noon."

"It's a lucky day," I say, adding this to the other good things that happened. One positive after another, dare I trust it?

Mike hurries through the door.

Frank gives me his card. "You show up next Saturday morning. I'll be there."

"Me, too, I'll be there."

"Mike, this is Frank who saved me the first night I arrived in New York."

"Hey. Glad you saved her. I'll grab a table. Order me a beer."

"Frank, you've become something of a guardian angel. Thanks. See you at work."

I bring his beer and my drink to the table. "Frank just offered me a part time job on the weekends. I'm amazed, grateful, too."

"Beautiful white woman, who wouldn't want you working for them?"

"What's with this white woman thing?"

"I'm a man whose Arabic genes are written across my beautiful face, which means I'm dangerous. Want ads don't want me when I show up. However, after many turndowns, I did get a job, nothing worthwhile, at a Broadway supermarket."

"Doing what?" He's slurring a bit. Is he on something? Maybe just tired after the job search.

"Security, of course, my army ranger past the selling point. I sit in a room and watch computers. Same hours as the last shit job, midnight to seven, and once they check my background, I'll be armed. Seems they've had several attempts at break-ins."

"I didn't think you'd want another job in security."

"I didn't. I don't. But can't find anything else. Also, the money will help me pay my half of the apartment I found this morning." Big smile.

My lucky day just crashed. "Mike, I'm . . . "

"Tessa, I know. It's another dead-end job. But man, I secured a place for us in lower Manhattan, unheard of. You wouldn't want me to lose it. I—"

"Mike, I can't move in with you. I can't share the rent. I can't."

"You're going home?"

"No. Don't interrupt. Let me explain." I tell him about Greg's offer, my roommate status, my free rent, how that and a part time job allows me to audit a photography class. His expression changes from a frown of disappointment to a tight expression of anger.

"You're kidding. You can't be that stupid. You trust some rich dude to keep his distance, are you fucking with me?"

"Mike, you don't know him. He'll be respectful, he'll be—"

"What world do you live in? Can you hear yourself? You're selling yourself for money or, no, for free rent. Don't you know men? Whatever the dude says he's going to go for grope as soon as he sees you settled. Shit. What am I doing here anyway? Give me a call now and then." He walks out, his gait unsteady. Ridiculously, I wonder if Frank is watching. Finish my drink and head out.

A light blanket of snow covers the ground, the wind has picked up and I walk with no destination. The cold concrete penetrates my worn sneakers. Mike's expression, I can't forget it, no, I won't. The depth of disdain, a well into which I feared falling. Of course he'd respond the way he did, what did I expect. Happy for you Tessa, what a break, I'd planned to live alone anyway. What bends my thinking is, what if he's right? The way he painted Greg, well . . . it's not Greg. How do I really know, Mike, in my head, asks? If Greg doesn't honor the roommate status I'll move out, but where? Mike isn't going to want me, and I can't blame him.

I handled it badly. As soon as Greg's offer was made, I should've told Mike so he wouldn't count on me to share an apartment. I didn't actually agree to share; it was more an out loud thought, obviously, not to him.

My cheeks numb, my fingers too, I'm freezing. Greg, the apartment, can't face either yet, but can't keep walking. A movie, doesn't matter what's playing, it'll be warm.

The doorman opens the lobby door, "Bad out there, isn't it?"

"Surely, cold," I say, heading to the elevator, the violent sound of the film's gunshots echoing in my head.

Greg isn't home. The apartment cold; someday I'll find the thermostat. I change into sweatpants and a heavy sweater, sit on the couch, close my eyes and try to reenter the happy hour with Kirsch, the lesson, the part time job, thank you, Frank. The buzz of the intercom interrupts.

"Yes."

"Mike to see you. I'm not sure . . . " his hesitance tells me more than I want to know.

"It's okay, send him up."

I'm not halfway done pacing the room before he bangs hard at the door. Do I even want to let him in? I open the door. "Mike?" The smell of beer is palpable.

"I'm stoned. I'm high. I'm pissed. And I'm not finished telling you what's on my mind," and he walks past me to drop his disheveled self onto the couch. His dilated eyes, slurry voice, and false bravado are too fucking familiar.

"What did you take, tell me?"

"Whatever I could: a few snorts, a couple tokes, some little green pill, some beers to wash away the bitter taste," his tone combative, daring me to object. "And you know what, Tessa, the drugs help, they really do. Disappointment disappears, the sun shines at night, and best of all, I no longer give a shit."

Where have I heard that before? Suddenly, I'm furious. "I'm so damn tired of all of you who take stuff to deaden reality. One terrible year in a war and you spend the rest of your life feeling sorry enough for your sorry ass to indulge in whatever whenever you fucking feel like it. And what does that get you? My friend Kevin came back and killed himself; I suppose he might've stayed alive on stuff like my so-called uncle Hack who never stops taking shit and will surely die before long. And for this you volunteered? My stepfather who can't relate to anyone has an excuse; he was injured. He can't work. But your limbs function and they're taking you straight to Stoneville. I'm not going to watch you kill yourself. And if you think . . . "

"Tessa, shut it, just shut it. You're on a crooked path. You think it's rent free, but you'll pay."

"Greg isn't a predator. He's a doctor, for shit's sake. Why can't you hear me?"

216

"Because I care too much about you. I don't even know why. I mean we know each other only a while."

Taken aback, I hear myself say "I care about you, too, except I can't, because it won't end well. It never does with drugs. Marla taught me that. I'll never get over her death. She didn't have to die. It wasn't her time. It's not yours either. I don't want you to die. I . . . I'm . . ."

Mike is off the couch, his arms around me. "Tessa, don't cry. Please, don't cry. I'll stay away, I'll—whatever."

"Don't want you to stay away," I mumble tearfully.

"Best if I go now," his voice low, weary. Swaying some, he reaches the door, which clicks shut.

The tears continue because he'll die, because he cares too much, because I care too, because I've seen it before, and there's nothing I can do to change any of it. I shouldn't have been dismissive of the war. It is terrible, and it does affect everyone horribly forever. And I want to text Mike and say so. A memory of Kevin bangs at my brain. It was a week before he killed himself. I saw him at the water's edge, head down, shoulders hunched, looking smaller than his six feet. I didn't walk down or call out to him. I regret now that I let the moment pass. I don't want to do that with Mike. But what can I do? Move in with him? Get a full-time job? Give up my class, my hopes, perhaps my future? And if he stays high, he won't listen to me, won't even hear me. My mother's stories about my father cling to my brain.

The phone rings. I plan to ignore it but it's Louise.

"Hi. Why are you calling? I mean . . . didn't my mother come in for the Saturday shift?"

"She did. Tessa, your mother's not doing well."

"I know."

"I suggested an antidepressant. But Nina said she wasn't interested in feeling better. I'm going to go out on a limb here . . . do you know about Peter?"

"Yes, what about him?"

"It was the last time your mother was happy. Thing is, Tessa, living at home isn't helping. Maybe you can do something for her. I was wondering . . . perhaps you'd consider asking Nina to live with you, just for a while. I know that's a lot at this time in your—"

"Louise, my mother would never agree to that. It'd go against her conviction to never depend on her daughters. But I'll try to talk to her."

"Tess, dear, hope I'm not being a busy—"

"No. I know how much you care for her. I'll call you. Bye." And lie down on the couch, my arm across my eyes, too spent to cope with thought.

I wake and it's dark, my leg is numb, prickling. I try to move it around, but there isn't room. I'm on the couch. Jesus, I fell asleep here. I dreamt about my mother. She was trying to get into the diner, but the door was locked.

34

Walking up and down West 75th Street I look for the address, but the building numbers are either missing or faded or simply not there. Maybe it's best to forget the idea and the letter, which I only just read. Marla's bravery, her certainty, that quickness with which she could make decisions, that's not me. But without her, the choice is mine alone. Yet who am I to tamper with fate? Maybe run it by Hack. Not fair, Scotty's his brother. Do something for your mother, Louise said. Would reconnecting with Peter help her? What if I find him lacking or no longer interested? I don't know. I don't know.

At a newspaper kiosk on the corner a man is adjusting piles of papers.

"Excuse me, I can't seem to find this building," and show him the return address on the envelope.

He points. "There, on other side of the street, only even numbers on this side."

"Thank you." I cross over. It's a three-story brownstone sandwiched between a Chinese restaurant and a shoe store. The building's front windows are gritty, shadowed by streetlight, impossible to see through from here.

Am I really going to do this? In my head, my mother's horrified voice at my interference. Somehow that doesn't matter, not when she isn't eating and has no desire to feel better. It doesn't take a rocket scientist to know where that's leading.

I walk up three worn, steep stone steps to an area with a chipped stone bench, and sit, the cold reaching through my clothes. The mauve sky promises more snow. What if Peter's with another woman, what do I say then? Just do it, Tessa, just fucking do it!

The names on the outside bells are indecipherable. Damn. I press one at random and wait. "Who is it," comes through a squeaky intercom.

"Lost one of my keys . . . Could you please—" To my surprise the buzzer sounds. Inside the hallway I search a line of mailboxes where the names are easier to read. I find Peter's, 1B. Jesus, right here where I'm standing.

Don't think, don't think, I press the bell.

"Yes?" Comes through the door.

"Hi. Um. You don't know me. I'm Nina's daughter."

The door opens to reveal a broad chested man, with shoulder length blonde hair, and a short trim beard, wearing sweatpants and undershirt.

"Are you Peter?" I sound like an idiot.

"I am." He sounds as confused as I feel.

"I saw your address on a letter you sent my mother who has no idea I'm here."

He pauses, "Really?"

"Why would I lie?" Then I hold out my hand, "Tessa," I say.

"Peter," he repeats, and his hand warms mine for a second. "Would you like to come in?"

There's enough discomfort to displace the air. "Well . . . " I hesitate.

"Are you hungry?" he suddenly asks.

"Why?"

"How's Chinese? It's a place downstairs, with lots of food. It'll take me a minute to change into something more decent. We can talk there. Won't you come in?"

I do. How could I not, me, a stranger arriving at his doorstep, unbidden and unknown? Anyway, my mother wouldn't have an affair with a pervert.

"Tessa, is your mother okay?"

"Sort of. I mean she's not eating much, but . . . " and suddenly mentioning my mother feels like a betrayal. "Yes, she's okay."

"That's an enormous relief. I won't be long." He disappears into what must be the bedroom and closes the door.

The blue-striped couch is comfortable. Though the furniture is old, fraying, the room is neat, more so than I'd expect from a man living alone. Of course, I'm still unsure that he is living alone. It's impossible to seek the truth about a person in the setup of a room. There are photographs, unframed, tacked to one of the walls, but the window light obscures them. A pile of magazines sits at the side of a round makeshift table, alongside a few books. I can't see the titles but am too nervous to touch anything.

Even more nerve-racking is that this is the man my mother loved. It isn't that he's off-putting, just new. What do I plan to say to him? I have no idea. Hopefully, the right something will come out of my mouth, though my brain hasn't yet let me in on what that might be.

Neither one of us speaks as we head out. It takes but a moment to reach the restaurant, which is small with a few tables and a counter, and none of the usual Chinese decorations, the food though smells temptingly familiar. I follow Peter to one of the tables and we sit across from each other.

The waiter hands us each a paper menu and waits.

Eating isn't possible, but ordering is necessary. "I'll have the fried rice."

"I'll have the same with shrimp," Peter says, as we return the menus to the waiter.

"Are you living with anyone?" I ask, embarrassed by the abruptness, but I need to know.

"No," he shakes his head. "Are you?"

"With a roommate."

"Ah, I see."

"Do you have a job?" Because why is he home during the day.

"Carpenter when I feel like it. What else?" his tone genial.

"My mom said she met you at the veteran's hospital."

"She did."

"Are you ill?"

"Not that I know of."

"Are you a vet?"

"Yes."

"I'm trying to find out about you," I say.

"Are you?" He smiles.

Out the bus window I wave goodbye. I like Peter, I think. How weird is that? A vet, but unlike Hack, he seems grounded and thank God, sober. Though at first uncomfortable his tone and easy responses put me at ease.

He asked about Marla and saw my hesitation—which was less a wish to keep secret than the fear of waiting sadness—and quickly said it was fine not to speak of it. But I did speak of it. I told him about the Miami trip through to trashing Marcus's room. The latter didn't seem to faze him. He knew about loss and death, about grief, he said, and how in the face of it, life changes occur.

Though he was careful not to probe about my mother, I did allow she seemed unhappy, and I hoped getting out to work the Saturday lunch shift at the town diner would help. What he'll do with that remains unknowable. But if I had to bet—

Getting off the bus, my phone rings. I hope it's from Mike, but it's a no-one-I-know call. I've tried to reach Mike several times, left messages. He's not responding, which is worrying.

❋

He watches until the bus turns a corner. Stunned! Nina's daughter here, to see him, how is that possible? Thing is, her arrival feels almost spooky; only a few hours before he'd booked a flight to California.

Thank God she didn't come to tell him that something bad had happened to Nina, just that her mother wasn't eating and seemed unhappy. None of that particularly upsets him, quite the opposite. It opens up hope, which scares him. For months, now, he's grappled with letting go of having a future with Nina, and relegated hope to only a dream; everyone knows dreams are just nighttime movies. Then this little fireplug appears. Even if Tessa hadn't introduced herself, he'd know that face, Nina's face.

Snowflakes drift lazily through the ashy air as he heads up the street, enters the narrow bar, and perches on one of the empty stools. He orders a double Scotch neat. The bartender, a large man, who moves slowly, says nothing, which is a relief to his overwrought brain.

If he goes to the town diner for Saturday lunch, how will Nina react? Sudden surprise can be overpowering, confusing, even cause disbelief, and remembers when his buddy was shot. He couldn't stem the bleeding even threw his body across the open wound. Another medic ordered him to leave, said his buddy didn't need company anymore. Weeks later his buddy walked onto the base on crutches. Peter thought it was an aberration, and when his buddy spoke, the voice exploded in his brain, deafening him. The shrink on base talked him down, explained that after witnessing too much loss, death, and destruction trust in what's real becomes muddied. Well, he trusts that Nina's daughter was here, and even if she didn't explicitly say why, he's not boarding the plane next week.

The bartender silently refills his glass, which to his surprise is empty.

35

Greg tosses his bag on the couch. "Going to shower, Tessa. Bought a cooked chicken, wine . . . in the kitchen."

"I also bought a cooked—" but he's already in the bathroom. Wine is perfect, the day's event still undigested. My mother needs to know; I worked myself into phoning her. She didn't pick up. I was relieved. Mom just had a meal with your ex-lover; he's very nice, talk to you later, not exactly the kind of message I'd leave on voice mail. Anyway, what's done is done; I console myself. Once more I try Mike, who once more doesn't pick up. I send him a text to contact me. If he calls during dinner with Greg, well, so be it.

Cutting up veggies for a salad, the faint staccato sound of the shower reaches through the silent apartment. It brings to mind stormy nights at home, which Marla slept through, but I'd wake, listen to the heavy sea winds slash at the windows, sure the glass would shatter, land on the bed, fearful child that I was. Am I still? Peter said loss and grief create life-changes. He may be right.

"Tessa. Hey," in sweats, his hair still wet, he opens the oven to heat the chicken. "Oh, you have one in there."

"I do. Let's keep yours for another day."

"Is yours free-range?"

"I don't know."

He looks through the wrappings still on the counter.

"Why does it matter, one is already heating?"

"It's not free range," he holds up a piece of wrapping.

"So what?"

"Tessa, the one in the oven isn't healthy, it's been fed antibiotics and cooped up, pardon the pun. Free-range chickens are better.

"What do you want me to do with . . ." I'm pissed.

"Toss it."

"What?" I can hear my family's disbelief. Once again, the difference between us calls out. Then soothe my ire: Greg's a doctor, knows what he's talking about. Still . . . there's no way I'm going to toss a perfectly eatable chicken; I take it out of the oven and slide the hot fowl into the fridge.

At the table, waiting for his chicken to heat, he uncorks the wine, pours a generous amount in each glass. "To you, of course," Greg toasts.

"How's it been at the hospital?"

"Awesome. Awesome. Awesome."

"I get the excitement, some details, please."

"Watched a delicate operation, a diseased kidney replaced with a healthy one. The surgeon was fantastic." He gets up, takes the chicken from the oven, places it on a platter, and brings it to the table, where he cuts it up expertly.

"Do you plan to go into surgery?"

"Honestly, I don't know. Other medical fields excite me as well. For now, I'm just absorbing."

"Your excitement is infectious." And we laugh at my choice of words. "What's it like to treat sick people?"

"I don't feel heroic, if that's what you're asking. A man who had been shot in the arm came into the ER. He had no insurance. Lenox is a private hospital. He was sent to another nearby ER. He put up quite a fight."

"That's upsetting, turning away someone in need. What did you do?"

"Nothing, really. I understand hospital rules. They're necessary to stem chaos."

"Sometimes you have to break rules."

"I suppose. But I fear I've been well schooled not to and wouldn't know how," and tops both half empty wine glasses.

A disappointing response, yet honest, but he's not unfeeling. Me? I'd have fought to admit the guy; I decide not to say.

"What've you been busy with?" he asks.

"My course in photography, took photos while visiting my mother. So, what do you think?" I ask.

"About?"

"My burgeoning career."

"Most fascinating."

"How do you mean?"

"I know little about photography, but learning about it must be invigorating."

"Invigorating, like watching a kidney transplant?" I smile.

"That's about life and death."

"And photography?" Why am I goading him?

"It's about choice, pleasure, creativity I imagine."

"Isn't medicine creative?"

"It's scientific."

"Isn't there an art to science?"

"Maybe," and looks at me quizzically. "You haven't eaten."

"I'm not hungry just tired and buzzed from the wine," and way too critical in this state. "Do you mind if I turn in?"

"Of course not. I'll clean up. Have a good night."

Clothing from Greg's unzipped travel bag is strewn across the couch. Well, it's his place, isn't it?

❋

She's alone in the kitchen, the men watching TV. Out the window dark clouds chase an early sunset. Hack's been doing a lot of the cooking; she owes him a night off. Though there aren't much pickings, she'll bake ziti, then heat whatever bread she can find.

Cutting up an old piece of garlic, remembers how Marla loved the pungent odor. At dinner once, all of them at the table Marla talked about garlic and health. Scotty chuckled with disdain. Marla became upset, angry, wanted to know what was so funny. Scotty wouldn't respond, just shrugged dismissively. His shrugs fill her days now. Whatever fond feelings they once shared, and they did, it's gone. Strangers again.

"Dinner," she calls, placing the plate of ziti on the table.

Her phone rings, Tessa. She doesn't pick up, but she'll have to sooner than later. It's the girl's monitoring that makes her uneasy. She won't make promises she can't keep or pretend she's suddenly "all better," a phrase the girls used when they were little. A mother's grief has no bottom, no end. How to, or even if to say that—well—she won't, at least not yet.

Scotty comes in, beer in hand, pulls out a chair to sit. Hack follows, steadies himself on the back of a chair, sniffs, "Smells like food." She takes the bread from the oven, places it on a dish, then on the table and joins them. For a few minutes they eat quietly. Not hungry, as usual, she munches on a piece of bread.

"Watch anything interesting?" she asks to say something.

"Scotty likes movies about rich people who get what they want, then die like the rest of us." Hack says.

"If you don't like the program, say so," Scotty mumbles.

"I don't disturb matter, haven't you noticed?"

"I notice everything, none of it's worth comment."

"Tessa called?" Hack asks.

"Yes. Didn't leave a message."

"I'll call her, just need to remember that I want to."

"You working tomorrow?" Scotty asks.

"Yes," she says. "Why?"

He shrugs.

After a few bites of the ziti she pushes aside her plate, "Hack would you mind clearing?"

"Why not?"

"Hardly touched the food," Scotty mutters. "A waste."

The early morning rain has ended. Strong, damp sea wind reaches around her bare neck as she heads for the diner. With gas being expensive, Scotty, too, rarely uses the car. If Rico wants him to bartend, he picks him up and drops him off.

In truth, though, walking to town is a chore. She's exhausted all the time. She knows it's part of the depression but also of having nothing, absolutely nothing to look forward to. She tries, she does, to help herself but the "what for" question won't let go. An anti-depression pill won't change her reality, so why spend money on it? Before Marla died, she had energy to spare, energy fueled by the satisfaction of meeting her daughters' needs as well as her own. Now even the few hours at the diner feel too demanding. Responding to customer requests, banter, or complaints seems beyond her. Once during her first marriage her stoned husband bumped into a table and upended her almost finished jigsaw puzzle, scattering the pieces all over the floor, too many to pick up.

Peter stands at the window, dressed since the day dawned. The early rain has stopped. It's been a week of day-by-day waiting for today to arrive, a terrible, restless week that should've been otherwise. Too many nights of sleep eluded him, his head besieged by foolish, sometimes, terrifying thoughts, scenes flipping from dire to romantic to whatever till he had to get out of bed and walk the 2 a.m. streets, which were fairly empty but not as pitch black as the country or the desert. Except for occasional traffic the quiet was comforting. He and Nina never walked anywhere post midnight; she always had to return home by dark. He did resent her other life, the one she lived without him.

It would be considerate to telephone her at the diner beforehand but can't risk Nina telling him not to come. No, he won't chance that. A lost opportunity would do him in. He's already been too slow with her. Should have asked her to leave her marriage earlier, maybe even done the ultimatum thing. It would've risked losing her. She was that determined to wait, but why? Maybe he'll get another chance to ask her.

In the adjacent windows a few lights come on. Its possible Nina won't even be at the diner today. Then he'll go again next Saturday. Now he knows where to find her.

The traffic is ridiculous, cars moving an inch at a time if at all, maybe an accident further up. His luck. The honking horns rattle his nervous system, which is already a fragile thing. Even if he wants to try another route, it'll take forever to get off this road. Wouldn't that suck, arriving after Nina's shift? *Stop*, he orders his brain. He left early; he needs to think less catastrophically.

When he arrives, he'll say, hello, my Nina. No, don't! Never rehearse emotions, that'll get him nowhere. Think aside, not ahead. He conjures up his recent, long put off phone call with his buddy Richie, who is doing better than Peter expected. His buddy's voice did trigger—way too vividly—the glorious hours he and Nina spent there. Still, it felt good to make the call, proof that taking action can turn out well. He's girding himself, isn't he?

Funny, the way life lines up its hours. Three days after talking to Richie, he made a flight reservation. A few hours later his doorbell rings and everything takes a U-turn. Though he has no faith in church or pagoda or synagogue or anything with a spire or a preacher—not after all he's seen—it does make one wonder about some universal puppeteer.

He spots a ramp in the near distance. He has no idea where the ramp leads. Jesus, have mercy. Don't let him get lost. Reminds himself he found his way in a sandstorm. Beeping and inching his car across lanes, he reaches the ramp, drives up onto a road that's amazingly uncrowded, what a crazy world. Stops at a nearby gas station. The attendant seems more than happy to spend time detailing how to get where he's going; probably would've spent another half hour describing the landmarks if Peter hadn't thanked him and gotten back in the car. He's met guys like that before, not just friendly, but needy for someone to hear them.

"All the lonely people," the Beatles sang, and every time he listened, he wanted to be heading toward Nina. And now he is.

Mama, maybe you are sending good thoughts my way. Doubtful. He switches on the radio, searches the dial, nothing pleases, switches it off. He prefers to be in his head just now. Why is that?

The town where Nina works is no different than the two-street towns that border it. Once upon a time, while still at the hospital he planned to leave the drab surroundings and head back to sunny California. Then Nina appeared and reordered the surroundings. Place is only a state of mind. He rolls down the windows lets in the sea wind that now shake the tree limbs.

He drives past the diner three times before parking. He gets out of the car nervous as an adolescent on a first date, takes a deep breath and heads up the street. A tiny bell tingles as the door opens.

36

Heading downtown to Kirsch's class, I'm ridiculously nervous. The other students have probably attended photography courses before this one. They'll be more knowledgeable, but I learn quickly.

Park Avenue is free of people, quieter than Madison or even Lexington Avenues. Mike hasn't returned my calls since the evening he left the apartment. I try him again, leave a voice message: "I must talk to you. Please call me," and try to sound urgent. His silence lays heavy inside me. I don't want rooming with Greg to end my friendship with Mike. I try my mother again. She needs to know I met Peter.

"Hey, Tessa girl." Hack's voice more slurry than usual.

"Did I wake you?"

"Don't think so. How you doing?"

"Okay, on my way to my first photography class, nervous."

"Scared is smart."

"I'm not exactly scared . . . "

"Heightens preparation," his voice weak, tired.

"Are you falling asleep?"

"A little fuzzy at the edges."

What that means, I don't dare ask. "Can I talk to my mother?"

"Louise called, said Nina's staying there a few days."

"Oh, that's a surprise."

"Yeah, maybe. Maybe not."

"Talk later, Hack."

"Definitely."

Good for Louise. My mother needs time away from that house.

As Park Avenue splits onto Broadway the scene changes from gray-white to Technicolor. Many shop windows are filled with colorful Indian fabrics and saris. Cumin and curry scents land on my tongue as I pass restaurants down short flights of stairs. Marla would've loved walking these streets, drawn as she was to all kinds of clothes. When we were little, it was she who insisted on playing dress-up, deciding for both of us who we were to be and from where we came. Sometimes it was France, other times China, but mostly it was India, where she could put together a sari in no time.

I count six of us on folding chairs scattered around the small room. Other than Kirsch, I'm the only female. Near the one window, there's a whiteboard for notes, I guess. Kirsch perches on the edge of a card table and waits for us to move our chairs to face her. "Welcome to all of you," her eyes take us in as if to memorize. "What calls you to photography?"

We are silent, thinking, waiting for one of us to respond and he does.

"I don't know exactly, but I always loved taking photographs."

"My parents only ever celebrate the views of their native country, and I'm going to prove there's beauty here, too," says another.

I'm not ready yet to disclose my thoughts though I could say taking photos gives me a sense of responsibility, but that seems too difficult to explain.

"Why is light important?" Kirsch asks rhetorically. "Without light there can be no photos. Light is essential either by sun, lamp, flash or fire to see what we want to capture. Add to this the lens of our experiences; I'll explain: A photo depends not only on how the light falls but also depends on our point of view. So we need to know or learn who we are."

A few hands go up, mainly making her reiterate what she's already said. I don't raise my hand; I don't know yet what I want to know. She talks some more about lighting and goes to stand in front of the window, her body blocking a chunk of the light, which she calls to our attention. She turns this way and that to demonstrate the way the light behind her changes what we see.

Listening to her talk, and she goes on for a while, it feels as if she wants us to know everything she knows, almost as if she has a need to rid herself of the information. What impresses me most is her concern that we know or learn who we are.

On the whiteboard she writes notes about lens settings and other aspects of the craft for us to copy and study. "That's it for today," she says, and it feels as if the session passed in a nanosecond. To my surprise, I agree to join the others at the coffee shop next door.

Walking back to the apartment, the enthusiastic chatter of the students still with me, Kirsch's words replay in my head: What we see depends on our point of view. Greg and I might not see much of anything the same way. Do I know that for sure? And Mike? Until this temporary breach, I'd say we saw eye to eye on most things.

"Morning," Greg offers, in the midst of pulling a T-shirt over his head.

"You're up early on your day off," I say.

"Habit. Why are you awake?"

"Have to be at my weekend job at six."

In sweatpants and barefoot, he walks around the table and looks at the photos that I'd spread out to study last night, the ones from back home.

"Nice," he says. "Why are they on the table?" Not a remark that satisfies.

Briefly explaining Kirsch's assignment on how to see, I gather them up.

"It's been a few very busy days away at the hospital. It's good to have a day off," he says.

"Why busy?" I place the photos in the briefcase that Kirsch suggested we purchase.

"ER for the last three nights . . . Murder. People come in for the weirdest reasons."

"Like?" Am I really interested?

"Bunions, loose tooth, nothing to treat at an ER, but takes up a lot of doctor time."

"People get scared when something doesn't feel right, don't you think?"

"Yeah, I do. So, listen, I was wondering . . . would you like to do something tonight, a movie or whatever you prefer?"

In a daze I look at him, "A movie sounds good."

"Great."

Why not, I think heading to the shower.

Frank's workplace is an old, creepy-looking warehouse squeezed between two First Avenue row houses. It has a rusty front gate and a dented metal door with a bell that I press.

"Hi, come in." Frank, bundled in a windbreaker and scarf, leads me through the long throat of a foyer to a door that opens onto a parking lot with a loading platform. A few medium sized trucks idle nearby.

"Cargo is brought here from over-booked trucking companies, and then reloaded onto my trucks."

Back inside, he takes me to a small side room that serves as an office with a desk, chair and phone. I'm to answer drivers' calls, take information about any problems, traffic, breakdowns or whatever, and with pins enter the locations on a large wall road map. Drivers who come in will check the map before picking up their loads.

Easy, I think but don't say, and simply nod.

"If you need me, I'll be in a hut out at the lot."

It's a little past noon when I leave the warehouse. With few phone-call problems, it wasn't very busy. The drivers who traipsed through seemed friendly enough, though names weren't exchanged, at least not yet. I head to the subway with more cash in my pocket than usual. Frank pays up front. Though hungry, destination beckons.

About to enter the subway station my phone rings: my mother. I can't talk now. I'll call her later.

On the crowded F train to Queens, even more people squeeze in at each stop. Many hands, including mine grasp the center pole for balance. It'd make an interesting photo, the hands, but the car lighting is wrong. It's taken a while, but I'm learning; I like learning.

Exiting the Jackson Heights Station, not sure exactly in which direction to go, I begin to walk. I've only been here once and that was with Mike. Shops are pressed between six story look-alike brick buildings. Trying to jostle my memory I search for landmarks. The store selling ethnic spices looks familiar. Christ, the racist graffiti still on Mike's building. Rain must've washed off our attempt to hide it. Once more I stare at the ugly words that not only malign Muslims, but also are disgustingly accusatory. Horrible!

For a moment I reconsider phoning Mike; he's probably catching some sleep. But why else have I come here? I phone. He picks up, "What?"

"I'm in front of your building. Come down or I'll come up. I'd love to meet your parents. You have ten minutes. Or I'll ring every bell till I find the Azadi apartment."

Keeping the entrance in view, I pace back and forth. It's cold and I'm chilled and I consider waiting in the warmth of the hall—

"Tess."

"Mike, how are you?" His sallow complexion, cracked lips, and the missing shine in his dark eyes tell me more than I'd like to know.

"You came all the way here to ask how I am?"

"Did you just get home from work?"

"I quit the stupid job like the other job and all the dead-end jobs to come. But to answer your question, I'm good, Tessa, amazingly well, sunny side up. Can't you tell?"

"Why didn't you respond to my calls?"

"Best not to be involved with someone involved."

"Can I buy you coffee? Please?"

"Why?"

"Come on, don't be like this and don't say 'like how.'"

"There's a bar up the street that serves coffee to us regulars. Pretzels, too."

"Lead the way."

He does, walking carefully like someone trying not to step on the lines.

It's a dim, musty place that splinters my determination and leaves me unsure how to continue. We head to a back table.

"I'll have a beer," he says. "Oh right, you're only offering coffee."

Ignoring the sarcasm, I buy two bottles of Beck and take them to the table. "Listen I get it, you're angry at me...."

"Tessa, stop."

I do.

"No deep talk. Okay?"

"Really? Mike I—"

"Don't want to hear that it's dumb or dangerous or any other resembling shit. Want to drink a beer and go home. I need sleep."

"I don't believe your dismissal."

"Your choice."

"You're being self-protective."

"How's the roommate situation?"

"Fine," I say.

"Well, it's been a real pleasure having you come by. Bu—"

"No. You stop this. You're important to me. I'm important to you."

"You're important to your roommate, too, I bet."

"You're so male. Is that all you can focus on?"

He grins. But Greg isn't the problem here.

"I don't know what you're stoned on, but you have vet privileges at a veteran's clinic. They'll help you get into rehab, even give you something to ease the comedown."

He takes a long drink of the beer, chuckles as if the joke's on me. "Where do you think I'm getting the shit? On some corner, I'm not that dumb."

"What are they giving you, and why would they?"

"Oh, that's right, never told you, I carry some shrapnel in the back of my neck, hurts like hell to sleep."

"I didn't notice that when . . . "

"Our intimacy was so short-lived."

"Does it hurt a lot?"

"Pain is subjective, right? I tell them it's an eight. The docs whip out their little white pads and send me to their well-equipped pharmacy on the premises, no hassle. After a few visits, I find another vet clinic, same story, same result. I'm an army ranger, man, that's a lifetime title. These places don't talk to each other. No one's really interested in us after we get out, so if we have the papers it's easy to toss a few Rx's in our direction, no sweat. You have to know how to use the system."

"Fucking proud of yourself, are you? Well, go ahead and bask in your little scheme to outsmart the grownups. It doesn't impress me. It'll be too late too soon."

"No, it won't. The pills quiet the jumping beans in my head that stream the same headline, no present, no future for a Muslim terrorist."

I lean across the table. "Let's not wait. Please? We'll go together to the clinic and then to wherever they send you for rehab. I won't leave your side, till you—"

"See you," he gets up and starts to walk out.

I follow him, watch his uneven gait put distance between us, and run to catch up.

"Mike, wait!"

"What? I made it clear, didn't I? Go home, Tessa. Have a good life."

"One pill leads to another, stopping becomes impossible. I saw it happen up close to someone else that I loved."

"Baby, you can't solve my life in this racist shithole USA. I mean it. Go—live your own. You deserve it."

"I'm not leaving you. I don't want to. I want—"

"What, Tessa, what do you want?" his tone as weary as an ancient.

"I want you whole, well and reachable, by me," my voice a whispery giveaway.

He slides an arm around my shoulders, my body subsides, my face pressed so hard against his shoulder I think he may topple, but he doesn't.

"Tessa, I need sleep." He eases me off him. "We'll talk more tomorrow. I'll meet you in front of your building."

"For sure?"

"What time?"

"I'll be done with work by noon. Let's meet at one." I watch until he disappears into the building.

Heading to the station, my brain on overdrive. Will he show up? Do I really think I can make Mike stop? Haven't I learned anything? Marla also didn't want to stop, and then she couldn't. The late afternoon sunlight does nothing to warm the chill that runs through my body. I've no desire to go to a movie with Greg. If he weren't a doctor, I'd say I didn't feel well. But he'll want to know where it hurts, which isn't explainable.

The waning afternoon light darkens the kitchen as we discuss movies. Nothing sad or scary or stupidly romantic, I don't say. "How about the Chaplin movie at the place uptown?"

"Chaplin?" he repeats without enthusiasm.

"So, okay, not for you, what—"

"Let's skip the movie, go out to dinner. I know a great place."

Of course he does, and he sounds so hopeful and I'm so frazzled.

His hand on my elbow, he steers me to the bar, where he orders a half carafe of wine by a name that I've never heard before. The bartender in elegant white jacket immediately places two glasses in front of us and in short order pours the wine. Soft sitar music emanates from somewhere nearby; an aroma of Indian spices fills the air; and the deep burgundy velvet-covered walls lock out the intrusive noise of traffic and sirens. An atmosphere promising relaxation aided by the golden-hued wine that goes down smoothly.

"I'm glad we decided on this," he says raising his glass. "Cheers."

"Cheers."

"It's good to be away from the demands of the hospital."

"You do work long stretches." I'm boring myself, no doubt, Greg, too, who is trying to engage me more than I him. It's hard to be charming with Mike in my head. Try, Tessa, I tell myself. Try.

"How was your work?" He refills our glasses. "Are you exhausted?"

"No, well, a little. I was only at work for a few hours, then—"

"They're signaling. Our table is ready."

The hostess in a gorgeous silky green sari leads us to a back table, and though the other tables are all taken, the space between them offers a sense of privacy.

"Tonight there is a buffet, if you wish. Something more to drink?" she asks softly.

Greg orders two bottles of Indian beer and another half carafe. "Do you want to take a peek at the buffet first?"

"Yes."

I walk the long cloth-covered table of hot and cold foods, placing dollops of this and that on my plate. Greg, too, fills a plate, but checks each food label before dipping in.

Two bottles of beer await us near frosted glasses garnished with slices of lime as well as another half-carafe of wine.

"So, Tessa, you were saying about not working all day?"

Do I want to continue or . . . ?

"If you'd rather not say . . . "

"I spent the afternoon with a friend trying to get him to go into detox."

"Boyfriend?" he asks quickly.

"Old friend, from childhood," I lie.

"Oh. What's he on?"

"I think opioids. He's a vet who was injured."

"Yeah, it's a real problem, I get it. Can I help?"

Could he? "I don't know. Mike is stubborn, but maybe if I knew of definite places for treatment I could—"

"Tessa, I have access to information. I can locate treatment centers specific to opioid addiction. Some are now starting to test various forms of antidotes, though most of those are still in clinical trials. Maybe, a clinical trial is where he should go, depending. If you want me to meet with him, help him decide . . . "

His tone now professional the way it was when he told Rhonda about her condition. It's a confident voice, which intends to reassure, "Greg, yes, any help would be appreciated, but my friend would never agree to meet with you. I'm grateful though. Thank you."

"Tessa, helping you pleases me. Being with you pleases me," his tone earnest, his eyes taking me in.

"That's sweet, Greg."

"No, sugar is sweet. I'm trying to tell you—"

"I hear you, but just now I can't—wouldn't—know how to respond. I hope you understand."

"It's just that I like you and have for a while now. Selfishly, I hoped that maybe you'd come to feel the same way, or perhaps let the idea of me settle in your thoughts."

"Greg, I'm touched by your words, really, but I'm at this place in my life . . . learning and hoping to soon begin a career. It's not the right time for me to consider any relationship."

"Hey, let's toast to a great evening," he raises the glass of beer.

"To a great evening," I say, and wonder what I'm closing the door on.

On the never dark streets of midtown, Greg leads me toward Central Park of all places, though he won't say why.

"I'm not great with surprises," I warn, unsure if Marla's ghost will follow me.

"I'll take a chance."

"Brave man."

"Not really. If you don't like, we won't do it," both of us a bit tipsy, having finished wine, beer and after dinner drinks.

"You seem much less serious than usual," I say.

"Oh, there are lots of parts of me that will become evident in time."

I laugh; suddenly giddy. "Is drinking one of them?"

"Absolutely, bourbon instead of formula. Kidding. However, I lived with six o'clock cocktail call all my life. My parents, with or without guests, would joke about the hands of the clock moving too slowly. I've developed a tolerance, I believe, having participated in their nonessential talk and essential alcohol since I was in middle school. Actually, no, I was boarding in prep then, but there were so many holidays . . . "

"You describe your wooden leg fondly."

He laughs. "Maybe."

The windy early March air still bites, but the alcohol warms me.

"Are you the only redhead in your family?" he watches me swipe hair out of my face.

"My mother," and realize I didn't call her back.

"Like yours?" he asks.

"Wilder, like her nature," is that true?

"So, you have her hair and her wildness."

"You think so?"

"You are so different from anyone I've ever gone out with. Also, I've never been good at flirting, and—"

"I wouldn't say that."

"Really? Anyway, my dates were often the daughters of parents who knew my parents, so yadda, yadda, yadda."

"Funny hearing yadda come out of your mouth, I mean you're so straight."

"Did you think I was gay? Is that why you decided to stay as my roommate?" he sounds troubled.

"I didn't think about your sexual preferences at all. I stayed because I had nowhere else to go," wine and truth telling, always a problem.

"There," he points. He takes my hand, leads me to a horse and carriage near the edge of the park. "Ma'am, may I have this ride?"

"Oh, this is my surprise, yes, of course."

He helps me up the rather high step into the carriage, comes in after me and throws a blanket across our knees.

Amazed to be riding through the park, where dim lamplight barely interrupts the darkness, and the clip-clop of the horse-hooves is strangely hypnotic; a warm coziness envelops me. Beneath the blanket, he reaches for my hand.

We head out of a wine bar on Lexington where we stopped for a nightcap at Greg's suggestion, both of us now under the influence as we head into the lobby, Greg keeping hold of my hand.

"Have a good night," the doorman says, his expression unsure.

Greg leads me to his room, which had been Rhonda's room and where I haven't been since she died. I notice his clothing spilling out of the open travel bag on the floor. Well, at least it's off the couch, I think. Greg falls back on the bed and pulls me down after him. I watch myself stretch out beside him.

Awakened by coldnessthe cold, my naked body twisted in a sheet, my mind the kind of blank that fears to see or know, I ease out of bed, grab clothes off the floor, and flee to my room before Greg can wake. Jesus, Holy Mother, I mutter eyeing the warn comforter, my head throbbing, my limbs rubbery, my memory wrapped in gauze. What the fuck have I done? Will I have to move out now? How else to avoid the minefield of expectations that I've allowed, perhaps encouraged? I don't even want to guess what Greg will think; it's best I leave before he appears. I'm not capable of dealing.

I dress quickly, hoping coffee will help clear the mud in my head. The hands of the wall clock inch toward six. Oh shit, it's Sunday. Work. I grab a jacket and hurry out. Coffee at the coffee wagon, I think.

Rushing to the subway, the chilly empty streets depress me. I've no idea if Greg's due at the hospital today. Fortunately, there'll be no time to see him before I'm to meet Mike. What to do if Mike doesn't arrive? What to do if he does come? What to do with my throbbing head?

I stop at the coffee wagon, order a cup for me and one for Frank, pluck the phone from my jacket pocket to tell Frank I'm on the way. There's a text from Mike: "Tessa, I'm re-enlisting. Don't shake your head. It's a good solution."

37

Gusts of early spring wind rattle the windows in Peter's car as she watches a darkening sky threaten rain. The last whirlwind days feel like a chapter in a corny, romance novel. Peter walks into the diner, she, shocked to stillness. Louise prods her out the door to be with him, offers to call Scotty. Peter drives to his apartment. They talk for days. They make love tearful with joy, amazed anew they've found each other again. End of story! Not quite, actually, not by a long shot.

Peter's hand moves off the steering wheel to squeeze her arm. They touch each other often to be sure it's still real: they are here together. She knows it will take more than real to erase or at least dim the past months of sorrow. And the loss of Marla won't ever be erased. The loss has also left her afraid, but unsure of what. Yet the stalking shadow of misery has been breached. His presence has grabbed hold, keeping her from further descent. But it's all happening so fast. Already, they've discussed the future. How is that possible?

Peter wants them to move to his California house, a place he's described many times. Being together in a new home evokes possibility, life opening to offer her a last chance. She can't make another mistake. And she won't sneak around anymore; she can't, her lies soaked in guilty tears that can't bring Marla back.

Peter drives up a ramp and parks atop a small incline that faces the beach. The rain comes down heavy, streaks across the windows, pounds on the car, a desperate stranger begging to get in.

"Why have we parked here?" she asks.

"I don't like talking and driving."

"We're only one exit from my house?"

"I know. Listen, I'm coming in with you. Has to be."

"Peter, I need to do this alone."

"You don't. It's safer if I'm with you."

"Scotty isn't going to harm me. But if he sees you, he'll just walk out of the room. That wouldn't help me resolve anything. Besides, it's not the right way to leave, not after so many years. I owe him that, Peter. He thinks I've been with Louise for the past few days."

"I'm worried he'll make you change your mind."

"Do you think I would?" she asks.

"You did once."

"No. I never changed my mind. My life changed. My daughter died. Nothing seemed worth anything. Can you understand?"

"I do. But Marla's still gone."

She slides her hand over his. "I won't leave you again. I promise. You and me."

"I'll park outside the house."

"Don't you believe me?"

"Has nothing to do with belief, just insurance."

"Okay, but for God's sake, don't beep the horn. It may take a while."

"You will pack, right?"

"Oh my God, I'm going to have to build up your trust in me. Yes, I will pack, and it will take a while. If you'd rather wait at the diner, I can—"

"I'll be parked outside."

Rarely are other people's cars parked outside houses in the boonies, she doesn't say.

Pelted by wind-slanted rain, not anxious to face the task ahead, she walks slowly toward the front door. She's already hurt Scotty once.

Thing is, after many years together, there's no good way to do this, though a part of her does wonder if he'll actually care.

In the entryway, stepping out of her wet shoes, she hears only TV voices and finds Scotty dozing in his chair; weather-etched lines track his forehead. Hack, semi-upright on the couch, may or may not be asleep. The TV volume is high, the room unlit and chilly to keep expenses down. She picks up the remote, powers off the TV, which wakes Scotty.

"When did you get in?" he asks with a hint of accusation.

"Can we talk?" her energy waning ahead of her words.

"Do you want me to . . . ?" Hack tries to hoist himself off the couch.

"It doesn't matter," and it doesn't. Hack will remain with Scotty and the thought is comforting.

"What?" Scotty stretches out his legs.

"Peter came by the diner and I'm . . . " her eyes on his face, which remains unchanged. "This isn't easy—I'm not sure how . . . First, I need to say that you've always been reliable, fair and how much I appreciate—"

"Cut the bullshit, Nina."

"I'm not asking for forgiveness. I'm not even . . . Just to discuss."

"What?" his voice impassive.

"Isn't there anything you want to ask me or say?"

"Did you think I'd beg you to stay?"

Is that a real question? Because she'd like to respond, fill him in on the reasons, yes, but also is ready to take the blame, indict her own action, and make her exit inevitable.

"No. Of course not, just that, well, I care about you, I mean—"

"Care?" his expression still unreadable.

"Scotty, we've known each other a long time. It might be better to—"

"Better for who?"

"Both of us."

"I'm not going to make you feel good. Why would I do that?"

If only he'd stomp out, or yell, roar, anything other than the disapproval that shuts her down and makes her second-guess herself. "Look I'm sorry for . . . "

"Sorry does nothing for me," his mouth a deep frown. Any further attempt to communicate will be fruitless.

"Peter is outside waiting for me. It's what I want." Then why doesn't she sound happier?

He stands. "Want a beer, Hack?"

Dismissed, she watches his long back stride to the kitchen. And glances at Hack, whose troubled expression adds to a sorrow she didn't expect to feel. It's not as if she wants to remain with Scotty; she doesn't. But it's harder to walk out than she thought it'd be.

"You will stay with him?" she asks Hack.

"Why not?"

"Are you angry at me?"

"I like you here."

"Why?"

"I don't do questions and answers, not since I shot the last man." His stoned eyes blink slowly as if waking in a too sunny room. "You'll be okay," he adds, and she holds it as a promise.

Walking through the long, narrow hall of a house that contains years of her life: her daughters' voices imbedded in the walls, their footprints across every floor, a scarf here a sock there, signs of their unquestioned existence. Even with Marla gone, the house holds all the years of her before. What happens to that after she leaves?

There's an old duffel bag in the bedroom closet, probably from Scotty's army days. Pulling clothes off hangers, carelessly stuffing them inside, as if they were going to the laundry instead of an unknown closet.

She gets that Scotty's hurt, disappointed, but why should his dismissal pain her? Did she expect them to remain buddies? Why couldn't he show some feeling? Though, when does he ever do that. In the last months he barely talked to her, not even about Marla's death. So why expect him to open up now? Still, he sees the inevitability of the ending, she's sure. Yet he won't allow her to explain, offer reasons.

Something else, too, that's always been there: her sorrow about his broken-ness. God knows she's tried to get him to talk about his past, to let her help him pick it apart, see what it contains: a man who didn't marry till almost fifty; a veteran who wouldn't discuss his war experience; a husband who could only hint at his life before her, allowing her sympathetic imagination to work it out alone. Is it compassion that's causing her guilt, or that his rejection negates the years together? They weren't all bad. It feels unfinished to walk out without being able to acknowledge that truth—except, it is finished.

Glancing at the old nautical flag in the closet, a memory comes too fast to deny.

It was cold the day they took a ferry across to New London, the little girls dropped off at her parents for a few hours. Holding hands, she and Scotty walked from one pier to another, investigated the boats made small talk with some of the men handling heavy lines. In a tiny museum, Scotty bought her the flag. They had drinks in one of the bars, the adventure coming to a close. On a bench waiting for the ferry back, the cold got colder. Scotty opened his coat, wrapped it around them, warming her even more than the alcohol. Ah, nothing is ever all good or all bad, is what her mother always said.

She looks at the duffel, which is almost full. There seems no way to leave without baggage.

Scribbling Peter's address and his and her phone numbers on a piece of paper, she tucks it into the dresser mirror.

The rain is coming down hard when I leave the warehouse and check my phone. Two texts from Greg asking how I am. He'll want to talk about last night. I can't. I won't, delay is best.

Clearly Mike won't be coming to meet me. Should I take the train to Jackson Heights, try to dissuade him from reenlisting? Is it better to die in the desert or here, in some drug den? No choice at all. Detox, rehab is the only way to survive. Right? Who better to ask than Mike, who won't talk to me?

Waiting for someone?" Frank asks, opening an umbrella over both of us.

"Undecided whether or not to visit my friend Mike, who wants to reenlist."

"Bourbon or coffee?"

"Bourbon sounds best, but I haven't eaten yet."

"I'm onto the diner now. Keep me company till you decide."

"Sounds good." Neither of us speak as we head to the bus-shaped diner near the East River. Silence doesn't bother Frank.

The long, narrow place is bustling with lunchtime customers. We sit at the counter, and each order a Reuben sandwich.

"Your boy was a Marine?"

"Army Ranger."

"He misses the life?"

"He can't seem to find a place for himself here." Saying so fuels my need to see Mike.

"You don't want him to go?"

"It's more complicated." Frank won't probe, but it feels good to talk about it. "As a Muslim and a vet, finding work has been a river too wide to cross."

"Nine-eleven has changed the bad to worse."

"It's what Mike says, too. But he's into drugs, just, maybe going back in would help him."

"Does he need help to make the decision?"

"I don't know, only that he's stubborn."

"Me? I decide nothing till I've had a good night's sleep."

Not sure if he means this as a message for me or for Mike.

We walk out together; the rain has stopped. "Thanks for lunch," I say, "See you next week," and walk toward the subway. The phone rings, my mother.

"Hi how are you?" And instead of the subway, I head back toward the river.

"Good, better, though sad about Scotty, after all the years . . . "

"What?"

"I'm with Peter, so thank you."

"What?"

"Are you having trouble hearing me?"

"No, of course not. What's—"

"Calm down, I'll fill you in. Peter came to the diner."

On the river path, the water busy churning up wake behind a barge, I listen to her voice hurry along as if she might forget something in the package of newness about her life that she's handing me. I can't take in all that she's saying except that nothing in my life sounds as daring or important as what she's laid out.

"California, mom? That's far. I mean, are you sure?"

"No, but Peter makes me courageous. He couldn't be more sure."

Suddenly I, too, want to do something daring, unexpected and need her to offer serious advice that I can climb like an escalator, because I'm very down.

"Mom, where are you now?"

"In the car sitting next to Peter."

"And you're sharing . . . ?"

"No secrets. Tess, Peter wants to say a word."

"Mom, no, not—"

"Hi Tessa, just wanted to say thank you for your visit that changed so much."

"You're welcome," I say, as Scotty comes to mind.

"Tessa, are you there?" my mother takes the phone.

"What did Scotty say?"

"Nothing, really. I hurt him again and it hurts me to remember that."

"What about Hack? Will he stay?"

"Yes, and you should call him. Tessa? Is this a bad time? Where are you?"

"I'm walking home along the East River."

"Why?"

"Mom, not important. I'm feeling a bit edgy is all."

"Does it have to do with that guy Mike you've talked about?"

"In a way. I care about him . . . he's still taking stuff, but I believe he can stop. Not everyone follows the same path."

"Tess, he won't stop. It doesn't work that way. I'm not going to try and convince you only remind you of what you already know."

Hack, Marla, and now Mike, and yes, my father, too: a list embedded in my brain. "Maybe you're right."

"We won't be leaving New York for a while but promise that you'll come stay with us in California. I can't go without knowing that I'll see you."

"Yes, of course you'll see me." I need this call to end.

"And you have to spend time with us before we go."

"I will."

"Okay, talk later."

My mother moving to California, how do I process that? So much to pull apart, taffy-like: She sounds less suicidal, but then her quick decisions to leave Scotty and Long Island? Peter seems okay, but has nil to do with my life. Scotty had little to do with my life, too, yet he is or was my true and honest stepfather. So am I supposed to miss him, mourn him, phone him and offer condolences? Clearly not the latter, which isn't Scotty's style. I try to conjure what Marla might say. But all I hear is the disdain for Scotty that never left her. Suddenly a wave of aloneness sinks me. Is it because my mom is going so far, or that my home as I knew it is gone?

I sit on a damp bench, wishing Mike beside me. Soon he too will be off to some godforsaken desert. I phone him. It goes to voicemail. "Mike, whatever you decide, I won't interfere, but don't you dare leave without contacting me."

A tourist ferry slowly passes, the deck crowded with onlookers, and what do they see: a woman on a bench, which tells them nothing at all about where I am.

Back at the apartment, my mother's news still spinning in my head, refusing to find purchase, a sense of disconnection leaves me feeling empty. I read Greg's note taped to the fridge: "Taking a walk, be back soon. We didn't do anything last night except pass out." Is that true? Why would he lie? Was I that drunk? Jesus, Tessa, didn't I warn you to be more careful? His parents would surely disapprove.

"Are you here," Greg calls closing the door behind him.

"Here," I say. "How was your walk?"

"Nice."

Which tells me nothing, but there's awkwardness between us, or is it just in me? Classic, isn't it? If you want to ruin a friendship, sleep together. What is our friendship? "We drank a bit much last night," I say.

"But it was a lovely evening. I enjoyed it hope you did. Want some tea?"

"No, I mean to the tea. Yes, it was a lovely evening." It's true, I realize, which confuses me more than I already am.

"Are you sure, I'm dipping in the tea bags," he says.

"Yeah, okay, tea sounds good."

Greg brings two steaming mugs to the table and sits across from me, "About last night," he begins.

"I'm horrified that I passed out," I say.

"I did as well and want to apologize."

"For what?"

"Tessa, you were next to me, and I didn't, couldn't . . ."

"Greg, it's for the best."

"Why do you say that?"

"This Mike I mentioned, he's not a childhood friend . . . well, I care about him and—"

"Oh, I see," his disappointment immediate.

"I'm in a weird state," I try to amend. "So, keep that in mind."

"If that's what you'd like."

The disappearing daylight darkens the kitchen. He switches on the overhead light. "I don't like dark rooms."

"Why?"

"Must be a reason but I don't know what it is. I'm going to do some studying, see you in a bit." His long legs cross the room in a few strides.

I've upset him. Do I care? I do, but why: Because he's a sweet guy and tries to please me, and I'm a grumpy, ungrateful recipient? Gazing at his untouched tea, my brain making decisions without alerting me, I go down the hallway, stop at Greg's half-open door, and push it open. He's lying face up on his mussed bed, no medical text in sight.

"Hi," I say.

"Hi," he replies, perplexed. "Are you okay?"

I perch on the side of the bed. "Yes. No. I don't know how to explain."

"You're confusing me," his voice low.

"I can do that to people."

"Is that what you've come in to do?"

"I think to apologize for being such an ingrate."

"Oh. Would you like to say more?"

"It's been an awful day, is what. I was afraid I'd slept with you while drunk, which I don't approve of. And my mother just left my stepfather and is moving to California with her lover, who is a nice guy, but . . . "

"Is it okay for you to come down here beside me so I can give you a hug?"

"That's kind."

"Doctors are kind, yes?" His arms open wide.

I have a fleeting image of Marla flat down in the snow, her arms wide, declaring, "Look, I'm an angel."

With his limbs wrapped around me, the mattress warm from our love-making, which was quiet, slow, and unexpectedly satisfying.

"Are you comfortable?"

"Yes, and you?" I ask.

"Amazingly."

We whisper back and forth though there's no one here but us.

The room is dark and the green clock digits blink 8:02. "Do you sleep with a nightlight?"

"Used to, not anymore. I've evolved. Are you hungry?"

"For steak and mashed potatoes," I say.

"We'd have to go out for steak. We have pork chops that I can prepare."

"What about the mashed potatoes?"

"A major problem, I can see. I could go down to the deli and—"

"Greg, I'll make a salad to go with the chops."

"Does that mean we have to get up?"

"Usually."

"But then I'll have to uncurl from you."

"You will."

"I'm not really that hungry."

I laugh. "Well, I am," and gently unravel my limbs.

I traipse to the kitchen, Greg close behind. The past hour, though more than pleasing, already doesn't sit well. Sleeping together while living here rent-free is a mistake, one that Mike predicted, one that I didn't mean to happen, one that I need to rectify. If there's a solution, and there must be, then finding my own place is it. Immediately the stress of not having money opens its biting mouth. It's too much to think about now—on the shelf it goes till tomorrow. I gaze out at a rain-filled, starless sky, listening to Greg's preparations behind me. Pull it together, Tess, there's work to do.

38

Exiting the unlit Longwood Avenue subway entrance, I'm struck once again by the number of people outdoors going every which way with intention. The place has stayed with me since I came here to check out that studio, which no doubt is long gone. I'm here for a different reason today. Kirsch assigned us to explore a part of the city through photos. I knew I'd choose the South Bronx.

I pass bodegas, mini-supermarkets, bars, pizzerias, and 99 Cents shops; stores selling furniture, shoes, and clothing are all so close to each other they must share walls. The smells of garlic, onion, and spices along with an almost sweet scent of decay are hard to miss. Slow-moving truck traffic offer foghorn beeps of impatience at the double-parked cars as they make their way to the Cross Bronx Expressway, which I read has cut through neighborhoods with a serrated knife.

Up a slight hill to a narrow street of six-story high brick buildings, I study the graffiti-covered facades. I take a few shots of naked windows peering down on uncovered, overflowing garbage cans below a perfect cobalt-blue sky.

On Southern Boulevard, passing several storefront churches, doors open, I peek inside one. Sunlight streams across the dusty floor sending hordes of motes into the air. Two people sit on folding chairs. The altar decorated with icons and candles. I don't dare disturb the scene with a click of a camera. But across the street from the church, I snap two shots of a storefront Methadone clinic, with grimy windows and people lined up waiting to get in. Thin, so thin, they look . . . and I shake Mike out of my head. He can't be in there now. I'm working.

The boulevard leads me uptown to the bustling Hunts Point Wholesale Market, where food is both sold and brought in for distribution. Customers bargain in many languages. No one pays me any attention as I take a shot of a pyramid of mangos piled higher than my head, and then aim the camera at workers in sweat-stained shirts lifting heavy crates from nearby vans.

After a long while of walking the cracked sidewalks, where rivers of debris run along curbsides, what calls out to me most is the diversity of faces and the vibrant voices that shout back and forth without caring who overhears. It's a swirling, crowded, always moving beehive of a neighborhood that is living and dying and can't be captured by one, two, or three photos, only the slow train of a film might do it justice.

As I head to the subway and back to the apartment, one last photo insists on itself: an open trash bin on fire, slim orange flames lick at the refuse as black smoke billows up toward a billboard advertising Caribbean vacations.

In the blue dusk, a shadowy figure leans against Rhonda's building. "Jesus! Mike?"

"Hey Tess."

"What are you doing here? Why didn't you answer my calls? Why—?"

"Whoa, too many questions."

Not nearly enough, I think, as I step closer. "Are you okay?" He's so thin. His beautiful lashed eyes glassy, his coppery skin yellowish.

"Fine as silk," it's Hack's slow drawl. Even if I wanted to, there's no denying he's stoned.

"Mike, I worry about you."

"That's a problem I don't want to have. Let's find a bar."

We head toward Second Avenue to search out a place. The fast clip of my thoughts silence me. Why is he here? What has he come to tell me?

Except for the ceiling, everything in the old bar is made of wood: counter, floor, paneled walls, the few tables and chairs. Dimly lit, dusty and uncared for, could we have chosen a worse place? No wonder we're the only customers. The bartender, flipping newspaper pages, looks annoyed when Mike interrupts to order two beers.

"I'm going to re-up," he announces as we settle in our seats.

"You already told me. But why?"

"Nothing here for me." His words cut like a shard of glass.

"Mike, just consider rehab and—"

"Never again. Went to one last week, just for fun, you know. Some asshole intake shithead said my Arab brothers flew in to kill his grandfather or some such crap. I didn't take it well."

"Oh Mike, that's awful."

"So, I'm leaving the free world."

"But you hate war."

"I'm a decorated Army Ranger, but you know what, no one cares. And you know what again? I don't blame them. Hey, not to worry, the Afghan people, they like me." He finishes off his beer, takes a pull from my untouched bottle.

"There are other kinds of jobs. You could try the police academy?"

"I hate those fuckers. Why would I become one?"

"Just a suggestion to keep you here?"

"Don't bother."

"Is that what you're doing, Mike? Giving up?"

"Yeah, maybe, so what?" he says, his hands shaky. "I'm getting more beer. You?"

"No," and watch his slow gait to the bar.

Whatever I say won't matter. He's too stoned to care. Anyway, it's not up to me, hear that, Tessa? Not entirely, I think.

"Thing is—" He places two beers on the table, both for him. "I'll have to detox before signing. The only way to get back to my unit."

"Good, Mike, detox is a really good move."

"Don't get excited. One of my buddies will put me up while I go through whatever. I can't do it at home. It'll freak out my parents."

"And then will you stay off the—"

"Probably not."

"Why not?"

"Give up the rush that chases away all the ugly and leaves me fine as silk? Why would I? It's magic."

"Why can't you just try?"

"Why couldn't your sister?"

"That's mean."

"Everyone knows what's good for me. They don't. You don't. Okay?"

"Far from okay. I'm not that easy to push away."

"That's what I love about you."

Aware of the hot button word, neither of us says anything. He finishes his beer and begins on the second.

Two elderly men come in and sit at a nearby table. Their presence feels restrictive.

"Let's go," Mike says, draining the second bottle.

"Where to?"

"The subway. You can walk me."

"Nice of you," the station being only yards away.

At the entrance, I stop myself from reaching out to hold him here, but he's already taken the first steps down. "Will you write?" my pathetic words depress me.

"If I have something to say. Okay?"

"Okay."

He takes the rest of the stairs carefully, holding on to the railing. I watch till only his absence remains. A woman about to descend into the station asks if I'm all right. And realize my hand is on my chest. "Of course," I say, which sounds as hollow as the moment and begin to walk, destination unknown.

He won't write. Staying in touch implies a promise he knows he can't meet, deceit and pretense not allowed. We're a lot alike and read each other easily. It's as if there's some kind of membrane connecting us. "Stick with your own kind," they said where I grew up. Mike would agree. If only he wasn't on drugs, but he is, big time, it seems. Unlike Marla, who was the fly caught in a web of dreams, Mike's addiction feels as deliberate as Kevin's gunshot. It frightens me.

Taking out my phone, I call the house and pray Hack will answer. He does. "Hey," I say.

"Tessa, girl," his voice low.

"My mother told me what's going on. How's Scotty?"

"Not saying anything he doesn't mostly say."

"What? Never mind. Can I ask you something?"

"Don't know till you do?"

"Why didn't you ever try to get off drugs?" Even as I ask, the question feels intrusive, but I need to know.

"To do what?"

"Have a normal life."

"No such thing."

"There is, Hack. Love, family, a job."

"I don't want to discourage you."

"Scotty believes life is a ball of shit. Do you?"

"I'm not suffering, not anymore, not after I pop goody-good drops."

"I know a wonderful guy, a vet who's beginning to take stuff."

"His pain is new. Mine isn't and soon he won't feel his."

This isn't helping. "Listen, tell Scotty hello for me. I'll call again."

"Yeah, we pick up the phone."

"Are you okay? You sound unusually tired."

"Must've been cavorting."

"Bye, Hack."

"Tessa in the city," he recites and clicks off.

Don't want to return to the apartment, don't want to chat with Greg, don't want anything to eat, don't want to sleep want only to rid my being of the invading pain of loss.

Manhattan lights blaze, unlike back home where the darkness stays dark.

Peter's gone to buy wine. She's alone in his sublet and the sudden quiet brings to mind the beach. How dark and ungiving it'd look at this time of evening. Outside his first-floor window people pass close enough to touch. Strange. Back home she'd—but it's no longer her home. She's without a home. Does she have it in her to make another? To change strange spaces into familiar rooms, which she did for her daughters and both husbands? She isn't sure she even wants to tackle that. So tired after the loss of Marla, can she call up the energy? Peter talks in heavenly words about his place in California; she believes him. But a place isn't a home. Twice now she's walked out of dwellings that she made into homes. Repetition scares her.

Peter wants to know her worries, what she's thinking, which isn't easy for her. She's always kept so much to herself; she had to. Even now admitting unhappy thoughts is to remember how much they still cling. She doesn't want to bring old misery or new doubt into their relationship. But she's not brave enough to enter a new life without fear or question. Yet she can't let it go, this chance for something better.

It's about trust, she understands. Peter calls it the trust that glues. He's right. But a man who's never married or had children carries different baggage. Her past is the backpack she wears.

Last night in bed he said she seemed pensive. She was. With so much change, her head was in a whirl, she explained. She didn't say that like the crumbs left after the cake is eaten, she can't quite brush off the remnants of guilt, which dog her. That Marla's death makes her question her right to a new life: How dare she be happy?

"You always give in to the should-s. You never do what you really want," Marla's scolding words come back to her.

She is doing what she wants, isn't she? She checks the time, grabs her coat. He's waiting at the BYOB restaurant down the street.

39

Stepping into the train, my briefcase in hand, which makes me feel important, I find a seat. The car rattles and sways and rocks me; I close my eyes. Unable to sleep these past nights, I'm tired, but no way would I miss today's final session. It's Mike's fault; he won't release my brain. As soon as I lie down images flash in my head: Mike crossing against the light, hit by a car, and I think, accident or deliberate? Mike shooting up in some alley, and I think, no, not there yet, but how long before he is? I blink away the awful scenes. But despite the deep breaths Sister Agnes intones, a fearful emptiness takes hold to keep me tossing and turning.

What wicked destiny sends me into the lives of people on drugs? I'm a failure at helping. I don't want the job, there's no payoff in feeling inadequate.

As Kirsch's session reaches its end, I share the collective reluctance to leave this teacher. I'll miss the students as well. Over these past weeks we've grown close. The classes, plus the coffee shop gatherings, plus the few hours of daily modeling had temporarily silenced my what's-next worries, which now raise their perky selves. Though our cells have recorded each other's phone numbers, I somehow doubt we'll stay in touch. Unlike me, they're going on to an advanced class, which no way can I afford. Modeling only allows for the audit of one course, which is now over.

But there's so much more I need to learn. The cocoon has been breached but no butterfly yet has emerged. Once I find a full-time job and a place to live, which could take a while, photography could end up sadly unattended. And this after Kirsch—by some indefinable magic—opened my eyes wider than ever before and made me believe that becoming a photographer is doable. Will there be enough hours in a day to work, study, and then roam the streets taking photos? Or will I be too weary to do more than stare at nighttime TV like so many where I grew up? It was Marla's fear, too.

"So, listen up," Kirsch says, stuffing papers in her briefcase. "I have some info to relate. In a short while I will be on the way to North Africa. My project grant has come through and I'll be photographing faces in several countries for the book of portraits I plan to develop."

We whoop and clap loud and long. We love this woman who has earnestly taught us so much.

"Thank you. And those of you that plan to take the advanced class let me suggest Tia Johnson. She's an excellent teacher and works with students out in the field. You are all invited to my place for cheese and wine on Saturday at three, the address there on the board. One more thing, Tessa and Jackson, please come up here."

Kirsch slides an arm around each of our shoulders, "Hey, you two, I submitted some of your photos to the Institute's yearly contest. Great news. Jackson, you came in second, and Tessa, you won first prize. Big congratulations!" More applause. We look at her, at each other, and Jackson says, "Wow," which I repeat like an idiot.

Too revved for the subway, I walk uptown. Not religious, not mystical, nor am I a believer in coincidence, yet there must be a force at work. Fate? Chance? Or is it the unstable universe? Mike needs to hear the news. He taught me how to use a camera. He had my first photos developed. He encouraged me to take photography seriously. He deserves to know first and foremost. Taking the phone from my pocket, I call him. It goes to voicemail. Though not a message I want to leave on a machine, I tell him that I've amazing news and to call me. He may already be in the midst of detoxing. Or is he ignoring me? The thought reignites the sadness that refuses to release me.

I remind myself that happy events don't erase sad ones, but live side by side, perhaps to offer caution. My mother is sad to hurt Scotty but glad to be with Peter. How does she manage that? A vivid memory of Marla during recess: she's running ahead to capture the seesaw, to climb it and stand in the middle her legs balancing the board, shouting, "I am up-and-down."

A drink to celebrate, I think. Clearly, the bar is where I've been heading even if I didn't know it. Funny thing the way the mind works. Will it sadden me to be at the bar without Mike? Probably. It's a test, I tell myself. Mike's leaving the country and I need to go on, don't I? Yes, but also, I need to know he's okay, and even as I think this it occurs to me that I may never hear from him again. Stop, Tessa, no torturing allowed, good day today, great day, I tell myself, remember that, please, I pray.

The bar isn't crowded. I look around, can't help it. The occupied tables hold no one I know. Then I see Frank up at the bar and I'm elated. It's an omen, I insist, a good one. He's the first person I met in New York and will be the first to hear my good news.

"Frank?"

"Hey, nice surprise," he says. "You waiting for your friend?"

"I came to have a celebratory drink," and maybe to feel near Mike.

"You're beaming, must be—should I guess?"

"No. You'll guess all the wrong things."

He chuckles. "Okay, spill it."

"I just won first prize and seven thousand dollars in a photography contest!"

"Bourbon or champagne?"

I laugh. "Bourbon, please. I should treat you." I slip onto a stool as the bartender pours the drinks.

"That's real money. Does that mean you're quitting the job?"

"No. That is, not till I find an apartment." And realize how crazy that must sound, but don't bother to explain further.

He lifts his glass.

I take it down straight, then call my mother to tell her the news.

Greg and I sit at a table for two on chairs high enough to climb. He looks weary. He's been on call, hasn't slept. But hearing my news he insisted we go out for a drink to toast my win.

"Here's to you and more such awards," is he surprised, I wonder?

"You're exhausted," I say.

"I am, but this win has to be given its due."

"You're sweet." And he is, and has been toward me since we met.

An elderly couple at a nearby table, heads bent toward each other, talk quietly, secretively, it seems, telegraphing an aura of together forever, or is that me thinking wistfully?

"What's next in your bourgeoning career?"

"The class is finished, the modeling work, too. I could go on to the advanced, but . . . I don't know, the prize makes me restless." Actually, winning the contest has made the usual feel like a waste.

"You'll figure it out."

"Greg, I'm thinking about getting my own place." The words out before I realize it's what I want to say.

"Why?" his shocked tone almost accusatory.

"My brain is a jumble, and having my own space may help me to decide what I want to do."

"Is it because we slept together?"

No fool, he. "I want us to get to know each other better, I do, but not while you're paying my expenses."

"Why does that matter?" Says a man who never had to worry about livelihood.

"I need to make my own way, and succeed at it." And the truth of it lands in my chest. "Does that make sense?"

"Not entirely, you have plenty of time and space in the apartment to think or do whatever, and . . . it's not me that's paying, it's my parents."

"Who probably don't know I'm in the apartment?"

"I guess. But, Tessa, if that bothers you, I can tell them. I don't care what they say about it. It's my life and—"

"That's just it, Greg. It's my life, too, and I need to own it, to feel how that feels, to experience the freedom of knowing that I can take care of myself."

"And then?" Greg's disappointment, perhaps anger, is apparent.

"We'll see. You're tired, we should go."

Returning to the apartment, Greg heads straight to his room. I can't blame him for not understanding what I've just come to myself. Causing him unhappiness doesn't feel good, but he had to hear it. I do want to get to know him better, that's true. What I didn't say is that I need my own space to grow my confidence, to know how far my edges can reach. A flash memory crosses my mind: myself at six or seven, trying to reach a high shelf to retrieve whatever, when my mother suddenly does it for me. Even now I remember the disappointment at having my near achievement short-circuited.

Still there are questions, too many to silence. Do I need a full-time job, or will Frank's job suffice? Find a cheap apartment first? Or use some of the money now to register for the advanced . . . How is it possible to suddenly have options yet feel stuck? Is this what happens to people who come into money? It's not as if it's a million dollars. That would send me traveling, camera in hand, to capture the contrasts between good and evil that exist everywhere. I'd also give my mother a bunch of money, which she, too, wouldn't know what to do with, never having dreamt of having excess. Rein it in, Tessa it's seven thousand dollars, a bit less than a million.

Peering down at the concrete slab of street I flash on the old cul-de-sac road. The sinkhole I'd scrabble down to be alone to day-dream, where only Marla knew to find me. It was a desolate road, but it led me out.

The buzz of the intercom startles me. It's late.

"Yes?"

"Mike is here, wants you to come down."

"Thanks. I'll be right there."

Grabbing my jacket, I close the door gently. Too impatient to wait for the elevator, I take the stairs down, my anxiety high. A night visit, this can't be good.

The doorman points outside where I go. Mike leans against the building, the smell of beer hard to miss, so, too his stoned, sleepy eyes. Seeing him so out of it suddenly infuriates me.

"It's late. Why are you here?"

"Hey, Tess," he slurs a bit. "So, what's the good news?"

"I won first prize in a photography contest along with seven thousand dollars. You taught me how to use the camera, developed my first photos, encouraged me toward photography." The words rush out dutifully, yet the truth of it softens my anger. How easy it was to forgive anything Marla did because I loved her. How did that help her?

"I take full responsibility," his words come slow as if he needs to pull them off some sticky paper. I should've known better than to expect him to shout hooray. It'd take more energy than he's capable of.

"We can't just stand here," I say quietly. Already, his presence threatens to erase the promise of the previous hours. And for the first time ever I wish he hadn't come.

"I suppose upstairs isn't an option," he says.

"It's not. Greg is asleep."

"Need to protect the roommate."

"Stop, Mike. Did you come here to upset me?"

"You beckoned, I came, though I did think I shouldn't."

"There's a twenty-four-hour diner on Lexington."

"You say, I obey."

And once more it's Hack's voice I hear, not Mike's.

It's a short block to Lexington. Except for two people at a back table the diner is empty, quiet, inviting of secrets, though for us it seems little is hidden. We head to a booth. "I'll get us coffee," I say.

I order two coffees and two toasted muffins, and wait at the counter. It's Mike, I remind myself, my Mike, who's come to celebrate my good news. Yet his disheveled self leaves me feeling sad and helpless.

"Coffee will be good for you, take it black." I place the tray on the table.

"Want to drink it for me, too."

"You haven't lost your humor."

"Not yet," and his desolate tone lands inside me.

"Are you done with detox," I ask, though clearly he's not.

"I stopped it."

"But you want to reenlist?"

"Except I don't."

"What aren't you saying?" my voice suddenly too loud in the quiet diner.

"I detoxed for two days, most unpleasant. The bastards at sign-up wouldn't have me, probably saw my shit face. So, why put myself through the rest of detox? For what: To kill my non-enemies? Came to my senses. That's the story."

"Your twisted tale makes sense up to a point. Have your parents—"

"I don't live there anymore."

"Where do you live?" my alarm clear.

"This buddy, that place, I manage."

Mike, homeless—"Listen to me, please," I plead, wishing and not wishing I had my own place for him to stay. "You must detox in rehab. It'll be easier. I'll go with you."

"You already offered, and I already said no."

"But Mike . . ."

"Tessa, it's ahead for you. You're primed. And I'm glad. Getting off drugs has no upside for me. Understand? I need them. I want them. I don't care about the outcome. Here's more truth. I'm tired, you can't imagine how tired."

I slide my hand across the table to grab his.

"Jesus, don't. Pity isn't helpful."

"It isn't pity."

"What then?" his sleepy eyes steady on my face.

I could say love. "Comfort."

He laughs, it's a harsh sound, and he removes my hand. "Why am I having this conversation? It's annoying. I need to go."

I don't try to stop him, maybe even want him to go, which confuses and upsets me more. "When will I see you again?"

"You won't." Is he reading my mind? Do I know my mind? A plummeting feeling turns my stomach.

"Why the surgical cut off?" I ask not sure why.

"You'd end up a caretaker. That would piss me off. I don't want to be pissed off at you." He gets up, shoves the uneaten muffin in his jacket pocket. I follow him out.

We walk the short distance to my building.

"How will I know if anything—?"

"You won't. Don't phone me, Tessa."

Close to tears, I hurry past him to the lobby.

Upstairs, thank goodness, Greg asleep. I tiptoe to my room, close the door gently, slip out of my jacket and lie on the bed fully clothed, unwilling to think about the last hour. Not possible. Mike's weary eyes, his thinner than thin body etched on my brain along with his definitive words that couldn't have been clearer. Perhaps it was the only way to help me separate. Did he know that? Do I?

It's strange to find herself at the VA hospital again. It's been more than a while. Still, she maneuvers easily through the hallways, which are quiet. It's late. The hospice wing isn't far from the cafeteria. The familiar mixture of food and medicinal smells remain as cloying as ever. Peter wanted to come in with her, but she asked him to wait in the car, that Hack was too ill for more than one visitor.

She enters a large room with two cubicles. Hack's the only patient, his bed near the window. He's propped up with copious pillows. She nods to Scotty who gets up from his chair and walks past her.

"Hack, going for coffee be back." He's out the door before she can thank him for letting her know. Yet she's relieved he's left; and wonders at the quickness with which the ties unravel. She sits in the chair he's vacated.

Hack's thin face looks older his sleepy eyes seem far away,

sedated. Not sure he realizes her presence she takes his bony, dry hand in hers, wants to clasp it, but fears to. "Hi Hack. I'm here."

"Me, too."

She smiles. Notes his cracked lips have been moistened. A nurse? Was it Scotty? "Are you in pain?"

"Waiting hurts."

"Waiting, Hack?"

"Finished with it," a whisper.

"Why?"

"Ready, aim, do it, done," his voice fading.

"I'm listening."

"Me and the demons . . . the long sleep."

"I think I understand."

"You, do." His eyes close.

She sits quietly, his hand in hers, not sure to leave or stay. He's witnessed so much in his short life, too much, that's always been clear. She remembers how Hack's temporary move in became permanent after Marla died. He did it without fuss. Hack never fussed. It was Hack who left food at her bedside all those weeks she lingered there, and who took back the barely touched plates without comment. Hack, who did what he could for her. He was her friend. He didn't judge her. It helped. Glancing at his still closed eyes, she leans over, lays a lingering kiss on his feverish forehead. "Thank you, dear Hack."

Sad to the bone, she takes the old route out to avoid going through the wards. She can't handle seeing more wounded vets. Back then this route led her to the lawn, to Peter. He'll want to know about the visit. She'll tell him about Hack's readiness to die, but how to communicate the loss of a shared past, she doesn't know.

40

Kirsch's place on Jane Street in Greenwich Village is a block away from the Hudson River. It's on a street of two- and three-story well-kept brick row houses with flowerpots on windowsills and steps that lead to glass-paneled front doors. Kirsch's apartment is on the top floor of the corner house. Entering the hallway, it occurs to me that after today I may never see Kirsch again, which saddens me. Since Marla died, I need to hold on to those I care about, though Mike let go of me, didn't he?

The door ajar, voices tell me I'm not the first to arrive. It's a studio, with a kitchen cove, bed, TV, nothing frilly about it. I'm guessing its home base to her comings and goings. On either side of a worn couch is a card table with chips and dips and several bottles of wine.

On another table, our winning photographs are propped against some books. Jackson's shots of old refrigerators on debris-filled lots tell the tale of a Brooklyn neighborhood, his title: *Waiting For Construction*. Alongside it is my South Bronx triptych, titled *Rumors of Life*.

All six of us have shown up for the party and cluster around Kirsch as she explains the origin of some of the photos, paintings, and tapestries that cover the wall.

"They are my memories," she confesses.

"What's the story of this one," Jackson points to a large, framed photo bathed in sun. In the midst sits a woman with a leathery face

269

and young eyes. Wrapped in scarves, she looks past the camera. Behind her tents and people are silhouetted by the sun.

"I took this on my first trip abroad. It's a refugee camp near Jordan, the misery so apparent it felt wrong to take any photos. In broken English, this woman said, 'Take it, show it, don't hide it.' So, I did, shot an entire roll. Sold a few of the photos to newspapers. That camp was the spark that sent me into photojournalism. So strange—this woman's misery the beginning of my career—a conundrum. To stop and help her or to first capture the shot, a photographer's dilemma." Kirsch shakes her head. "Come, let's eat and celebrate our great discussions."

But, still, we cluster around her.

"How old were you on your first trip overseas?"

"I think, twenty-one or two, but hardly experienced. Becoming a photographer was a portal into life."

"Are you going to North Africa in a group?"

"No, just an assistant."

"Are you excited?"

"Traveling to places I've never been makes being a photographer newly gratifying."

"What countries?"

"Morocco first, still working out the others," she says, urging us to try some of her very own dips.

I don't ask any questions but hold tight to her responses.

It's after six when I leave the party. I stayed a while longer than the others to help Kirsch straighten up. Kirsch went on about much as she often does in class. Her experiences always excite me, yet today they created a yearning that leaves me with feelings that refuse to explain themselves. Is it that the class is over, Kirsch no longer available, or even that my mother, too, will be thousands of miles away? No, it's something more than missing them, a mash of fear and confusion, and I don't know why. It's uncomfortable. I head to the river.

Though not serene, the river is calmer than the turbulence inside me. Dead leaves, sticks, other refuse ride the short, choppy waves of the current. No boats are near, the water a black and brown patchwork. I lean over the rail to see what I can see in its depth. Yes, I see it now. Kirsch's excitement about her upcoming trip, the pleasures and satisfactions she anticipates filled me with envy and longing. Marla would understand. Sitting in Marcus's king size bed, her hair mussed her smile easy, the beginning of the end for her, but that's not the message of the memory: it's Marla declaring, no warning, that unless we do something outrageous we'd end up living the same unrequited life as everyone else around there.

Warm enough to park on a bench with jacket intact, I gaze at the sky for a sign. Only I don't need one. I already know what would be outrageous: going to North Africa with Kirsch as her assistant. Different cultures, people I'd never meet otherwise, so much to see, to learn. How do they cope? What will their faces tell my camera? Do they, too, succumb to addiction? What are their reasons? I know too well the connection here between being trapped and drug use. But what of elsewhere—it could teach me more than any advanced class. Such a trip would . . . *Stop, Tessa, get real.*

Why would Kirsch even consider me? What experience could I offer? Winning a contest isn't enough. And traveling would use up the prize money. And then I wouldn't be able to afford my own place. And how long would it take to find work? And if I were gone for weeks, would Frank be able to hold open my job? And blah, blah, blah. Anyway, she's no doubt already chosen an assistant.

You don't know that, I can hear Marla say. Why pass up a chance to do something amazing? So, this is how the dead live inside us.

Once more on Jane Street, I gaze up at Kirsch's windows; the lights are on. I need only walk up the steps to the front door, press the bell. But lead fills my legs and panic fills my throat. Just standing here I feel like an intruder. There's no one else on the street. If by chance Kirsch were to look out her window, see me loitering here . . . too embarrassing. Go home, girl.

Walking to the subway under a darkening sky, the thought of what's next feels empty. It's how Mike feels, too, isn't it? And Hack won't go near what's next; Kevin simply gave it up. Marla would never have given up if drugs hadn't stopped her. Of that I'm certain. On the phone, my mother said it seemed I'd found my footing with photography. It's true. I want to show and tell what's hidden and uncomfortable to see. But what my mother meant was that now I could settle down. No, there's more to a life than settling down.

Across the street I notice a thin, dark-haired young man who looks like Mike. I cross over to see him better. Jacket unzipped, jeans frayed he's barefoot in old sneakers. It's not Mike, but it could be. How does one even contact a homeless man?

The station appears too soon. At the top of the stairs, my jaw clenched tight, I take out my phone and call Kirsch. It rings a few times, then goes to voicemail. Her serious message blanks my mind ahead of the loud beep. Then with eyes squeezed shut as if not to see what I'm about to do, I say quickly: "Hi, it's Tessa Boyce. If you're still interviewing for an assistant, I'm interested." For a moment, the audacity numbs me.

I forego the subway and walk uptown. Passing through streets, skirting people, crossing one avenue after another with little attention to where I'm headed; my usually too-active brain eerily quiet as if refusing to absorb what I've done. In the garment district, I dodge ancient-aged men wheeling racks of clothes, their faces as unrevealing as my thoughts.

At 72nd Street, the Papaya frankfurter store wakes my brain with a vivid memory of my first night in Manhattan. Hungry, cold and tired, I wandered for hours. How many moons ago was that? Though I'm still fatherless Tessa from a nowhere town, much has changed since then. Absurdly, one of Hack's rants comes to mind: "See, Tessa, I take the action, no expectation, then if I'm not dead, sweet calm." I'm far from sweet calm, yet whatever the outcome, a sense of possibility begins to take hold. Is this why people climb mountains?

Beneath a streetlight, I take out my phone and text Greg. "If you can break for dinner, I'll meet you at the hospital." He'll be surprised, but no more than I am. Hospitals spook me. I'm not even hungry, not for food, that is.

It's nearly eight and dark out as I approach the hospital entrance. The lobby is quiet; a few people sit silently. The gift shop is shuttered. I look out the plate-glass window at a street of modest buildings.

"Is everything okay?" Greg approaches, concerned.

"Yes, fine." I point to his white coat and stethoscope around his neck. "Impressive."

"I have about thirty minutes, not enough time to change and—"

"It's okay, Greg."

"There's a cafeteria on the sixth floor."

"Perfect."

A few white-coated men and women still linger at tables, though the place is about to shut down, food being packed away.

"I can still get us sandwiches. Do you know what you want?"

I shake my head and watch him go behind the long cafeteria counter. My phone rings. My heart jumps. It's my mother. I'll call her later.

"I'm glad you stopped by." He places a sandwich in front of me and begins to unwrap his. "I've been thinking about what you said the other evening. You're right. This roommate stuff is bewildering. It would be better to see each other without all the baggage that it implies."

What baggage, I wonder, but asking might sound like a challenge. "Thank you for understanding."

"I intend to do whatever I can to hold onto you. Is that obnoxious?"

"No, Greg. Not at all." I mean it, though whatever does or doesn't develop, I'm glad to know him.

"Have you decided about the advanced class?"

"The prize has muddled my head. I think my reach exceeds my grasp, to badly quote Browning."

"You read him?"

"Don't sound so surprised. No, actually, but the quote was on the wall of my high school."

"I really need to deal with that snobby side of me," he shakes his head.

"It's okay, I know where your heart is."

"Do you?"

"I believe so."

"How is your friend, the one on drugs?" his tone less curious than wary.

"Mike's still on drugs, doesn't want help doesn't want my friendship, either."

"That makes you sad?" He persists, neither of us eating.

"Very."

"Can you say more? Please?"

"Mike wants us to go our separate ways, and me to get on with whatever."

"Are you?" A plea?

"If I could change Mike's direction, I would, but I've learned the hard way it isn't up to me. Does that speak to your concern?"

"I think so."

Clearly, it doesn't, but what more can I say? To change the subject, I tell him about Kirsch's upcoming trip. How I'd love to go to North Africa as her assistant; that no doubt she already chose an assistant, and even if she hasn't, why want inexperienced me?" The speedy words threaten what little sanity I've reached.

"In medicine you need facts to make predictions. When did you fall? Where does it hurt? How is your appetite? Do you . . . "

"I hear you. I did leave her a message I was interested, and now feel both foolish and glad for doing so."

"Very human," he says solemnly.

Leaving the hospital still edgy and restless, I'm reluctant to return to a vacant apartment. Get some sleep, I think, the night will pass, it always does. My phone beeps: a text from my mother.

Immediately, Hack appears in my mind's eye: stoned, yes, but sweet, kind as always. More honest than anyone, he hides nothing, including his anguish. Hospice, her text said, everyone knows what that means, but does it have to? It's a vet hospital; they treat many patients like Hack, don't they? There must be some who move back to regular whatever. Unconvinced by my thoughts, I want to go straight out to see him. Except it's late, getting a train . . . by time I get there probably wouldn't let me in. I'll go first thing tomorrow after work. What if he dies tonight? Last words matter, Marla taught me that, too, didn't she? It isn't only the loss of what Marla might've said, but what I never had a chance to tell her that hurts.

The street traffic is noisy. I step into the nearest building lobby to hear better, stand just inside the door, and call. Scotty picks up. "Hi, it's Tessa, can you give Hack the phone?"

"It's Tessa," I hear him say.

"Tessa in . . . " A whisper.

"I'm going to miss you so much." I blurt out.

"Be happy."

"But, Hack, I'll—"

"For me."

"Okay."

"Do it, girl."

"What, Hack?"

"Whole thing."

"I'll try, I mean, I will. I'm coming to see you tomorrow."

"Won't be here." No, wait, I pray, but he doesn't want to, and hasn't, not for a long time.

"You're my Uncle Hack. You'll always be my true and best uncle."

"Better than medals." A breath.

"Yes, I hear you,"

"He's asleep," Scotty takes the phone.

"Thanks, Scotty. I'll call you." I will, of course I will, the hallway cold, dismal, silent.

I slip the phone in my pocket. It beeps a text, which I ignore.

With phone in hand I stare out the open blinds into moonless darkness, then reread the text for the umpteenth time: "Come see me tomorrow at four." I still can't believe my eyes: Kirsch, Molly Kirsch. My God, I think, tomorrow? What will Kirsch want to know, what questions will she ask? What am I meant to be doing in preparation? I can't think! Hack's breathy voice still alive in my head. Do it, he said, I will. I'll bring my briefcase of photos. Why would she want to see work that she's already seen? Tessa, calm, it's just an interview. But I can't hear myself.

I glance at the bed. How to get through the next hours? Marla and I would sometimes fantasize the next day's possibilities to help us sleep, but fantasy now feels dangerous. I remember the little white sleeping pill Marla scrapped from my sweaty palm. Never could decide if I did the right thing that night. But she was so needy, in pain; I could see it. I'm not in that kind of pain. I don't know what I am, my mind in a twist of sadness and excitement.

Greg won't be home till late. I wish he were here to distract me. I'd tell him about Hack, a vet, and an addict, who is my best uncle, whose weird wisdom kept me listening. I'd tell him Hack is in hospice. I'd tell him Hack is dying. I'd tell him about the interview.

I could call my mother; we'd talk about Hack, but I'd not mention the interview. She might say North Africa, no, too far, too daring, too whatever. That's a laugh. She left a long marriage, is moving to a place she's never been, with a man she's only begun to live with full time. Daring, I'd say. Maybe, just maybe I've inherited some of it.

I leave a note on the fridge: My uncle in Hospice, my interview tomorrow.

It's still dark out when Greg taps at the bedroom door, opens it partway. "Are you awake? I'm leaving in a few minutes, saw your note, wanted to wish you luck at the interview today."

"Thanks. I'm about to get ready for work."

"Sorry about your uncle."

"Do people get out of hospice?"

"Tess, they're usually placed there when they're terminal."

"Yeah, I knew that."

"I brewed coffee. I'll bring you a cup."

"Really?"

"Don't sound so surprised." My words tossed back at me.

"I'd love a cup."

Well, I think, that's a good omen and slip out of bed. A few hours at Frank's but then what? Won't be able to see Hack till after Kirsch, not enough time to take a train out and back. I slip into the black dress I wore to my interview with Rhonda. Though not superstitious, I am shaky.

Leaving Frank's I head to the bus-shaped diner for lunch. It's crowded and I sit at the counter. Though I order a sandwich, only coffee will go down. Time is barely inching along. A movie? Killing time in a darkened theatre is even less appetizing than the sandwich. I pay and walk uptown, though it's downtown I'll need to be.

Entering Central Park, I head toward the carousel, the sky unhappily gray, the few people on benches stare at me without interest. That's so New York, I've discovered. Back home people stared, too, but with an air of suspicion: What have you come to take away from me now?

The carousel is shuttered, no music plays. I sit alone on the facing bench and can almost see us on the moving ponies. How we laughed. Marla was stoned, yes, but I wasn't, and yet we were both enjoying the carefreeness of abandon. I could use some of that now.

My phone beeps, a text from my mother, which I don't want to read, but do: "Hack is gone, honey. It's what he wanted." It's true, I know, but heavy sadness sinks me. Those goody-good drops he popped never did give him peace. A memory of him sitting alone at the kitchen table comes to mind. It was late when my mother and I walked in holding Marla upright, the three of us frightened. Though stoned as ever, Hack told us what steps to follow to revive Marla. We obeyed. She revived. I think now how together he must've once been before his tours. Oh, Hack, I want you here. I want to tell you about the interview, what results. I want to hear you say, "You take the action, no expectation, then—" I want to remember and take in your weird outlook, a kind of strength, actually: Things matter but they don't. Enjoy it as it comes, it's here and then it's not. I'll try to hold on to all of it, Hack, I will.

41

In the coolness of twilight, relief and more relief follow me down the front steps of Kirsch's building. It's done. I was her last interviewee, she said. She'll make her decision by Monday.

Though I wore my anxiety like a red shirt, maybe my sadness, too, she did her best to put me at ease. She chatted about the institute, said what it was like to work with different students. Said this would be her first trip with an assistant, as if we both would have much to learn. Then slid into questioning before I realized I was answering: Have I done much travelling? No. Do I like people? Yes. Was I afraid of animals, insects, bad weather, would sleeping in strange households freak me out? No, to all that.

Kirsch said her growing up years were far from the best ones, and asked about mine. I described where I grew up. She probed for examples of difficulties I'd faced, called them once in a lifetime happenings. I wanted to say, being there with her. Instead told her about losing my sister, panhandling for money in hot Miami, and my naïve attempt to run away with a gang that never showed up, though I waited all day on the beach.

What was it about photography that called to me, she asked? The answer came easy: It gives me a voice and a responsibility to bring into the light what others can't or don't want to see. Maybe it was her welcoming smile, her nodding head, but I found myself telling her much more than I'd expected, including today's loss of

Hack. I needed her to know that I've already been on a long, difficult journey.

Seeing me to the door, she asked did I feel capable of dealing with the unexpected? The reply, a whisper in my ear, was that my sister's death tested me in ways that I could never have known otherwise, that it prepared me for as yet unknown challenges.

"Yes, and here you are," she mused.

Yes, here I am, I think, and resolve never to lose Marla's voice. If Kirsch chooses someone else, I'll register for the advanced class. If that means taking a night job to pay the rent on a place of my own, so be it. Point is, one way or another I know what's next.

I head uptown to meet my mother and Peter for dinner. No doubt we'll share stories about Hack, supposedly to enlighten Peter, but really just to talk about him. It's how memories are made. I won't mention the interview yet. Greg, though will surely ask how I did. "Well," I'll say, "I did well," and I did, didn't I?

It's staying light out a bit longer now.

42

Late for work, the camera strap over my shoulder, I stride toward the warehouse. As soon as he sees me, the coffee wagon man pours two cups of coffee, one for me and one for Frank, and places them in the cardboard tray. There's no way to pass without stopping for a word or two.

"Will it be a good day," he asks, a smile deepening the weathered lines in his face.

"Do you think I know?"

"No. Young people don't know what old people can feel in their bones."

"And what do your bones tell you?"

"Maybe a little sun."

"You're usually right."

"That's encouraging."

"Need to hurry."

"Enjoy everything before it disappears."

"I'm trying."

"All you can do," he says more to himself.

Hurrying past the strange sight of still darkened windows in tall buildings and sidewalks awaiting people, I marvel at the silence. The big, promising city is, for the moment, all mine, and I take it in with every breath. One more day till Monday.

As I turn the corner, the first blood streaks of sun appear in the sky. Though late, I stop to watch the darkness fade away.

ACKNOWLEDGMENTS

My profound gratitude to Dan Simon, the publisher of Seven Stories Press, for your continuous belief in my work, and for the thought and care you have always made available to me. Thank you. Thank you.

Thank you as well to each and everyone at Seven Stories Press for the close care and nurture of the novel: as always my deep appreciation for your amazing work to usher into the light a beautifully designed book and cover. Thank you Corinne Butta and Tal Mancini for the careful copyediting that smoothed out the wrinkles.

And to Ruth Weiner, intrepid Director of Publicity and so much more at Seven Stories Press; I'm forever grateful for your careful attention to my work, past and present, which has made all the difference.

My deep appreciation to my three first readers whose astute critiques made the novel more real: Jane Lazarre, talented writer and constant friend, whose knowledge and devotion to my work never fails to spur me on; Prudence Glass, my six-time Emmy Award friend, who took the time to give me daily insightful updates; and to Liz Gewirtzman, whose close reading, detailed talks and intelligent insights, were invaluable.

Thank you Jan Clausen and Farah Jasmine Griffin, two extraordinary authors, who read scenes from my novel and offered detailed, nuanced and insightful commentary, and never failed to cheer me on.

Thank you Tom Engelhardt for the constant support and ongoing belief in my work, and for being there from the beginning. Thank you as well to *TomDispatch* for publishing and disseminating my essays and supporting my books.

To my dear talented friend Elizabeth Strout, whose concern, care and advice are always spot on, my love and appreciation.

And, as always, thanks to my wonderful agent, Melanie Jackson, a national treasure.

For urging me on and being there to offer support I'm grateful to Vicki Brietbart, Prudence Glass, Barbara Schneider, Rina Kleege, Joanne Nagano, Jennifer Birmingham, Wesley Brown, and Marsha Taubenhaus, whose nightly phone calls keep me afloat.

A special thank you to Denise Campono whose insights enhance my work and so much more.

And to those who aid and abet in ways too numerous to describe, I thank: Cindy Harford, Anika Dobson, and Peggy Belenoff.

To Pat Walter, thank you dear friend and fan for your generosity and time.

A special thank you to Martin Baskin, MD, whose intelligence and patience and good decisions have gotten me through.

To my family for their never-ending love and support, I am grateful to Robert and Sam Trestman, Judi Gologorsky Brand, Sam and Carmen Wiggins, and to Dr. Kenneth Trestman for his brilliant council. Thank you to my granddaughter Maya for keeping me constantly amazed.

To the memory of the late Charlie Wiggins whose unfailing belief in my work sustains me.

As always thank you Georgina, Dònal, and Maya, the lights and loves of my life, you make it all matter.